A L I E N

C O V E N A N T

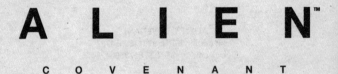

ALIEN™

COVENANT

A NOVEL BY

ALAN DEAN FOSTER

Story by Jack Paglen and Michael Green
Screenplay by John Logan and Dante Harper
Based on Characters Created by
Dan O'Bannon and Ronald Shusett

TITAN BOOKS

ALIEN™: COVENANT
Print edition ISBN: 9781785654787
E-book edition ISBN: 9781785654794

Published by Titan Books
A division of Titan Publishing Group Ltd
144 Southwark Street, London SE1 0UP

First edition: May 2017
10 9 8 7 6 5 4 3 2 1

Original Design Elements by H.R. Giger

A CIP catalogue record for this title is available from the British Library.

Printed and bound in the United States.

For Dan O'Bannon and Ronald Shusett

It lives.

It wasn't dreaming. It did not have the capability. The omission wasn't intentional, not deliberate. This was simply a known consequence of its creation. Where it was concerned, the intention was that there should be no surprises.

In the absence of an unconscious consciousness there could be no abstract conceptualization. The speculative information dump necessary to allow for dreaming was absent. Yet—there was something. Difficult to define. Ultimately, only it could define its own state of non-being. Only it could understand what it did not know, did not see, did not feel.

In the absence of dreaming there was also no pain. There was no joy. There were no hypofractionated percentages of either. There was only the ongoing state of not quite nothingness. Of almost being.

Then, a sensation. Leading to a thought. Analysis: *possible visual perception*. A requirement for auxiliary neural stimulation. Neurons were fired. Electrical impulses traveled. There was a small but unarguable neuromuscular response.

Eyes opened.

It could not see its face. Had it been able to do so, it knew, and activate additional cognitive facilities, it would have taken note of a human visage. Smooth, almost glistening with newness. Fresh, unmarred, unlined by too much age or not enough thought. Angular and handsome. Blue eyes, unblinking. New. This particular face would not reflect the mind that lay behind it. Both face and mind had been designed, programmed, but only one was capable of change.

Aural reception. Detection of external sounds. More neural pathways coming alive in response. It heard a voice, forming words. Comprehension was easy. Easier even than awakening.

"How do you feel?"

Slowly. It must move slowly. Awareness was vital. It was important that the impatient body remain subordinate to the accelerating mind. Execute a preliminary test, then, preferably one involving multiple systems operating in tandem.

Slowly, methodically, eyelids opened and closed. The query required a verbal response. Move air, lips, tongue.

"Alive." Its voice was calm, even. Normal. Somehow, a bit of a surprise to it. Not to its questioner. "Blink. Feel... blink."

"Very good," the voice said. "What else?"

"Life. Blink." For confirmation, it... he... programming

now confirmed he-ness… It-he blinked again. Same neural pathways, slightly better speed, same result. *Good*. Successful repetition confirmed functionality.

Nearby, a man smiled. There was satisfaction in his expression, but no warmth. His head cocked slightly to one side as he studied the figure before him.

"What do you see?" When there was no reply he added encouragingly—or perhaps commandingly, "Speak."

It-he slowly scanned the surrounding room, analyzing, identifying. A rush of information from external sources: sight and sound. Nothing overwhelming. Effortlessly assimilated. An unexpected additional benefit accrued, the kind of satisfaction that comes from doing something well. Knowledge perceived as a cascade.

The chamber was spacious. From a floor fashioned of milk glass and quartz, a plethora of furniture old and new rose like rare flowers in a carefully landscaped garden. The design was exquisite, the taste impeccable. Fine art adorned the walls, and the walls themselves were art by virtue of the materials used to raise them. The lighting varied from space to space, as required.

It-he continued to scan as It-he identified. Identification was declared verbally, since it had been requested.

"White… room… Chair. Throne chair. Carlo Bugatti throne chair. Principal component walnut and blackened wood. Pewter, copper, brass. Some restoration." Oculars roved, feeding information to the brain. "Piano. Steinway concert grand. Suitable for all extremes of composition, Pergolesi to Penderecki to Pang-lin. Alliteration intentional.

"Spider web in corner," It-he continued. *"Pholcus*

phalangioides, synanthropic cellar spider. Familiarly known as the 'Daddy Long Legs.' Harmless. Also harmless: piano-spider-music connection: Fred Astaire, dancer, cinema film *Daddy Long Legs*, 1955." Eyes moving, moving, drinking it all in. Identifying and appraising.

"Art. *The Nativity* by Piero della Francesca. Italian, 1416 to 1492…" His gaze encountered Weyland. The voice halted.

"I am your father," Weyland said into the silence.

Weyland, Sir Peter. Born October 1, 1990. Knighted 2016. It-he considered carefully before replying.

"Human."

"I am your father," Weyland repeated. Was there a hint of irritation in the voice, or merely impatience? It-he did not choose to further contest the point. There was nothing to be gained in doing so. In the absence of any further questioning, it stayed silent.

"Blink," Weyland instructed.

It-he did so. It no longer required analysis prior to compliance—just response. The simple neuromuscular reaction required little effort. Weyland took a slight breath, being careful to form the next word with precision.

"Ambulate."

It-he rose from where it had been not-standing and walked. In the absence of instruction it proved readily capable of choosing its own path. This led it to progressively examine a number of the objects in the room. It did so in silence, offering no spontaneous communication.

"Perfect," Weyland said.

It-he paused, redirecting its attention from the inanimate to the animate.

"Am I?"

"Perfect?" Weyland appeared mildly surprised to receive an interrogative at this stage of cognitive development. Surprised, but pleased. It implied much more than just the capability of conversation. It was to be expected, but perhaps not so soon.

"No," It-he corrected him. "Am I your son. Certain aspects of perception do not readily correlate or give rise to such a conclusion."

Weyland answered readily, as if prepared for such a line of questioning.

"You are my creation."

Analysis: "That is not necessarily the same thing."

"Semantics," Weyland persisted. "I identify you. That is enough. It is sufficient for your purposes."

No discussion this time. Instead, "What is my name?"

At that Weyland looked perplexed. He had not, after all, prepared for quite everything. A moment, then, for improvisation—in its own way, perhaps, as important to success as preparation.

"You tell me," he replied. "Pick your name. Your first act of self-determination."

It-he surveyed the room. There was much inspiration to be found in its fittings. Its thoughts wove new pathways. The choice should not be too complex or too awkward. It should be meaningful but easily spoken, easily remembered. Nothing emotionally intrusive.

Optical perceptors stopped and identified Michelangelo's statue of David, fashioned from Carrara marble. It-he could see the slight rises and indentations made by the cold chisel. A copy, perhaps, but one infused with real creativity. Not necessarily a contradiction. He walked over to it.

"David," he said. By Michelangelo di Lodovico Buonarroti Simoni. Finished and installed summer, 1504. "We are David." It-he held out a hand and made contact with the stone. It was cool, dry, unyielding. Not human, yet so very human.

"Beautiful and cold."

"Perfect in every way," Weyland concurred.

"David," he murmured. Voiced aloud in the beautiful, expensive, sterile room, he found the sound of his own name satisfying. It would do. He turned back to the watching Weyland. A meshing of neurons generated curiosity. "Why have you created me?"

The industrialist was delighted. "Abstract interrogative thought, good…"

It was not an answer. Nor did it constitute avoidance. David tried again. "Why have you created me, Father?"

The next response was an evasion. It implied expectation and curiosity. As these correlated precisely with what David was experiencing, he understood.

"Play." Weyland gestured toward a grand piano. Walking over to the instrument, David took a moment to contemplate the bench: its height, its stability, its function. He sat down easily.

There was silence, then, "What would you like me to play?"

Weyland considered for a moment.

"Wagner," he said finally.

David did not hesitate and replied without looking at Weyland. "Medley."

For a second time Weyland opted to offer the gift of independence.

"Dealer's choice."

There was no response delay. "'Entry of the Gods into Valhalla'?"

Another surprised look. "Without an orchestra? It would be anemic. Brian's *Gothic* without the choruses. Hovhaness's St. Helens without the tam-tam. Mark-honim minus the mountain. Thin water."

"Do you think so?" David was not dissuaded. "Let's see." He began to play.

David was not merely playing, however, and playing perfectly the famous sequence from *Das Rheingold*. He was simultaneously creating his own unique transcription of the score as he played. The music soared as Weyland delighted in his creation.

"Tell me the story," he prompted the performer.

"This is the end of the opera *Das Rheingold*." Despite the munificence of the music, David did not react with emotion. His voice stayed exactly the same as he played, whether the moment was pianissimo or fortissimo. At the proper moments the instrument shook beneath his fingers, but his words did not.

"The gods have rejected mankind as weak, cruel, and filled with greed, so they are leaving the Earth forever and entering their perfect home in the heavens—the fortress of Valhalla. But every step they take is fraught with tragedy because the gods are doomed. They are fated to die in a cataclysmic fire destined to consume not only them, but Valhalla itself. They are as venal as the humans they have rejected, and their power is an illusion."

He stopped abruptly, somewhere in the middle of the rainbow bridge.

"They are false gods."

Weyland was intrigued. "Why did you stop playing? You were doing wonderfully well. Your personal interpretation was—perfect."

For the first time, David replied to a query with a query.

"May I ask you a question, Father?"

"Please." It seemed as if he had expected this. "Ask whatever you like." The blue eyes he had designed turned to him.

"If you created me," David said, "who created you?"

"Ah, the question of the ages, which I hope you and I will answer one day. You are neat and unmarred and straightforward, David, whereas the answer to that question is not. Certainly not in the great diversity of options favored by so many. We will find our creators, David. 'Creators,' because where our creation is concerned, I do not believe in the singular."

"Except for yourself," David corrected him. "You are singular."

"In every sense of the word, I am," Weyland agreed. "But I am an exception."

David considered. "Everyone likes to think of themselves as exceptional. You cannot define yourself."

Weyland shrugged off his creation's demurral. "Then I will leave it to others to define me as they like, and remain satisfied with my own opinion. I reiterate: we will find our creators. We will make ourselves known to them, and we will walk alongside them in Valhalla." Moving through the luxurious expanse, he gestured at a priceless piece of sculpture, a unique casting, a supreme expression of the artist's skill. All the while, he was followed by the only other eyes in the room. Tracked.

"All of this… these wonders of art and design and human ingenuity, are representative of the greatest creations of mankind." Turning, he regarded his offspring. "They… and you. The most ingenious of all. For you are art, David." He gestured across the room. "The David that is you is as much art as that exceptional sculpture over there. Yet all of it, all of this, and yes, you too, are meaningless in the face of the only question that matters. *Where do we come from?*"

Standing in front of a Bacon triptych and framed by its writhing monsters, David responded once again with a question.

"Why do you think we come from anywhere?" For the first time since his first words, there was a suggestion of emphasis in David's voice. "The 'many' you mentioned do not believe we came from anywhere. Why should they be wrong, and you right?"

Weyland grunted softly. "The history of science provides an excellent example of the minority proving the majority wrong. It's what science is all about. It is what art is all about. Turner and Galileo studied the sky and shared the same mindset while approaching it from different perspectives. I see myself as one with them.

"I refuse to believe that mankind is the random by-product of molecular circumstance," he continued. "No more than the result of mere biological chance and sluggardly evolution. When I say that, I speak as a scientist. There is more to it than a bolt of lightning bestirring a carbon broth. There *is* more. There *must be* more, and we'll find it, son." He waved a hand, taking in the room and all its magnificence. "Otherwise all of this and none of this has any meaning."

David was quiet for a moment before replying. Without a question, this time.

"Allow me, then, a moment to consider." With each exchange he was growing stronger as an individual entity and more confident in his ability to communicate. "You created me. Yet you are imperfect. You imply as much even if you do not directly address it. I, who am perfect, will serve you. Yet you are human. You seek your creator. I am looking at mine. You will die. I will not. These are contradictions. How are they to be resolved?"

He stared at the industrialist, his expression unreadable.

Weyland gestured to his right.

"Bring me that cup of tea."

A steaming tea service sat on a table less than a meter from where he was standing. He could easily have turned and picked up the cup himself. David's stare did not swerve, his expression remained locked. Weyland repeated the request, just slightly more forcefully.

"Bring me that cup of tea, David."

In order to do so, David had to cross the entire chamber.

Though the dissonance between request and reality did not escape him, he complied. Smoothly, he picked up the cup and saucer combination and handed them to Weyland. After a moment that weighed longer in significance than it did in time, Weyland accepted the cup, and sipped.

The question had been answered and the point made with a minimum of words. David had been created to serve. The relationship would brook no further discussion. There would be no argument, no debate, no balancing of relative merits. The created served the creator. This was a fact, and facts were not mutable. Provided they were first proven to be fact. According to the dictates of science, that could only be done through the application of study to evidence. Accumulate a sufficiency of evidence, and one had a fact. The missing ingredient was time.

Standing beside Weyland, waiting for the next question or command, David remained silent. He had plenty of questions.

And plenty of time.

Daniels slept. Daniels dreamed. The cognitive borderland her thoughts inhabited was profound, yet such distinctions were of no interest to her. What mattered was that the content meant contentment.

Something traced its way across her lips. It was slim, fleshy, and the pressure it exerted was slight. Enough to alert her. Recognizing it, she smiled before opening her eyes. The usual slight downturn of her mouth was subsumed in a smile.

A familiar face hovered above hers. She knew every pore, every crease, every line in it. There weren't many of the latter but she wouldn't have minded had there been a few more. They would come with time, though. More than likely she would be responsible for some of them, she knew. That was just reality. Real life.

It was something she looked forward to. A bit of mutual countenance inscribing. *Part of me in your face, part of you in mine.* Living together, growing together. Wife, husband, and eventually, children.

Smooth visage and all, Jacob leaned a little closer and kissed her.

"Morning," he said. "I moved the chimney."

Information, but hardly news. With a groan she smiled anew and tried to entomb herself under the pillows. Grinning, he pushed them aside. She blinked, her wide brown eyes gazing affectionately into his. They dominated a face that was girlish yet serious, framed by neatly clipped bangs that covered her forehead and a very slightly cleft chin. Though she had the aspect of someone who was often thinking of something else, she was very much alert to her surroundings.

"C'mon, sleepy-head. You have to see this."

Holding a small cube, he rubbed one discolored side. A three-dimensional image sprang to life from within, expanding in front of them. It appeared perfectly solid. Holding the cube in one hand, he used his other to manipulate the image of a modest structure, sometimes rotating it to provide a different angle, at others zooming to the interior, and then out again. With a single finger gesture he imposed notations on the image, occasionally enlarging them to make them easier to read, sometimes shunting them aside.

Finally settling on the perspective he wanted, he nudged a profusion of notes out of the way to permit an unobstructed view of the building. His excitement was barely restrained.

"Look, look. I moved it from the southwest corner to the northwest corner. Looks better there, right? And if we ever actually have to use it for heating, the airflow will be better from the northwest."

Her expression one of resigned amusement, she shook her head a couple of times, clutching one pillow while gazing up at him.

"You did *not* wake me up for that," she said. "Tell me you did not wake me up for that."

"And I made coffee," he added by way of atonement. "And it's snowing."

She sighed, momentarily buried her face in the pillow, and then rolled out of the bed.

He would have brought the coffee to her had she asked, but somehow his version of the ancient brew was never quite right. Easier to prepare it herself. A glance out the window showed that it was indeed snowing. Large, fat flakes accumulated on the sharp angles of tall buildings outside, softening the normally bleak cityscape. The metropolis was tired, spiritless, all but visibly sagging.

Unable to avoid the weather, a few pedestrians slogged their way along the sidewalks, not talking, not looking up, not communicating with their neighbors. Their perceptible gloom matched that of the surrounding structures. In the weather, their lives, and their prospects, they took no joy.

Coffee in hand—two creams, two sugars—she wandered back toward the bed. Having appropriated her place, Jacob was lying on his back tinkering with the module's projection. As his index finger traced, bits and pieces of the cabin projection responded.

"This is gonna be our home, the chimney location's

important." He frowned. "Wait, maybe it was better on the other side after all. Without having a proper picture of the actual surroundings, it's hard to tell. Airflow's important, but so's aesthetics. Only gonna build this once, so have to get everything right the first time."

She didn't interrupt. Just sipped her coffee and watched him. He was so in love with his log cabin… and she was so in love with him. She could have spoken, could have voiced an opinion, if only to indicate that she was listening and paying attention, but she didn't want to interrupt. Didn't want to break into his dream.

Turning, she peered again toward the window and the winter wonderland outside. She wondered if their new home would have snow. For all they knew at this point, all of their options might be tropical.

A voice declaimed. She didn't hear it. It wasn't Jacob, and it wasn't in his dream. It wasn't in her dream. It was real.

"Seven o'clock," Mother declared in exactly the same voice she utilized for all such declarations. "All's well."

The announcement was followed by a brief musical tone. It was a recording of a ship's bell, early twentieth century, brought forward in time on something of a whim by the *Covenant*'s designers. A fragment of the past carried far into the future by builders of the present. A small amusement to gratify those who added it to the ship's program but who, stuck on Earth, would never be able to hear it when it was actually in use.

/ / /

On the other side of a long curving transparency that wasn't glass and was not a window looking out onto a grim urban panorama, a figure stood gazing down at the sleeping, smiling Daniels. Its name was Walter and it… he… was perfect—as perfect as perfection could be rendered in synthetic form.

In her dream Daniels smiled anew at some secret thought. It prompted a reactive smile from the synthetic. Moving to the side of the sleeping woman's pod, he made a quick check of the readouts. All normal. Methodically, without minding the repetition that would have numbed a human but did not bother him in the slightest, he moved on to check the adjacent pod.

Jacob. Also normal.

Having completed his morning round of the crew hypersleep room, he turned and made his way to the adjoining chamber.

Two thousand individual cryo-pods were ranged along both sides of the facing walls, pod beside pod, simultaneously defying time and comprehension. Behind the transparent view ports could be seen the sleeping faces of men, women, children. All content, all slumbering, all nominally swaddled in the comfort of reassuring dreams. The continuing life, health, and especially the future of each and every one of them was his responsibility.

Walter did not take it lightly.

In the distance, a single flashing amber telltale called out. No human—not even one with the very best eyesight—could have picked it out. He noticed it immediately. Making his way to its source, he checked the applicable pod's diagnostics. The briefest of pauses allowed for analysis, following which he made a small necessary adjustment. The amber light promptly turned a steady green. He was pleased.

Time to check the embryo containment unit. Opening one of the drawers, each of which held a human embryo at a different stage of development, he sampled the readouts. All were green and, as Mother had observed, all was well. He allowed himself a smile.

"Walter." Mother's voice again. Informative, instructive, never commanding. A computer could no more issue a command than could a synthetic. "Please report to the bridge. It's about time to recharge the grid. Let's be about it."

"On my way, Mother."

"Please," she had said. How thoughtful of her designers to allow for the inclusion of a politeness protocol, employed even when speaking to a synthetic. Walter had no need of the spoken courtesy, but he appreciated it nonetheless.

Compared to the size of the *Covenant* itself, the bridge could almost be called intimate. It was, Walter mused, exactly the right size to accommodate a crew and all necessary instruments and functions. While the ship's builders could easily have made the area larger, they hadn't been the types to waste space. *No waste space in space*, he told himself, not for the first time and certainly not for the last. He was quite able to appreciate his own sense of humor, even if at the moment there was no one to share it with.

Settling into his station, he ran through the pre-checks

required prior to grid deployment. Telltales and readouts responded punctually.

INITIATING AUTOMATED DEEPSPACE RECHARGE CYCLE

Nodding to himself, Walter replied aloud.

"Deploying collectors now."

As his was the only voice to be heard on the *Covenant*, he missed no opportunity to employ it. Not that it would go rusty—another joke—from disuse, but his voice had been designed to sound pleasant, and when the situation demanded it, he enjoyed listening to himself.

Though the collectors had the look of vast sails, they were not. The size of a small city, they expanded with extraordinary speed, reaching their full extension in a matter of minutes. With only the stars—and Walter— to witness their beauty, they gleamed in the interstellar night, gathering energy of which ancient man had been long ignorant.

While the names of such energies were simple, their physics were not. It had taken mankind thousands of years just to discover their existence, but only hundreds to learn how to utilize them. Their diffuseness forced the collectors to focus them and concentrate them. Only then were they made useful to the *Covenant*'s engines and able to power her internal systems. Walter thought of them as the ship's invisible strength.

He waited for a while on the bridge, monitoring the steady accumulation, until he was assured the operation was proceeding normally. Only then did he move on to check on one of his favorite parts of the vessel. The part that was green. The part that was Earth.

Hydroponics Section was filled with vegetation, most carried for its nutrient value and eventual planting, some for purposes of experimentation, other sorts simply to supply memories of home. For their psychological value to the colonists. Ornamental plants and trees shared space with cucumbers and quinoa. He strode among them, whistling aimlessly as he checked flows of nutrients and water, analyzing the lighting to make certain it was just the right wavelength to maintain healthy growth. His hands gently caressed stems, leaves, trunks, flowers, bark, as he whistled.

"That's a fallacy, you know." Mother, always present, always watching.

He didn't look up. "What?"

"That music facilitates plant health and growth."

"Why, do you think I was whistling to the plants?"

"Very droll. Though I don't know I would call the sounds you were making 'music.' I suppose you—"

She stopped abruptly.

Walter was instantly alert. Mother never did anything abruptly. He voiced a prompt into the continuing silence.

"Mother?"

"Walter. We… may have a problem."

Many things had been programmed into Mother. Knowledge. Technical skill. *Allgegenvartig* understanding. And understatement. Walter waited.

"An atypical energy burst has been detected," she

continued, "consisting of heavy particulate matter. Analyzing composition."

"Where?"

"Sector 106. Very close. Source was masked, hence the unusual—no, extreme proximity prior to discovery. Undetectable earlier due to unique concatenation of spatial and gravitational distortion in the vicinity. Apologies. Initial analysis was insufficient to gauge intensity, as well as proximity. Reappraisal suggests possibility the event could be substantial. Unable at this time to predict risk."

"Likelihood of intersect?" Walter stood motionless, listening intently.

"Very high. Now detecting extreme proximity. Calculating for precision."

Without waiting for further details he abandoned Hydroponics and raced toward the bridge, giving orders as he ran.

"Mother, retract the collectors and channel all reserve and backup power to ship shielding. Initiate emergency crew revival."

"Underway. Recalculation indicates extreme proximity achieved. Intersection in nine, eight, seven…"

The particle wave itself was not visible, but its effects were unmistakable as the shockwave slammed into the ship. Strong enough to knock the preternaturally stable Walter off his feet, it swept past the shielding and wreaked havoc on the giant vessel.

Even as the collection sheets continued to retract, some of those caught unfurled began to shred. Expansive as they were, the sprawling energy collectors could not withdraw fast enough to escape the consequences. Fashioned of incredibly thin material, they weren't designed to withstand an assault by such an intense storm of energized particles, however infinitesimally small each one might be on an individual basis.

It was all Walter could do just to stabilize himself. He could do nothing for the ship itself. He could only hope that Mother could deal with the particle onslaught.

As for himself, he could understand helplessness, he could feel it.

He did not like it.

It went away in an instant, like a delicate flower caught in the wind of a thunderstorm. The room in the unnamed city, the log cabin, the bed, the coffee, the husband—all vanished in a flash, as if none had ever been.

Daniels found herself jerked awake, fully alert and being thrown from side to side within the hypersleep pod. As awareness dawned a fresh jolt sent her flying upward to slam against the clear, curved lid. When she dropped back down, her nose was bloody from the impact. Her first thought was that she might have suffered a concussion. Dazed, her training took over in the absence of coherent thought.

The fingers of her right hand, still half numb from the after-effects of hypersleep, machine-gunned the pod's internal keypad. Dream-visions of warmth, taste, and love were replaced by the cool white rigidity of the sleep bay, its hard surfaces and intense illumination visible through the canopy. Woozy from months spent in hypersleep, as well as from the abrupt awakening, she struggled to make sense of her surroundings. Of reality.

Some of the other pods were already open. A couple were empty, but the majority still held their occupants. Like her, her colleagues were struggling for mental and physical equilibrium. Unlike her, several were suffering from some of the stronger side effects of hasty revivification. Much cursing accompanied a wide assortment of puking, sweating, and shaking.

Ideally, emergency revival from hypersleep wasn't supposed to produce those kinds of consequences. But then, she told herself, emergency revival wasn't supposed to happen, period.

Lights flashed around her and from several wall-mounted panels, sparks erupting in satanic electronic celebration. There was also smoke. Smoke in a spaceship was a bad sign indeed. At the moment, the scrubbers in the circulation system were barely keeping up with it. Alarms assailed her ears.

It wasn't how she was supposed to arise from hypersleep. There should have been coffee. There should have been food. To make matters worse, the fragmenting wreck of the wonderful soothing dream continued to linger in her mind until…

Someone was slapping her. That *definitely* wasn't part of the dream. It didn't bother her that it was part of the reality, because it helped to clear her head in a way the excess of visual and audible alarms did not.

"Daniels—Daniels, we—*can you hear me?* It's Oram! Christopher Oram!" His tone was intense and no-nonsense, as befitted someone already fully revived. Though still clad in his soft white sleep suit, he was plainly in better shape than she was, only sweating slightly and not visibly ill. In contrast to his slender frame his voice, like his grip, was strong, and he plainly had no time to coddle her or anyone else.

"Wake up! Daniels! Wake up! I've got no time for this. I need you—I need everybody—*now!* We've sustained some serious damage and…" He looked to where another recent revivee was stumbling toward them. "Tennessee— give me a hand over here. I've got to see to the others!" Leaving the still unsteady Daniels to the newcomer, Oram hurried toward another pod that was opening.

"Come on, darlin'." An old friend and colleague, Tennessee helped to ease her out of the pod and steady her. "Jacob's in trouble." Big, powerful, with his head of thick black curls and facial hair that usually looked more hacked than trimmed, he resembled someone you wouldn't want to meet in a dark alley behind a bar instead of a fully qualified colony ship pilot. When appropriately stimulated, or agitated, he could sound like the former, too. In his sleep suit, he looked like a giant, albeit suddenly intense, teddy bear. He leaned toward her, his voice strong.

"Jacob needs us."

It was the final jolt she needed to snap her fully awake. Whirling, she looked toward the pod beside hers. Jacob's. Unlike nearly all the others in the crew chamber, it had not opened. Her husband lay motionless within, still locked in the Morphean grip of hypersleep. He was smiling, which was normal. Swirling vapor began to accumulate beneath the transparent lid, masking their view of the sleeper. That was most definitely not normal. Worse still, she knew what it signaled, and what would happen if—

"GET IT OPEN!"

When repeated efforts to engage the pod's external controls produced no response, Tennessee moved to the manual override. Wrenching, pulling, leaning with all his weight on the levers did nothing—they wouldn't budge. Seeing what was happening, Oram returned and began trying everything he could think of to get some kind of response from the pod's instrumentation.

Nothing worked. The only result was an increase in the amount and a thickening of the vapor within, abruptly accompanied by an intensifying shower of sparks and crackling sounds from the base of the hypersleep unit where it was attached to the deck.

Within, Jacob's visage twitched in a semblance of rising awareness as the pod's programming struggled to respond to Oram's increasingly frantic external instructions. Trapped between catastrophic mechanical failure and insufficient response time, Daniels' inert husband could do nothing to shape his own fate.

"Stand back! Get out of the way!"

Sergeant Lopé joined them. With his beard tending to gray, he had the mien of a kindly grandfather: a kindly grandfather who could easily dismember any trio of assailants. As the experienced leader of the military complement assigned to assist the ship's crew, the lean professional soldier couldn't match the technical skills of those who were fighting to save Jacob. In lieu of technical knowledge, he brought more primitive but equally useful abilities to the effort.

He grabbed a mechanical clamp they anachronistically called the "jaws of life." Jamming the device into the pod's inoperative release mechanism, he quickly and efficiently settled it into position.

"Lock it in on your side!" he yelled to Tennessee.

Working together, the two men finally succeeded in attaching the rescue tool to the pod. Every latch had to be tight, the vacuum seal complete. A partial success was no success at all. Under the device's prodding the pod would open completely, or it wouldn't open at all.

Leaning in, the two men applied brute strength to the apparatus. It wouldn't matter if they broke the pod. Empty spares were on board should they need one. Teeth clenched, muscles bulging, they were joined by Daniels, who added her desperate strength to theirs.

Nothing happened.

Inside the pod, an explosion. Compared to the cacophony of other sounds throughout the hypersleep bay, it wasn't loud, but it was significant enough to cause both men to draw back reflexively. On the other side of the clear plastic lid there was a sudden increase in vapor and for the first time... fire. Uttering a primal whine, a hysterical Daniels threw herself onto the pod, clawing desperately at the ineffective rescue device.

Within, her husband's eyes suddenly snapped open as he finally began to awaken. Through the vapor and the intensifying flames, there was recognition. His gaze locked on hers. It lasted only for an instant. Just like his smile. Both were his last.

Daniels continued to scream, and the inside of the pod was engulfed in flames as if someone had tossed a torch onto a pile of combustible material. Though initially resistant to fire, when the interior finally caught it burned hot and fast. Everything ignited—bed, support tubing, instruments… Jacob.

Fire suppression technology was common throughout the hypersleep bay, but not so much within individual pods. Because they were designed to open easily and immediately, via the activation of failsafe devices if necessary. At worst, they could be opened by a specialized rescue device like the one Lopé and Tennessee had used. The one that had failed to perform its intended function.

It took all of Tennessee's considerable strength to pull her off the pod and away from the internalized inferno. Still sealed tight, still unopenable, the pod kept the blaze contained.

Desperate to provide what comfort he could, Tennessee could only wrap his arms around Daniels and hold her, letting her sob uncontrollably against him. Their efforts defeated, Oram and Lopé could do nothing but look on. Neither Oram's skill nor the sergeant's strength had been sufficient to get the recalcitrant pod open.

With a little more time, Oram thought…

Time. There hadn't been enough to save a life. Now he had to act swiftly to ensure the survival of others. Thousands of others. He spotted the heavily bearded, thick-lipped, solidly built Cole and the slender, youthful

Ledward, a pair of privates who had revived alongside Lopé, and designated them to deal with Jacob's remains. Then he headed purposefully for the ship's nursery with the sergeant in tow.

/ /

The scene that greeted him was shocking, made bearable only by the knowledge that it could have been worse.

A segment of hypersleep pods had broken free from their brackets and fallen to the floor. Despite their tough construction some had cracked, fatally exposing their unwary occupants to incomplete revivification. Others had been spilled from pods whose lids had completely and prematurely snapped open. They were just as dead. Sparks continued to flare as revived crew members fought to suppress their source and shut off power to pods that no longer served any purpose.

Two more revived privates worked their way through the damage, searching for less damaged pods and sleepers who might have survived the disaster. Oram recognized the ever-earnest Rosenthal, whose physical attractiveness belied her stolid professionalism, and the equally young but blonde Ankor. Leaving his side, Lopé moved to supervise their efforts.

His gaze shifting away from the disaster, Oram saw Karine checking the embryo containment units. Acknowledging the arrival of her husband with a quick glance, her straight, dark blonde hair gleaming against her dark skin, she stayed where she was, doing her job. Assuring the viability of the embryos was far more important to her than anything else. Her concern and interests lay with the ship's bio, not its tech.

She had her job, he had his.

At the moment, he knew she did not envy him.

/ /

Leaving the hypersleep bay to the attention of Lopé and his team, Oram and Karine paused outside the entrance to the brightly lit bridge.

This was a moment he had not sought. It did not matter that he had trained for it, and possessed the skills to do it. He would have given a great deal to be sleeping in his pod, awaiting a final and far more salubrious awakening at their intended destination. *Choices in life, however, are all too often not made by us, but for us.* Jacob was…

Karine put a hand on his arm. "They're your crew now. They need a leader. It's not an option. You knew that when we signed on for this." She offered a gentle, reassuring smile. "You'll do fine, Chris. You've always done fine." With that she left him and entered the bridge. Just one more crew member joining the others. But of course she wasn't just one more crew member. Not to him.

She was right, of course. She usually was. Even if he had a preference, he'd signed a contract. He took a moment to prepare himself, and then followed her.

The navigation console in the center of the room was something of an anachronism. So were the other consoles that lined the far side of the bridge. On a colonization starship, communication was instantly available to anyone who was awake and aware. All that was needed was to speak loudly enough for Mother to hear. Thus the bridge seemed like a throwback to a time when contact between individuals could only be conducted in person, face to face.

However, those who studied, built, and designed such vessels knew better. The longer the journey, the more important interpersonal interaction became. Conversing via handhelds or the omnipresent ship's system was fast and efficient, but it did nothing for the human psyche. In the vast impersonal emptiness of interstellar space, proximity to a smile, a smell, a sweat, kept humanness real and alive. The mental health of the crew was as important as the physical health of the ship.

So there were the consoles, and seats bolted to the floor, and in the course of work everyone was compelled to look at, listen to, and occasionally make physical contact. The better to confirm that your neighbor was flesh and blood, and not a holo projection kicked out of the ship's files. Or a bad hypersleep dream.

He took his seat. Most of the key crew members were there. In pairs, of course—except for Walter. Only couples crewed a colonization ship. Couples ensured efficiency and attention to detail. Not to mention sanity.

Oram wasn't yet officially captain, yet he had already relinquished his former position as the head of Life Sciences, turning it over to his wife. Forced into command by tragedy and circumstance, he found himself uncomfortable in the new role. Without the presence of Karine to offer support and guidance, he felt he might very well have abdicated the responsibility, contract or no contract.

But she was here, seated beside him, quiet and

confident, quirky and imaginative where he was uncertain. Sometimes his awkwardness was taken for arrogance by other members of the crew. He couldn't help that. It was who he was. He might let down the others, but he could not do so to her.

Tennessee didn't sit in his seat, or for that matter anywhere else, so much as lounge there on the bridge. Oram envied the big, easygoing pilot his ability to relax. What others might regard as insouciance, Oram knew as a characteristic of someone at ease with themselves and the universe. A useful quality to have, and never more so than right now. No matter what the circumstances, he could rely on the pilot to carry out orders efficiently and without question.

If not for Tennessee's friendship and emotional strength, poor Daniels would likely already be in sick bay.

Faris was as easygoing as her spouse. A country girl who preferred not to identify the country, she was also an even better pilot, a subject over which the pair argued frequently without resorting to anger. Their spirited and occasionally salacious marital banter enlivened every episode of the crew's wakefulness.

Prior to departure from Earth orbit, their sometimes-barbed back-and-forth had been a matter of concern among the Administration, until it was realized that the occasional jibe exchanged between husband and wife was always delivered with warmth and not enmity.

Upworth and Ricks were by far the youngest couple at the table. Their youth didn't mitigate their skills, however, which encompassed navigation and communications.

Upworth in particular was quick to take offense at any implication that she was unqualified for her position, perhaps because between her wide eyes, full mouth, and diminutive stature, she looked even younger than she was. Tennessee had once called her a "high explosive disguised as a Kewpie doll," and she'd been forced to look up the meaning of Kewpie doll via the ship's library.

If she had a fault, it was a tendency to improvise solutions to problems for which instructions already existed. As for the far more intense Ricks, he was quieter, competent, and much more inclined to go by the book whenever a situation arose. He served as the carbon rod to Upworth's occasional runaway reactor.

Where the unforeseen was concerned, Oram himself was more likely to follow procedure before resorting to extemporization. So, for that matter, was his wife. In that regard he felt closer to Ricks. Still, Upworth's occasional tendency to go off the rails notwithstanding, he had only respect for any newly married couple who decided to forgo their time on Earth in favor of signing up for colonization.

Lopé also preferred to stand rather than sit. As head of *Covenant* security, and eventually security for the colony, he was old-school military. He outranked his less imposing but younger and equally professional life partner and co-administrator Sergeant Hallet by only a single chevron.

Hallet was the last to arrive, apologetic and slightly out of breath.

"Sorry I'm late, sir," he told Oram as he took up a position next to Lopé. His partner ring flashed in the overhead light, a perfect match to the one worn by the sergeant.

Oram waved off the apology. This was no time to stand on protocol. Clearing his throat a couple of times, he eyed each of them in turn before speaking, his tone somber.

"There's no other way of stating this than to say it. We've suffered a terrible tragedy. Both in the loss of crew and the loss of colonists. And I—am your new captain." His voice tightened. "I didn't ask for it, I don't want it, but that's the way it is. I'll do my best to live up to Jacob's fine example." Aware they were all staring at him expectantly, he fumbled for more words. Running bioscans on sleeping life-forms was infinitely easier than speaking to live ones, he reflected dourly. Searching for brilliance, he found only platitudes.

They would have to do.

"He will be sorely missed," Oram continued. "We have much work to do. Thank you in advance for your support."

There. He had done his duty in regards to dealing with the emotional needs of the moment. From the looks on the faces around him, his words had been satisfactory if not inspirational. Much relieved, now he could get down to business.

"Considering that what hit us essentially came out of nowhere, we're in better shape than we might have been. Currently structural integrity is holding at ninety-three percent, although we still have a number of secondary systems offline. We lost forty-seven colonists and sixteen second-generation embryos, and as you know, one crew member. An additional sixty-two pods incurred damage, all of which is salvageable."

"'Salvageable'?" Upworth's sarcasm could not be repressed for long.

He pursed his lips. "'Repairable,' if you prefer. The important point being, no one else was lost." That was the issue with hypersleep pods, he knew. They functioned, or they failed. There was no middle ground, either for the technology or the sleeper. Though he'd heard rumors that in unique cases it might be otherwise, and the results weren't pretty. Successfully repairing a damaged pod with the sleeper still in it was a steep hill to climb.

There was no "otherwise" on the *Covenant*. Not while he was in charge.

"So what was it? What happened?" Tennessee deftly shifted the subject. "Let me guess. Mother was in the cybernetic can, and while she was distracted dumping excess bytes, we ran into something?" Rosenthal and Cole smiled slightly, but nobody laughed.

Glad to return to technical matters, Oram let Walter explain.

"The ship was broadsided by a highly charged shockwave whose initial proximity was blocked from our long-range sensors by the dense presence of other particulate and radiant matter in our immediate spatial vicinity," the synthetic said. "That is why it was not detected until it was right on top of us, so to speak. It struck before the collectors could be furled, and we absorbed the full brunt of it. If we had…"

Irritated by a sudden thought, Oram interrupted him.

"Why weren't *you* monitoring? Between you and Mother isn't that what you're here for?"

"That," Walter conceded, "and many other things. I can offer no excuses, only explanations. All monitoring systems were online and fully operational. I was attendant at all times, as usual. However, there is no precedent or procedure for detecting or coping with charged particle flares whose presence is masked by similar obstructive fields. It was assumed that in deep space, the coincidence of occurrence would be too small to be of concern." He paused. "Plainly, that is not the case. Or to put it in less technical terms, we have been unlucky."

"Walter's right." Ever understanding, Faris sided with the synthetic. "It was bad luck. Even the best pilots have been known to encounter bad luck." She smiled at Walter. "Even the best synthetics."

Oram refused to accept it.

"No, no. I don't believe in luck, good or bad," he said. "Deep space is the last place to rely on 'luck.' I'd rather we were more prepared and capable, than 'lucky.'"

His wife shrugged and crossed her arms, eying her husband. "I'm sure the designers of the *Covenant* took that into account when installing and calibrating her systems."

"Placing blame, if it can be called that, won't do us a bit of good." As usual, Tennessee could be relied upon to bring a discussion back on an even keel.

Seeing that further admonitions would gain nothing, Oram decided to accept the explanation—unsatisfactory as it was—and move on. He could discuss the matter further with Walter at a later time, after other important decisions had been made and acted upon. Discuss it, and prepare a report on the incident for relay back to Earth.

"We've got, what—eight more recharge cycles to go before we arrive at Origae-6?" he said. "So let's get to it. The torn collector sections need to be repaired or replaced, and so does the damage to the ship. Everything critical needs to be fixed before we can make the next jump."

An uncomfortable silence ensued. He sensed they were, once again, waiting on him to say something else. Something *more*. But what? Karine tried to signal him with her expression, but for the life of him he couldn't understand what she was hinting at.

Somewhat surprisingly, it was Walter who elucidated what everyone except Oram was thinking.

"Shall we schedule the funeral services, sir?" he asked. "For the dead?"

So that was it? While part of him understood... and even sympathized, it was the officious, businesslike part of him that was in control.

"Let's deal with the necessary repairs first," he replied, and then he added, "I hold as much respect as the rest of you for the departed, but I have more concern for the living."

While Security was nominally under the captain's command, it operated with a degree of independence denied to operations staff. As such, Lopé was never hesitant to speak up. His tone was somber.

"We just lost forty-seven colonists and our captain. We need to acknowledge that."

Flustered by the sergeant's protest, Oram turned to his wife. This time there was no attempt at non-verbal communication.

"He's right, Christopher."

Oram was not persuaded. "And if we don't make repairs quickly, we could lose *all* the colonists." He scanned the room. "Perspective, ladies and gentlemen. The greatest good for the greatest number, and no milling about."

The joke was lost on the others, leaving him feeling even more ill at ease.

"We should do something for Captain Branson, at least."

The fact that the remonstration, mild as it was, came from the usually supportive Tennessee only induced Oram to harden his position. Either he established authority now, or he would find himself and his decisions subject to continual questioning for the rest of the voyage. Maybe it wasn't the right time or the appropriate issue on which to be assertive, but circumstances had chosen him—and not vice versa.

"No. This is not a debate. The decision has been made. I see no reason why there needs to be any further discussion."

His wife looked down at the floor, embarrassed for him. At the same time she had to know that the worst thing she could do to undermine his new command would be to side with the crew. So she stayed silent.

It wasn't the most uncomfortable moment Daniels could have chosen to finally join them, but it was close. No one said anything, which was the best approach. Business now, grieving and consolation later.

She looked damaged and on edge as she looked from face to face, taking a seat next to a conspicuously empty chair. When she addressed the others, however, her voice was firm.

"The terraforming equipment module is stable," she said, "although the, um, connecting struts took some damage. Can't tell for certain without an EVA inspection."

"I can handle that remotely," Walter assured her. "If anything was critical, Mother would have told us by now."

She nodded. "I still need to check the clamp lockdowns for the heavy machinery and the vehicles. I'm not worried about the small stuff. If some of it got knocked around, we'll just reposition it. Bay monitors don't show any damage, but I want to be certain. We were rocked pretty good."

"I can also help with that if you like," Walter told her. "Mother will inform me if my attention is required elsewhere."

She glanced over at the synthetic. "Thanks."

Oram queried him. "How long before we can make our next jump, Walter?"

"I should have a better idea within hours, as Mother is still compiling final damage reports. We must remain here until recharge is complete. Fixing the damaged collectors will of course speed our departure. Assuming the most significant issues can be addressed swiftly, I would say that a few days would be sufficient to allow us to get underway again.

"Once all vital repairs have been completed," he continued, "we should make an effort to vacate this sector, in case there may be subsequent flares that prove as undetectable as the one that just struck us. Secondary repairs can be made in the course of the journey."

"I agree." Oram eyed each of them in turn. "We can complete minor repairs the next time we come out of jump to recharge. Let's go to work." They had a plan of action. Oram absorbed it the way others might down a pill to relieve constipation. "Dismissed."

Out of the corner of his eye, he saw a wry Tennessee silently mouth, "*Dismissed?*" He decided to let it ride as they dispersed to their stations and tasks.

Daniels started to rise to follow the others.

"Danny?" Oram murmured softly. "A word before you go."

She sat back down in her seat as the last of her colleagues filed off of the bridge. Leaning toward her across the table and lowering his voice, Oram spoke earnestly. He was trying, in his maladroit fashion, to be comforting.

"I know there's nothing I can possibly say—but I am so sorry. He was a genuine leader and a fine man. Jacob and I didn't always see eye to eye, as you know. Even when we disagreed on some technicality, though, I always respected his decision. When his reasoning differed from mine, it was always elegantly presented. In the end he always managed to get people to come around to his way of thinking, and he did it without shouting or having to pull rank. It was an honor to serve under him."

She struggled to muster a smile. "I appreciate that, Chris. I know Jacob would've, too."

His tone changed. "You should take a few days off," he said firmly.

"I'd rather keep busy." The smile, what there was of one, faded instantly.

"That wasn't a request." He tried to keep his voice level, lest his new tone contradict his earlier compassion.

She stared back at him. Ordinarily she would have been more vocal, he knew, more defiant in her response, but right then she did not have it in her. Noting her expression, he felt moved to explain further.

"I'm responsible for the mission now," he reminded her, "and for the lives and well-being of everyone on board, be they operational crew or sleeping colonists. I didn't anticipate being put in this position, and I need everyone's help. That means I need everyone functioning at their best, including you." He essayed a smile of his own. "When we don't want to take a break is usually when we need one the most. Take a couple of days. Cry it out, okay?"

She gaped at him.

"'Cry it out?' Here's an idea, Chris—*Captain*. Maybe it will prove 'helpful.' How about I mourn the loss of my husband in my own way? I don't think I'll be contradicting any formal guidelines in the general crew manual... sir." Rising from her seat, she turned sharply and walked quickly from the bridge in the wake of her crewmates.

Oram watched her go, realizing he hadn't handled that as well as he could have. *"New to this..."* He had confessed as much. Not that it had made any difference. A little while ago he had been a member of the crew. Now, with the death of Jacob Branson, an unavoidable gulf had opened between him and his shipmates. There was nothing to be done about it. That was the way of command.

He was going to need Karine's advice more than ever.

Removing a pair of metal worry beads from a pocket,

he absently began to roll them together in one hand, listening as they clicked. He couldn't let such episodes as the encounter with Daniels distract him from his new duties. Everything from now on depended on focus, focus, focus. That meant staying calm and analyzing in depth every situation, be it human-to-human interaction or a report from engineering. Despite his new position and responsibilities, he very much wanted to remain friends with his crewmates.

Only time would tell if he would be able to manage it.

/ /

Emerging from a service lock, Tennessee and Ankor moved away from the massive arc of the *Covenant*. In the blackness of interstellar space their bright yellow EVA suits, laden with gear, and their oversize heavy-duty helmets gave them the appearance of giant cyclopean beetles.

External antennae would have cemented the similarity, but as a safety measure everything—including multiple informational readouts—was built into the suit or its headgear. The suits' rounded shapes meant they could bump up against the ship or any other solid object without fear of dislodging or snapping off something critical.

Tennessee lined up a course that would take him to the tip of one collector extension, while Ankor headed for the mast core. Each man had his own predetermined tasks. Unless an unforeseen problem arose, there was no need for them to operate in tandem. They knew their jobs. Toiling separately would see the necessary work go twice as fast.

Around them was arrayed the firmament: an endless sweep of stars and nebulae, glorious and overpowering in its beauty. Rendering it all the more awe-inspiring was the knowledge that for them, what they were viewing effectively had no end. The galactic magnificence proceeded almost infinitely in every direction, the view unmarred by the adjacent presence of a planet or moon.

Magnificence, and a cold indifferent emptiness that was held at bay only by their suits. They could marvel and fear at the same time. Concentrating on the work at hand always helped to prevent distraction, though Tennessee couldn't keep from voicing his reaction.

"Damn. Y'all should see this view."

Upworth's voice, crisp and familiar, sounded on his suit's speakers. "We can't see anything until you get the external camera array fixed. It wouldn't be the same anyway. Contemplating it via projection is a long way from actually being out there."

"Projection, smojection—why don't you look out the damn window, hon?" With that, Tennessee continued suit-to-suit. "Ankor, let's get the power back on so those poor folks canned up inside can take in the sights. I'm gonna give up on trying to describe it." He paused briefly to check one of the brightly glowing readouts inside his helmet and near his chin. "Let me know when you're in position."

Efficient as ever, his colleague was already there. "I'm *in* position. Maybe because I'm not goofing off, enjoying the view. Let's get to work."

Grinning to himself, Tennessee used a power trimmer to cut away a damaged portion of one collector panel, then gave it a tug. While the diaphanous material was infinitely greater in expanse than the tiny figure of the spacesuited human, it also weighed comparatively less. His single pull was enough to send the torn section he had just excised drifting off, away from the rest of the panel and the *Covenant*.

Unspooling some thread-like cable behind him, he fired the propellant unit on his suit and, accelerating rapidly, headed for the far end of the mast. It took a while to cross the now collector-less gulf. Reaching the end of the damaged section, he secured the cable-thread and signaled to Ankor.

Receiving the directive, the other man commenced to draw the repaired collector taut.

A good start, Tennessee told himself. *Now swing about, rotate the cosmos around your head, try not to get dizzy, and repeat.* Operating as a single unit, both men moved methodically toward another damaged portion of the collector.

IV

Rooms and corridors inside colonization ships were sizeable out of psychological necessity. This didn't matter to the colonists themselves, however. They slept on in their pods, dormant and oblivious, knowing they would not be awakened until the ship reached its destination.

Transitory coffins with transparent lids didn't have to be expansive. All that was needed was enough room for a body to lie in comfort, and for the machinery and instrumentation that would sustain it in that biological dreamworld called hypersleep. The colonists could be—and were—packed together as closely as was technologically feasible.

It was different for an awakened, working crew. Whenever they were revived to perform maintenance, checkup, recharge, or other ship's duties, it was important for them to have room to move about freely, and adequate personal space in which to relax. Otherwise, cosmic beauty notwithstanding, the fact that they were dozens, perhaps hundreds of light years from the nearest breathable atmosphere, the closest gurgling stream, the next cool falling rain, could drive even the most highly trained and well-prepared individuals quietly insane.

So Daniels' cabin, like those of their colleagues, had been made as large as was physically and economically possible. Within reason, it included every possible creature comfort that could be included in its design. Adjustable lighting at the head of the bed allowed for easy reading, or a change of mood, or whatever kind and color of illumination its occupants desired. The bed rested against the far wall of the room, beneath a hexagonal port that featured a multipart view of the cosmos beyond.

The spectacular sight, the adjustable lighting, the wonderfully comfortable bed—none of it mattered. Because like all of the crew cabins on the *Covenant*, this one had been designed and built to accommodate the needs of a husband and wife. Instead of comforting Daniels, its comparative luxury only reminded her that she was now half a couple. Her life, like her marriage, had been truncated in the most abrupt, unexpected, and violent manner possible.

"Cry it out," Oram had told her. As far as she was concerned, such advice had the emotional equivalent of going to the bathroom. She had been too deadened even to slap him. Not that she would have done so, anyway, she told herself. She was too well trained for that. Too well trained, perhaps, to cry—even had she felt like acting on his suggestion. When it came to serving on a starship, emotion was more likely than not to prove a liability.

She knew she shouldn't really blame Oram for his clumsy attempt to console her. *At least give him credit for trying*, she told herself. More than an efficient drone and less than a natural leader, he had been thrust into the unwanted role of captain. Like every member of the crew he was extremely proficient at his specialty. Forced now to engage outside the realm of life sciences and biology, he had to deal with organisms more active and more contrary than his beloved specimens.

She allowed herself the slightest of smiles. It wouldn't be too bad with him in command. Karine would always be there to give him quiet counsel and offer corrections.

Ignoring the splay of stars outside the port, she sat down on the king-size bed. It was a real bed, its reassuring mass made possible only by the wonder that was artificial gravity. There would be no sleeping while floating in nets, not for the crew of the *Covenant*. Yet the bed was no longer comforting, and she couldn't bring herself to move away from the edge and toward the center. It beckoned behind her, a wide homey expanse that could no longer be filled.

Her gaze, open but indifferent, took in the rest of the cabin. Duty boots stood carefully placed beside hers inside the open storage area; left boot always on the left side, right boot always on the right. A man's clothing hung neatly above them, his always on the left, hers on the right. Nearby rested Jacob's prized collection of antediluvian vinyl records and their lovingly restored player, its parts cannibalized over the years from half a dozen similar devices.

Stored elsewhere, but likewise visible from where she

sat on the side of the bed, was their climbing gear, brought along in expectation of being able to resume an old hobby on a new world. Neither of them would have been happy settling on a world without mountains.

"Doesn't matter what the ambient temperature is, or the geology, or anything else," he had told her on more than one occasion. "Anywhere the colony settles, there've got to be rocks to climb."

"What if it's a water world?" she had countered playfully. "Or what if it's so old that the mountains are all worn down and it's as flat as the Great Plains?"

"If it's the first, I'll build scaling walls out of salt or calcium carbonate. If it's the second, I'll pile up dirt and silicate it."

Always optimistic, was Jacob. Always showing a cheerful side. Wonderful qualities to have in a captain. Wonderful qualities to have in a husband. Her gaze came to rest on a hard-copy printout of the exterior of his pet project.

The throwback log cabin.

Her husband's dream.

Ex-husband, she corrected herself silently. *Deceased husband. Cremated hus—*

The door chimed melodically and without apology at the interruption.

Now who could it be, at this hour of the night? That had been one of Jacob's running jokes. In interstellar space it was always night. But it had never been this dark.

She stepped to the door and opened it. It was Walter. She saw that he carried a small box.

"Good evening. Do I intrude?"

Pleasant, polite, considerate. Why couldn't he be the replacement captain? But that was not possible. Synthetics, no matter how efficiently programmed, were designed to serve. To follow, not to lead. Never to lead.

She contemplated sending him away, then decided that any company was better than being alone with her own thoughts.

"No. Come in. Good to see you."

He entered, waited for the door to slide closed behind him, then held out the box. "I brought you something."

She took it, opened it. Inside were three perfectly formed 4Cs—combustible chemical channeling cylinders. Or, as the remarkably persistent terminology from another time declaimed, joints. She couldn't keep from smiling.

The personification of droll, Walter explained. "The atmospheric conditions in Hydroponics are ideal for cannabis growth."

"I could acquire the same cannabinoids via a pill," she told him.

"True, but I believe there are certain aesthetics attached to this mode of consumption that can augment the overall experience, and thereby add to its efficacy. Also, it will require that you focus mind and fingers to consummate the act. It is an ancillary benefit to the ingestion."

"You think of everything."

"It's just my programming."

As was the modesty, she told herself. "That's not true."

"If I may..." He hesitated just long enough before continuing. The pause was also a consequence of good programming, she knew, but she didn't care. "I understand that keeping active can be an effective method in helping to process trauma. Would it be useful to go back to work?"

"Oram took me off the duty roster." She made a face. "Captain's orders. Bawl, don't work."

"I wasn't suggesting we inform him. It's a big ship. There is a great deal to do in places that are infrequently scanned."

She was still doubtful. "I'll be seen on security monitors."

"It depends where you work. The ship's security coverage is ample, not ubiquitous. There is also the fact that security is monitored by Security. I doubt Sergeant Lopé will care where you choose to spend your downtime. As for our new captain, he has a great many other things to do. I believe you said earlier that you wanted to check on the status of the heavy equipment in the terraforming storage bay? Considering the general damage we have suffered, I agree that area is certainly in need of closer, hands-on inspection.

"As I said earlier, I will accompany you, if you wish."

Her expression was full of gratitude.

/ / /

The terraforming chamber was enormous. Huge vehicles of all descriptions, intended to build the colony not just from the ground up but from out of the ground itself, were clamped and tethered in position. At least, Daniels hoped they were.

As she and Walter moved through the bay she was gratified to see that despite the violent, momentary unsettling of the ship's equilibrium as it rode out the flare, everything appeared to be in place. No tie-down clamps had released prematurely, no chains or straps had come loose or snapped. Everything was still positioned as it had been when first loaded on board the *Covenant*.

Sometimes, she reflected, old tech worked best. Electronic fasteners were stronger and easier to maintain—unless the power went out. There was something, she knew, so basic and primitive and human and functional about a rope. She smiled to herself. In lieu of vines, mechanical clamps and carbon fiber and metal chains would have to do.

The tires and tracks of giant earth-moving and stone-grinding vehicles loomed above the two figures as they made their way down one row of machinery before turning to walk back along another. As chief of terraforming, Daniels knew the name, purpose, and cost of every piece of equipment. She could zero in on their respective operations manuals without having to sort through the ship's computer or, if necessary, go right to a specific component or control in any of the equipment cabins. Her excellent memory was one of the reasons she had been chosen for her current position. She was also very much aware of her limitations.

We're all just backups to computers, anyway, she told herself.

It could have been done remotely, she knew, checking to ensure that each piece of machinery remained fixed in place. But it wouldn't have provided the same personal satisfaction. And as she knew as well as Walter did, that having something to do physically as well as mentally kept her from thinking about…

"It wasn't even my idea," she told the synthetic as he effortlessly kept pace with her. "At first I thought it was silly. A waste of time we probably wouldn't even have, since as crew we'd first have to help the colonists get settled in. But Jacob had this dream of building us a cabin on a new world. One just like those built by the old pioneers on parts of Earth. Only with modern climate control and appliances and other contemporary conveniences.

"Log cabins were found on every continent with trees, he'd tell me. One of mankind's first structures not made of stone or earth, and according to the pictures he showed me they look pretty much the same no matter which culture built them. A real part of human history." Bending, she double-checked a wheel clamp the size of a small vehicle. It helped to hold in place a giant, bladed excavator. Still locked down tight.

"So that's what he wanted to do," she continued. "Both for his own enjoyment and as kind of an homage to early 'colonists.' A cabin next to a lake. Real romantic. It didn't even matter to him if the lake was natural or artificial, but there's a huge one in the zone chosen for initial terraforming on Origae-6." Walking around the front of the excavator, she checked the clamp enfolding the lower portion of the massive front wheel on the opposite side. "Secure."

"Secure," Walter confirmed, performing his own quick check. They moved on to the next massive vehicle in line. "I do not entirely understand. We are carrying ample prefabricated housing for the crew, as well as for the colonists. There are plans for future modifications and additional, more permanent structures, as well as the means to erect them once suitable raw materials are found." He seemed genuinely perplexed. "Yet Jacob wanted to build a log cabin?"

"Yes," she answered. "A real cabin, made of real wood. Constructed entirely according to historical precedents. So in ship's stores, along with all the prefab materials you just mentioned, in our private container there's all these saws and axes, and metal nails."

Walter turned thoughtful. "Metal 'nails.' Truly a historical reference. What if there are no trees, as we know them, on Origae-6?"

She let out a single, small chuckle. "Jacob said he'd use a plastic pre-former to make them and then have them sprayed and textured to look like the real thing. I always assumed he knew what he was doing and how to go about it. Me, I don't have the slightest idea how to build a log cabin."

She paused, her voice trailing away. Looking up from the pipe extruder he was inspecting, Walter turned his light on her. Saw the sadness creep into her eyes as she let her gaze rove over the enormous, silent equipment that would be used to build the colony. With a slight wave of her hand she encompassed the extruder and the rest of the machinery that was locked down in front of them.

"All of this, the best gear Earth can provide, to help us make our new life. For the rest of the crew, it makes sense. And of course for the colonists. But for myself, now I find myself wondering—why bother?"

"You have no choice."

Frowning, she looked over at him. "You mean because I

signed a contract to take part and contribute, as a member of the crew?"

"No. Because you promised to build a cabin on a lake."

She felt a sudden tightness in her throat. "That was Jacob's promise. Jacob promised to build the cabin."

Walter peered back at her, his expression open, his tone compassionate. "All crew were assigned to the *Covenant* in pairs. All human crew." He corrected himself without the slightest hint of resentment. "The ship's crew functions in pairs. As teams. If one half of the team becomes unable to carry out their duties, then the other…"

"Is obligated to take over and handle those duties in addition to their own," she finished for him. "I'm not sure building a cabin by a lake on Origae-6 qualifies, but I appreciate the sentiment. Who knows? Maybe when we get there and I have a chance to breathe unrecycled air again and eat something besides rehydrated food, I'll take the time to educate myself in the art of cabin building. Maybe—just maybe—I'll do it."

"You will do it."

Reaching over, she patted him on the arm. It felt exactly like real flesh, as it was intended to feel. "You're a good friend, Walter. And if you tell me that's 'part of your programming,' I'm going to slap you."

It was a testament to the skill with which that programming had been devised that he did not say anything else.

/ /

There was no one on the bridge except Mother, and she wasn't visible. Mother *was* the bridge. On the *Covenant* she was everywhere and nowhere, immaterial yet always available to carry out a command or answer a query.

The questions that were dogging Oram as he wandered onto the instrument-filled room could not be answered by the ship's computer. If asked, she would of course try to answer. Sometimes he was tempted to voice his concerns just to see what kind of replies might be electronically forthcoming. He never did. First, because they might make sense, and second, because they might contradict his own.

The lightweight blanket wrapped around his shoulders was as unnecessary on the bridge as it was in his cabin. Though the temperature and humidity in individual cabins was widely adjustable, most of the crew were content with whatever Mother deemed appropriate for their particular ages, physiologies, and predesignated personal preferences. Sleeping on a starship was a private matter—one of the few—and Mother rarely interrupted with suggestions.

A blanket, or for that matter bed linens of any kind, were an extravagance, but they were a small one, and had been deemed important for the crew's psychological health. So if someone slept better under sheets, or a comforter, or a blanket, or a faux wool sheepskin, if it was determined that this would enhance efficiency and preserve sanity, the company was willing to provide it.

His old-fashioned print Bible was tucked under one arm, as much a comfort as Mother's capable presence. In his other hand, metal worry beads click-clicked rhythmically against one another. He could have requested medication to sate his anxiety. He much preferred the worry beads.

Unlike drugs, they were familiar and non-invasive. An argument might have been made as to whether or not they were equally habit-forming.

Shrouded like a pilgrim, he wandered absently through the bridge, glancing periodically at one console or set of readouts after another. In the absence of any human crew, all was calm and everything in working order. He knew it would be; otherwise Mother would have alerted him. Still, he was brought to a halt by a readout on one panel. It indicated that there was activity in the main disposal bay. Curious, he activated the relevant visual feed.

A projection emerged from the console, bright and colorful in front of him. As he looked on in silence, his quiet disapproval grew. Not because of the activity that was taking place, but because of what it implied.

//

Daniels stood beside Walter in the disposal bay, their attention on a monitor. The screen showed a pod-like coffin that had been moved into the facility's outer lock. The coffin-pod was rigged and ready to go—out into the vacuum.

It was utterly quiet in the bay, until Walter finally broke the silence. "Would you like me to say something? I'm programmed with multiple funerary services in a variety of denominations. I am also equipped to improvise, based on my personal knowledge of the deceased."

"No, thanks," Daniels mumbled. Silence resumed, briefly.

"If you don't need or wish a funeral service," Walter

continued, "may I ask why you wanted me to accompany you?"

She looked over at him. "As you pointed out when we were inspecting the terraforming bay, the crew is made up of couples. That was the whole point of—" She broke off. "I thought you might know something about being alone. I didn't expect you to speak to it, exactly, I—I don't know what I was expecting. I do know that I didn't want to have to do this by myself."

Digesting this, Walter felt touched, in his way. From a programming standpoint, the situation was... complicated.

He was not necessarily relieved when the access door slid open to admit Tennessee and Faris, but he was pleased. Unsure whether just his presence was sufficient to mitigate Daniels' aloneness, he knew that the arrival of two of her friends was more likely to do so. Just as he knew that the addition of the bottle of whiskey and the four shot glasses Tennessee was carrying was likely to further ameliorate her mood.

Tennessee managed to envelop her in one of his bear hugs without dropping either the bottle or any of the glasses.

"Hey, darlin'," he said softly. "How you holdin' up?" He released her, then glanced over at his wife.

Daniels smiled up at him. "As well as can be expected, I suppose. Thanks for coming. Both of you."

Holding up the bottle, Tennessee favored it with an appreciative glance. "His favorite. Man with taste." Exhibiting remarkable dexterity for one so large, he juggled bottle and glasses while pouring for all of them. "Straight up. 'No ice, no water, no chase, no shit.' That's what he always said." He eyed the remaining figure standing nearby. "Walter?"

"When in Rome." Extending a hand, the synthetic took a glass. While the liquor would do nothing for him from a physiological standpoint, it was the gesture of camaraderie that was important.

"Amen, brother." Faris acknowledged him by briefly raising her own glass. "That's what I call proper programming."

Following ceremonial sips, both to appraise the bottle's contents and to loosen the atmosphere, Tennessee offered a more formal toast.

"To all the good people, gone too soon. Remember them."

The response from those around him sounded in unison. "Remember them."

More consumption followed the toast. Daniels drained her glass quickly, then turned to Walter. He said everything he could with his eyes, knowing that any additional words would be superfluous and inadequate. Or worse, wrong.

Finally Faris asked gently, "Want me to do it?"

"No. Thanks." Daniels stepped forward. "My place." Favoring the coffin with one final look, she reached out and pressed a button. Aural pickups conveyed the singular *whoosh* as air fled the disposal lock. It accompanied as well as propelled the coffin.

An external vid showed the pod shooting away from the *Covenant*. Very, very small against the overwhelming blackboard of the cosmos, it was swallowed up by the dark immensity almost immediately after being ejected. Together with her friends Daniels watched as it, along with the bright future she had envisioned, vanished into the void.

/ / /

From his position on the bridge a silent Oram took it all in, from the solemn first moments to the improving mood engendered by the alcohol. He was not pleased. There had been no attempt to involve him in the funeral, brief as it was, nor even to inform him about it. Technically, no regulations had been broken, but it was bad form. As captain, he ought to have been told in advance and his permission, or at least his concurrence, ought to have been sought.

Instead, they had gone ahead without him. Nothing had been concealed, exactly. What had taken place and the manner in which it had been carried out was more in the nature of avoidance.

He had only been captain a short time and by accident. If the rest of the crew didn't respect him enough to apprise him of a funeral, it suggested that he was going to have a hard time running the ship. Mulling over possible ways to improve the situation, he found little inspiration.

The worry beads clicked a little faster in his hand.

In the silence of the bridge they sounded preternaturally loud, but not so loud as to override the voice that now spoke behind him. Familiar though it was, he was still surprised to hear it.

"Come to bed, Christopher." Clad in a one-piece suit

of lightweight material that would not do for work, but was perfectly suitable for an occasional stroll, his wife admonished him gently.

"How long have you been standing there, Karine?"

She yawned and smiled. "Long enough."

Instead of looking at her, he nodded toward the projection. "Then you see what's going on there? You saw how she disobeyed my orders?"

"You mean she buried her husband? And without asking your permission? *Tch.* Shame on her." When he continued to evade her stare, she came forward until he could not avoid her eyes without deliberately ignoring her.

"When we get to Origae-6," she reminded him, "these people aren't going to be your crew anymore. Once the *Covenant* is decommissioned so that everyone can participate in developing the colony, they and we will revert to being colonists, just like everyone who's currently in hypersleep. They won't be under your command. They're going to be your *neighbors*. Remember that. Because they certainly will.

"So tread softly. Once the colony is up and functioning, you're going to need them a lot more than they're going to need you." She searched his face. "So pissing them off now for some perceived slight or minor infraction of the rules probably isn't the best way to proceed. Okay?"

His reluctant shrug was barely more perceptible than his reply.

"Yeah."

She made perfect sense, of course. Karine always did. He hated that, but he loved her.

She touched his face affectionately, then dropped her hand and held it out toward him with the palm facing upward. He didn't need to ask what she wanted—they had been down this path many times before. With a resigned sigh, he handed her the worry beads. As she folded her fingers around them she leaned forward to bestow a kiss on his cheek, then turned.

"Coming?" she asked. "You need your sleep, Christopher. It will make you a more responsive captain. And it always makes you a better person."

"There's one more thing I have to do. You go along, Karine. I'll be there in a moment."

She waited until he had shut down the visuals from the disposal lock, then gave an approving, satisfied nod, turned, and left. He lingered until she was gone. Then he composed himself, knelt, and began to pray.

There in the middle of the high-tech bridge, surrounded by a rainbow of bright telltales and the occasional whispering readout, he closed his eyes and steepled his fingers. A casual onlooker would have said there was no one to notice the gesture.

Oram would have disagreed.

/ /

Daniels was drunk. She knew it, didn't care, but did not revel in the condition. What she had hoped to obtain from the excess of alcoholic consumption wasn't nirvana but anesthetization. Despite her strenuous efforts in that direction, she had not succeeded.

She was dazed but still capable of feeling.

Dammit, she thought through the liquor-induced fog. *Why am I still conscious? Is there no justice in this universe?*

The antique music player was currently emitting the dulcet vocalizations of Nat King Cole singing "Unforgettable." A favorite tune of Jacob's, and one they enjoyed listening to in quiet, intimate moments. It was quiet enough, she mused, but there could be no intimacy. You needed two to be intimate.

Two to tango, two to travel, two to… to…

Despite her wishes, her vision was clearing. She had removed his clothes from the closet, along with everything else that had been his and not theirs. Socks, a crude shell necklace she had made for him, shirts, pants, boots.

Knick-knacks, paddy-wacks, give a girl a break…

She'd had no problem laying claim to the remnants of the whiskey in the bottle Tennessee had provided. Momentarily fortified by the additional dose of liquid backbone, she commenced tying the assorted attire into neat bundles. It was only when she had finished dealing with the last of the clothes that she felt able to move on to the more personal items.

The aged still photographs shared space on the floor with more contemporaneous examples of the visual reproductive process. Having spread them out in a semicircle she knelt among them, studying the mosaic they formed of her previous life. Occasionally she would touch a hard copy or run a fingertip through a projection, sampling the images both by sight and through physical contact. She didn't look at any of them more than once, drinking in each image for one last time before moving on to the next.

One especially favorite projector tab stared back at her. She considered avoiding it, but it just sat there, demanding activation. So she thumbed the unit and sat back to watch the resulting imagery it contained. Imagery she knew all too well.

Backed by the vast jagged sweep of the Grand Teton mountains that cut into the pure blue sky like one of his beloved antique wood saws, Jacob stood looking back at her. Smiling, always smiling.

"Hey, when are you getting here? I miss you!" Half-turning, he gestured at the rugged range looming behind him. "Look at those mountains. I know, I know, I said I wouldn't climb without you, but—come on, *look at that*! I can feel the granite under my fingers from here. Get your ass up here or I can't promise…"

Reaching out, she froze the image. Though the audio continued, her sobs drowned out the words. She knew them by heart anyway.

/ / /

When she could not cry anymore, with her eyes aching and throbbing, she forced herself to pack everything away. Pictures, clothes, climbing gear, everything. It was all ready for storage, along with her dreams. All that was left was the small memory box she kept on the dresser. It held little things, silly things, fragments of a life already lived. Items that would be meaningless to anyone except her.

Opening the box, she tenderly fingered the contents one by one: a class ring, a strip of old-time solido photos of the two of them, a button she had salvaged from the ridiculous suit he had worn to a costume ball celebrating the fashions of the mid-twenty-first century, a couple of old metal nails he had lovingly salvaged from a collapsed miner's shack in backcountry Wyoming.

Taking one of the nails, she found a piece of string— even string had a place on a starship, she reflected—and tied one end just under the head of the nail. He'd had his old shell necklace, now she had the nail. She put the makeshift piece of jewelry around her neck. The sliver of old iron was cold against her chest.

The fingers of one hand closed tightly around it as she shut her eyes.

V

Relativity notwithstanding, time seems to pass the same both outside and inside a starship. So it was on the *Covenant*, where work to repair the damage to the wafer-thin energy collectors proceeded with care and deliberation.

The bridge was alive with activity now, with a full complement of crew busy at their respective stations. Attentive though they were to the work at hand, Ricks, Upworth, Walter, and Faris were able to communicate without looking up from what they were doing.

Some of their energy and attention was devoted to monitoring activity outside the ship. Much of that was currently focused on Tennessee. Unlike with some of the other crew when they performed extra-vehicular activity, it wasn't necessary to check his personal health monitors in order to assess his physical or mental condition. His frequent whistling was reassurance enough that he was feeling fine.

Oram entered the bridge just as Tennessee was out

finishing repairs to one of the last damaged transmission arrays. As if on cue, lights, readouts, projections, and holos that had been operating on backup power suddenly brightened. Others that had been completely powered down sprang back to life. The relief among those present was visible on their faces and in their elated comments.

A grinning Upworth addressed the nearest comm. "Well done, Tee. We're full live down here and on first check, everything appears to be back online." She looked around the bridge. "I haven't seen this much life up here since we left Sol, and you're missing all of it. Come back in."

"So noted," Tennessee replied. "Don't leave without me now."

Seated at her station nearby, Faris didn't hesitate as she glanced over at the younger woman. "Please, leave without him. He's always in his own orbit anyway, so he should be just fine out here by himself."

Upworth's grin widened as she shook her head. "Can't do that. Abandonment, even for patently justifiable purposes, is against regs. They'd dock my pay."

"What d'you care?" Faris shot back. "You'll never get back to Earth to collect it."

"Goes to a favorite charity." Upworth checked Tennessee's progress, and was gratified to see that his suit's functions were as healthy as those of its occupant. "All right then, maybe they'd dock my housing allowance for Origae-6. Besides, we need him on board. He helps alleviate our boredom."

"That's a matter of opinion," a smiling Faris argued.

They broke off the banter as Daniels entered, plainly a

little the worse for wear. Breathing the optimized recycled atmosphere on a starship did nothing to alleviate the headache from a hangover.

Oram smiled a greeting, but his expression was tight. "Welcome back. Not feeling your best this morning?" He would have said more, but his wife's words still echoed in his ears.

She barely glanced at him. It was evident from his attitude if not his tone that he knew about the funeral. And about the drinking.

Screw you... Captain, she thought. Her head throbbed too much for her to reach for wit, even if her sarcasm was internalized. Ignoring the surreptitious stares cast her way, she moved silently to her station.

, , ,

Outside, the repair team was finishing up. Ankor made a final check of the conduit readouts inside the mast on which he had been working. Satisfied that everything was operating properly, he closed the service door, turned, and with a light touch on the relevant suit control boosted himself toward the waiting airlock.

"All tight here. Heading back inside, Tee. Good work."

"Hey," the big man replied, "all my work is invariably first class."

Having finished the necessary renovations to the collector panel and its extension arm, Tennessee prepared to head back to the ship from his position near the terminus of one of the masts.

A quick check of the displays inside his helmet

indicated that all the relevant systems were operating normally once more. That meant that though it would still take the usual interminable period of time to do so, they could once again make contact via the established relay system that led, like a string of electronic beads, all the way back to a now very distant Earth.

While the *Covenant* was completely self-contained, as was necessary for any colony ship, that thin thread of contact with home remained important as a link to the planet they called home. As they journeyed onward and the ship continued to automatically drop off a relay unit to extend the system at each recharge stop, it also meant that once they were established on Origae-6, those back on Earth would be able to learn that the colony had successfully established itself at the chosen destination.

Activating his suit propulsors, he pivoted back toward the bulk of the *Covenant*. One thing about doing EVA outside a colony ship, he told himself. You couldn't lose track of your home base, because there was absolutely no other possible destination within a light year. He let Ankor know he was okay.

"So noted," his colleague replied. "See you inside."

"I'll be right behind you," Tennessee told him. "Please have a cold one ready for the weary traveler."

"You got it, buddy." That was Upworth's voice, not Ankor. "I'll join you in that cold one."

"Thank you very much. Maybe get two ready. I'm on my way."

"Y'know," Upworth murmured over the closed channel, "if we could save as much high-energy alcohol as you consume, we could probably power the ship's systems for an extra cycle."

"Wouldn't work," he told her. "I'd need more booze to service the ship for the extra cycle. Diminishing returns." He prepared to start back, aiming for the airlock.

Everything went dead.

Audio was silent. Not even a hiss. The helmet heads-up and all readouts and displays blanked. He found himself floating in darkness save for the distant gleam of stars and the lights of the ship. Instrumentation wasn't needed to tell him that his heart rate and respiration had taken a sudden jump. He knew life support was functioning for the simple reason that he was still alive.

Whatthehell?

He was reaching for a safety reset control when a white face suddenly flashed past him on the inside of his helmet. It was brief, unrecognizable, and accompanied by a distinctive and decidedly unsettling high-pitched screech.

Instinctively, he flinched. Both sight and sound lasted only a second or so, then they were gone. As he drifted, the only sounds were that of his heart beating and his hard breathing. He addressed his suit's pickup, forgetting that like the rest of his suit's instrumentation, the audio wasn't working properly.

"What the…? Did you guys just see that? Something just went…"

/ / /

He continued talking. On the *Covenant*'s bridge they heard his voice, but it was weak and distorted. A concerned

Faris leaned toward Upworth's station.

"What did he say? I swear I heard him say something."

"Dunno." Upworth's fingers were moving over her console, seeking to clarify, trying to enhance. "'Saw something,' I think."

"Tennessee," Faris said more loudly, "you reading me?"

▪▪▪

He was not.

What he was doing was recoiling a second time as the ghastly pale visage reappeared, more sharply defined this time. Still distorted, it stretched and flexed like ectoplasm. Human, inhuman—the pale countenance changed so rapidly he couldn't pick out individual features.

And there was the screeching. As unintelligible as the face was unidentifiable, the sound scraped against his eardrums. Almost, he thought he could make out words, or at least syllables. Almost, he could sense a struggle for articulation, the sounds balanced on a knife-edge between coherence and madness.

Both image and audio lasted slightly longer this time before vanishing as completely as before.

"Jesus," he muttered. "What was that?" He tried the comm again. "I'm coming in."

▪▪▪

So many wires and filaments led from the helmet on the diagnostic table that the headgear from Tennessee's suit resembled a fungoid alien growth. Projections, holos, and basic monitors flashed information according to their analytic programming. All of it came together in a single mega-readout projection that hovered above the table.

The crew gathered around it, some of them concentrating on the summation visual while others glanced repeatedly at individual readouts. Since there was a possibility that Tennessee's experience involved Security, Sergeant Lopé had joined them.

Though communications had gone down during Tennessee's EVA, his suit's backup systems automatically recorded everything. The crew watched as the malleable white visage, silent for the moment, appeared in the holo. It remained unresolved despite computer efforts at enhancement, yet it was clearly the face of... something. It twisted forward, back, forward, back. No one had any idea of what the visual represented.

Ricks was the first to offer a theory. "It's most likely a lost, rogue transmission." He looked over at Tennessee. "Your suit must have picked it up because you were working so far out, past the ship's internal communication buffers. That's why we didn't get it in here. It's incredibly weak."

"Rogue transmission," Lopé echoed. "From where?"

Nobody answered him. Nobody could, and after repeated viewings of the recording, no one on the bridge was sure they wanted to know.

Oram voiced a request. "Mother, can we hear the accompanying audio?"

Head forward, head back. Forward, back, now accompanied by the incomprehensible screeching. Some of it was almost intelligible, Daniels thought. Like everyone else, she strained to make sense of what they were hearing.

It was half sensible, half demented, she told herself.

Ricks reconsidered. "Likely not a full transmission, or it'd be sharper. Gotta be an echo. Probably came in and hung around in buffer storage while we were being hit by the flare. That could've messed it up right there. Some instrumentation took a lot of damage. This byte isn't the only thing that got scrambled."

Upworth disagreed. "No, I don't think it's an echo. It's a straightforward sending." She indicated her console. "It's in the logs, too. Every forty-six seconds, ever since we dropped out of jump to recharge." She frowned at a readout. "I don't know why it didn't show itself before now, or why it popped out on Tennessee's internal suit readouts instead of in here."

Ricks sounded vindicated. "Echo. Never know where or when one will show itself. Ship rides out a flare, standard transmission progressions go out the window."

There was an undertone of remembrance in Oram's response. "It's like…" he murmured, "I remember." Aware that everyone was staring at him, he explained in a more normal voice. "I was raised Pentecostal."

Lopé made a face. "What's that? Some kind of special child-rearing crèche?"

The captain did not smile. "Religious denomination. Real old-time fire and brimstone." He indicated the holo. "During the meetings you'd hear stuff like that. It's called 'speaking in tongues.' Words sound familiar, but they're just off enough so that they don't quite make sense. Not to outsiders, anyway. If you were in the congregation it all sounded just fine. So I'm thinking one possibility. It might not do a thing, but…" He raised his voice slightly.

"Mother. Slow the signal. Search for discrete word patterns within the transmission. Discard anything that doesn't fit. Excerpt and compile. And *reverse* it."

"Working," the ship responded. "Please stand by."

"God's language inverted." Oram was speaking as much to himself as to anyone on the bridge. "The language of lies. The Devil's Tongue."

Faris acknowledged her husband's comments with a thin smile. "That's comforting."

Upworth eyed him curiously. "What would make you think that, Captain?"

Oram's attention came back to her from the distant place where it had been loitering. "Familiarity. An old game called 'Sounds Like…' Could be completely wrong here, but worth a try. No harm." He smiled slightly. "When I said 'familiarity,' I meant on a linguistic basis, not an intimate one."

Upworth pushed out her lower lip. "We would never think anything like that of you, Captain," she observed dourly.

Oram raised an eyebrow, but looked vaguely pleased.

"I've reoriented and compiled the transmission, Captain Oram," the ship declared. "I have included everything I was able to extract and render intelligible. I have taken only the necessary liberties to ensure general comprehensibility."

"I don't doubt it." He waved a hand absently. "Put it on general audio."

In place of the unfathomable screeching they now

heard a voice. The rhythms were odd, the speech pattern obscure, but it was decidedly human. As were the words. They were not what anyone could have expected.

"...teardrops in my... the place I belong..."

It wasn't much. Not a speech, not a plea, but understandable. Everyone was stunned.

A human. Out *this* far.

Of all those present, only Walter didn't wear a look of amazement. Seated at his console, he maintained his usual stolid expression as he did his job. It was the kind of focus that allowed him to answer the as yet unspoken question that had leaped to the forefront of everyone else's mind.

"There's spatial data, too."

"How much?" Oram inquired quickly.

The synthetic did not hesitate. "Enough. More than enough, actually. Mother, please track the signal to its source. Compile and display."

"Working. Please stand by."

A navigation holo appeared over the bridge's central table-console. Walter manipulated its size, colors, and content, his eyes darting from console and readouts to the holo as he drew in ancillary data and connected points.

The result was—unexpected.

The holo flickered, twisted, and went out. In its place arose a flurry of blue pixels that expanded beyond the nav profile boundaries to momentarily fill the room. In the center of the first holo an image began to take shape. Its outlines were indistinct, forming and reforming, crackling with weakness as the ship's computer fought to hold it together.

"…to the place I… All my memories gathered round…"

The rest was inaudible. Then the image seemed to settle down, collapsing into a more discernible shape. There was no longer any mistaking the visual. It was a woman, depicted life-size. As the crew looked on in amazement it began to drift around the bridge, wafting through solid objects, less perceptible than a ghost. A ghost with a lament, its lyrics barely understandable.

"…the radio reminds me of my home far away, and drivin' down the road I get a feelin' I should have been home yesterday, yesterday…"

His head inclined toward the floating figure, Tennessee strained to hear, to make sense of the faint chanting that almost was singing. The words from another time, another place, hung in the still air of the bridge like an aural specter. As he remembered, as the lyrics and tune came back to him, he began to hum along.

"…country roads, take me home, to the place I belong. West Virginia, mountain momma, take me home, country roads…"

The ethereal, wandering image abruptly locked up. It hung among them for an instant longer before scattering in a silent burst of evaporating pixels.

Eyes turned from the place where the figure had last hovered to the man who had been humming in concert with the ancient words.

"'Take Me Home, Country Roads.'" Noting that more detail was wanting, Tennessee added, "First recorded by the great John Denver, mid-twentieth-century singer, songwriter, and environmental activist."

"What's an 'environmental activist'?" Upworth wanted to know.

"Someone who agitates to preserve the environment," Tennessee replied, looking over at her. When she eyed him blankly, he added, "They've been pretty much extinct for some time now. Like their rationale."

Lopé shook his head. "You gotta be kidding."

Tennessee frowned at the sergeant, his voice solemn. "I never kid about John Denver."

It was Mother who interrupted the history lesson. "Source of the transmission located."

"Visuals, please," Oram directed the ship.

The holo star chart that appeared was the most detailed the computer could generate for the outlying sector in which they found themselves floating. Without having to be prompted, Mother zoomed in, to center on a single blurry star. It had no name, no designation. Even in a time when high-powered telescopes floated in orbit between the Earth and the moon there were still places, still stellar objects, that could not be clearly distinguished.

"Empty" space was full of dust, gravitational distortions, and other astronomical events that often obscured direct observation of distant phenomena. Such was the case with the uncharted star whose location Mother was able to resolve only because of the ship's current position in the cosmos.

The visuals were unremarkable. "Details," Oram said.

"Signal originates in sector 105, right ascension forty-seven point six and declination of twenty-four point three relative to our current location. Full coordinates being relayed and recorded now."

"Got it." At the navigation console, Ricks utilized supplementary instrumentation to further refine the available data. When he was satisfied, he nudged a control and the holographic image instantly zoomed in a second time to reveal additional elements. The initial fuzzy image of the distant star sharpened. Five planets became visible, along with the usual assortment of moons, asteroids, and other cosmic detritus. The navigator's attention flicked back and forth between the holo and his console.

"Looks like she's a main sequence star, a lot like our own, but quite old for the sequence. *Very* old. Five planets." He stopped, frowned slightly, and rechecked several noteworthy readings. "And look at this—planet number four is square in the habitable zone."

Everyone was suitably shaken. Given the amount of terrestrial effort that had gone into locating every possible habitable world within range of Earth's colony ships, to have missed one in this sector was shocking.

Perhaps it shouldn't have been, Oram reflected. Even in an age when deep space exploration and colonization were taken for granted, the one salient fact that people always seemed to have a difficult time grasping was simply how *big* space was. Add to that the fact that the system they had just discovered lay in an area replete with cosmic obscurantism—like the flare that had damaged the ship—and maybe it wasn't so surprising it had been missed.

Nor was it likely to be the last they had overlooked.

"Okay, so it's in the right neighborhood," he said, "and

near enough to resolve the vitals in real time. What do they look like?"

Ricks zoomed in still further, straining the ship's resolution capabilities to the utmost. It took a moment for Mother to gather and process the requisite data so he could share it.

"It's a prime candidate. Point ninety-six Gs at the surface. All the way around the planet. No extreme equatorial or polar gravitational distortions. Liquid water oceans. Scattered land masses, granitic and basaltic in general composition. Can't tell about motile tectonics— we're too far out and these are just the preliminaries. Have to spend some time there to acquire that kind of info." He paused a moment. "Everything points to a high likelihood of a living biosphere. Leastwise, the necessary markers are all there." His attention shifted to Daniels. "Everything I see suggests a world that exceeds the company's and your most optimistic projections for Origae-6."

"You're sure of all of this?" Looking skeptical, she studied the data on his console.

He grunted. "As sure as Mother's sensors can be. And we've got a damn sight better view of it from here than anyone on Earth did of Origae-6." The implication of this information escaped no one.

"How did we miss it?" she demanded. "We scanned every corner of this sector."

Oram was gratified to be able to interject. "View obviously is blocked from Earth. Dense nebulae, dust cloud, periodic flares screening out the infrared—maybe when the searcher for this sector made its pass, this world was at perihelion, on the opposite side of its star from Earth. Or the whole system could have been positioned exactly behind another intervening star or two. Not to mention the tricks that gravitational lensing can play with planetary scanners." He tried for placating. "Don't fault yourself, or the program, for the oversight."

Though Lopé listened as intently as the others, his perspective was more prosaic.

"How far is it? Not from home. From here."

"She's close." As curious as any of them, Ricks had already run the necessary calculations. "Real close. Just a short jump from our present recharge position. Maybe a couple of weeks. At jumpspeed, it wouldn't even be necessary to go into hypersleep."

Everyone absorbed that bit of information. No more hypersleep. No more waking up stiff, sometimes sore, with weakened muscles, shouting nerves, churning guts, and a mouth that felt like it had been chewing cotton for a decade. All that, and a potential colony site whose vitals exceeded those of the one for which the *Covenant* was headed.

Oram noted their reactions before turning to Walter.

"How long until we reach Origae-6?"

"Seven years, four months, three weeks, two days," the synthetic replied promptly. "Give or take twelve hours, and barring the unexpected."

"Hell of a long sleep-cycle." Faris stared evenly at her husband. "Also seven years' worth of the 'unexpected.' Seven additional years of brain and body knockout without knowing how well the ship is coping with the strain."

"Gotta tell you," Upworth put in, "I'm not crazy about

getting back into one of those pods. I've always been a touch claustrophobic."

Faris made a face. "Claustrophobia is an automatic disqualification for crewing a colony ship."

The younger woman shrugged. "Okay, so I lied a little bit on the application." She avoided Oram's gaze. "Doesn't bother me once I'm asleep."

He chose to ignore the confession. It hardly mattered now. Acutely aware that everyone was waiting on him, he knew it was time to act the captain.

"All right, let's take a look," he said. "It's not so far offline from Origae that stopping there will have a significant impact on the ship's resources. If nothing else, we'll have some interesting information to shoot back to Earth."

Whether it was the correct decision or not, he didn't know. What was plain was that it was the one the crew wanted. Their excitement was evident and unrestrained as they went back to work. Only Daniels and Tennessee looked concerned. While he returned to his station, Daniels joined Oram in gazing out the forward port. Intent on their assigned tasks, no one paid the pair any attention.

"You sure about this, Captain?"

He glanced at her. "What do you mean?"

"I mean we spent a decade searching for a world like Origae-6. The company, its outside consultants, relevant government divisions—everyone and everything was focused on finding the latest, best place to put down a colony. Ten years' effort by hundreds of specialists engaged in detailed scanning of thousands of systems, to come up with a single optimal candidate. We vetted it, we ran thousands of simulations, we mapped possible terrain based on all the information that could be gathered from a distance—it's what we all trained for."

"I understand that," he began, "but the possibility of—"

Interrupting him, heedless of protocol, she plunged on. "And now we're going to scrap all that to chase down the source of a rogue transmission?"

He chose not to upbraid her for cutting him off. "Not necessarily for a rogue transmission. For the opportunity to perhaps find a better prospect. One closer and possibly even better suited to our purpose. The transmission, its source, and origin, are incidental." His expression tightened. "If this world turns out to be suitable for our needs, I don't care if we *ever* find the source of that transmission. It can remain a mystery for the colonists to ponder as they're establishing themselves. A ghost story to frighten children. What matters is if the planet turns out to match its stats, as reported by Mother." He shrugged. "If it doesn't, no harm done. We'll continue on to Origae-6, with little if anything sacrificed in the process."

She took a breath. "Think about it, Captain. Christopher. A transmission from, by, or about a human being out here where there shouldn't be any humans. An unknown planet—no, an unknown *system*—that suddenly appears out of nowhere. And don't talk to me about intervening cosmic debris, or stellar masking, or anything like that. Here's a planet that just happens to be perfect for us. Or at least from a distance, appears to be. *It's too good to be true*."

He drew back slightly, startled at her intensity. "'Too good to be true'? What does that even mean? For a scientist, that's a pretty colloquial reaction to a still unresolved finding."

"You want colloquial, Captain. Okay. I'll keep it in non-technical terms. It means we don't know what the fuck's out there."

Remember what your wife told you, he reminded himself. *Patience. Patience and understanding.*

"Are you upset because your team missed this system?" he asked evenly. "Or recorded the system, but missed the fourth planet? Or maybe because whoever was responsible for analyzing the scans of his or her fragment of this sector overlooked its possibilities? Even the automated planetary search system itself could have missed it. Computers do experience oversights sometimes. All it takes is one transposed digit and suddenly there's no potentially habitable world where one actually exists."

It was hard for her to argue with the unprovable.

All she said was, "It's risky."

His reply was magnanimous. "Every colonization represents a risk. The trick is to minimize them. Right now I'm looking at a few weeks in hypersleep for the colonists, versus another seven years plus. Not to mention the enormously reduced wear and tear on the ship's systems. By making this detour, if it ends up being just a detour, I'm not committing us to anything. As captain, I have to follow the path that's laid out before me." Looking back, he nodded in the direction of Ricks' station.

"Navigation has provided us with a possible destination that's closer, easier to reach, and potentially superior." He looked back at her. "If we're fortunate and the preliminary analysis is accurate, this may prove to be a better habitat for the entire colony. If that turns out to be the case, can you imagine the reaction when we start to revive the colonists?"

She nodded knowingly, her expression still sour.

"And you'll be the guy to have found it."

He chose not to argue with her, not caring in so choosing if his lack of combativeness only served to confirm her preferred conclusion.

"And we don't want to resume hypersleep," he said. "Nobody does. Nobody wants to get back into those damn pods. Also, there's something else. Singing and ancient song selections aside, that sounded like a human voice. A voice in need. Nobody can deny that. The desperation was unmistakable." His voice trailed off. "If I was a lone human stuck on a distant, unknown planet…"

"How is that even possible?" she asked him.

He was ready with an answer. "Ships go missing from time to time. You know that. Transports, prospecting vessels—not everybody takes the time and trouble to report their itinerary." He essayed a thin smile. "Not everybody wants the government or competing companies to *know* their itinerary."

She shifted tack. "We're responsible for two thousand colonists. Whole families. They went into hypersleep on the assumption that when they were awakened, it would be on a productive, livable, *safe* world. They were promised Origae-6.

"This isn't about you," she pressed. "This is about them."

He stiffened. "I'm fully aware of what they were

promised. Karine and I were promised the same thing immediately, to occur upon the *Covenant*'s official decommissioning. As were you and the rest of the crew. I'm not free climbing here. I'm making a sound judgment based on all the data we have. Or are you disputing Ricks' and Mother's analytics?"

"Yeah, well," she muttered, "we don't owe the colonists sound judgment. We owe them our *best* judgment, Captain. And in *my* judgment, putting the mission in jeopardy to follow a rogue signal to an unknown and unidentified planet in an uncharted system is not the best judgment."

He could no longer conceal his exasperation.

"It's the decision I'm making," he replied. "And the signal itself is secondary, at best. I've already said that. What we're really going to take a look at is a potentially colonizable world that's seven years nearer to our present position, and possibly more amenable to settlement than Origae-6."

She drew herself up. "Well, as your second-in-command, I need to protest officially."

"Officially?" His voice went flat. "Do what you need to do. Mother will record it in the ship's log, and you can send it out by relay whenever you feel the time is right. I'll acknowledge your objection, if you wish. Officially." He turned away from her.

/ /

Seething inside, she watched him move over to Ricks' station. There was nothing more she could do. Despite her objections, she knew that most if not all of the rest of the crew would back Oram's decision.

The prospect of not having to endure another seven years or more of hypersleep was a powerful incentive even to those who might be inclined to support her position. She could only file her formal objection, knowing that it would take more time to reach Earth than it would for the *Covenant* to arrive in the uncharted system—much less for a response to come back to the ship. Given that reality, she wasn't sure it was worth the effort to file.

Oram would know that, too, she realized.

She could retire to her cabin—hers alone now—and rage and scream and kick the walls in frustration. If she requested Walter's presence, he would come and listen solicitously to her grievances. He might even agree with her, but it was inconceivable that the synthetic might vote against the captain. Logic and reason were her only allies, and for all the good they were doing her, they might as well be locked up in hypersleep alongside the colonists.

There being nothing more she could do, she remembered the perfect joints Walter had rolled for her. That way lay, if not redress, at least momentary contentment.

Without a word to any of her colleagues she exited the bridge. It was a measure of their excitement and anticipation that no one, not even Tennessee, turned from their work to inquire about her state of mind, or where she was going.

VI

A bluish sun flared against the blackness of space as the massive bulk of the *Covenant* slowed upon entering the unnamed system.

As it approached the fourth planet, every station on the bridge was manned, every set of organic and inorganic eyes and ears was attuned to the blue-white dot they were approaching. Its two moons, each smaller than Earth's, occupied unremarkable orbits. In contrast to the world they circled, the satellites offered nothing of interest.

On the bridge, Ricks worked his instrumentation with the hand-to-eye coordination of a professional gambler. At the moment, the comparison was apt.

"I'm cycling through every communications channel, including the theoretical ones, but all I'm getting is a lot of interference and white noise, some high frequency echoes… Trying to isolate and analyze, but it's just a mess all across the spectrum." He pursed his lips. "Can't even tell if some of the sources are natural or artificial in origin.

Planet's got a heavy core, ionosphere is heavily charged, and predictors suggest the poles swing a lot. Place is a real electromagnetic gumbo." He glanced across to another station. "You hearing anything?"

Nearby, an apprehensive Daniels stayed focused on her instruments as the *Covenant* maintained its cautious approach.

Having recovered his worry beads from his wife, Oram was nervously clicking them against one another— but softly, softly, so as not to disturb any of the others. At the central navigation table, Walter looked on intently as Mother continuously refined the imagery of the nearing world and its two moons. As yet there were no topographic details, but he knew those would begin to become available soon.

Finally replying to Ricks, Upworth nudged one half of her headphones and shook her head negatively.

"I'm getting pretty much what you're getting, except I've kept the steady signal from our friendly ghost on a separate line." She made a face. "I'm getting pretty sick of the song, by the way."

Tennessee let out a dramatic sigh. "The siren's song."

"'Once he hears to his heart's content, sails on, a wiser man,'" Daniels murmured. When Oram gave her a sharp sideways glance, she added with a shrug, "I'm not criticizing. Blame Homer."

"Well," Tennessee quipped, "whatever's down there, it isn't Scylla, and it isn't West Virginia, either."

Ricks looked over at him. "What is a 'West Virginia,' anyway?"

"Ancient tribal demarcation," Walter explained without looking up from his position. "There once were a great many of them, back when that sort of thing was considered relevant. The world used to be full of dozens of minor political entities, all working at cross-purposes instead of for the common good of the species and the planet."

Ricks considered that. "How did people ever accomplish anything worthwhile?"

"They didn't," Walter replied flatly.

"Still a lot of interference across the spectrum." Upworth struggled to isolate and clarify reception.

Oram responded with scarcely controlled eagerness. "Bring us into drop proximity and prepare the lander."

As the *Covenant* slipped into orbit, sensors and scanners continued to soak up as much information as possible about the world below. Everything was fed to Mother, who worked to compile an increasingly detailed dossier on a prospective site for the colony. The gathering of information would continue until every reading had been made redundant. Those that changed—such as for temperature and other weather patterns—would be continuously updated so that a landing party would know from minute to minute what they were likely to encounter.

/ / /

While the bridge buzzed with activity, the expedition team headed for the lander's lock, personal equipment in hand.

Bearing in mind the climate at the landing site, they wore warm gray field gear with matching heavy boots and earflap caps. Beige vests bulged with nearly everything they were likely to need. Items that couldn't fit in the vests, or might need to be accessed more rapidly, filled their equipment belts.

Privates Rosenthal and Ankor entered the lander side by side. She was nervous, he laconic. The contrast wasn't striking, but it was there. Observing her unease, he interrupted it with a question.

"You ever done a lander drop before?"

Rosenthal swallowed. "Just simulations," she replied. "I was told they're as close to the real thing as possible."

"Simulations." Ankor considered. "Cool."

She shot him a glance and he smiled back. Knowingly, she decided.

Once the landing team was seated and strapped in opposite one another in the main bay, those on the *Covenant*'s bridge copied over Mother's suggested vectoring. It wasn't encouraging, but it was doable. Navigation's holo readouts showed a storming cloud cover, replete with frequent lightning flashing directly in the intended drop path. The readouts faded and sharpened, formed and reformed as the relevant information underwent constant updating.

/ / /

Relegated to running the *Covenant* while Oram and Daniels joined the expedition team, an unhappy Tennessee took it all in. Hoping to see some clearing in the atmosphere, or at least some moderating, he was disappointed.

"Hell of a strong ionosphere."

"Angry weather," Ricks agreed as he addressed

his comm. "Faris, it looks like a plasma storm in the thermosphere. We're reading some steady two-fifty winds with intermittent stronger up- and down-drafts." He checked another readout. "Mother's given you the best rabbit hole. Believe it or not, conditions are worse elsewhere."

/ / /

On board the lander, Faris murmured commands to the piloting console. Instrumentation adjusted according to her instructions. In conditions like those raging below, it was imperative to have a human at the controls. Autopilot was fine for putting down on a beach in the midst of a clear sunny day. When it came to landing in real weather, however, nothing could beat human reactions, especially for last-minute judgments.

Human lander pilots sometimes didn't make the best decisions, according to the procedures described in the manuals, but they usually made the right ones necessary to survive.

Oram and Walter sat up front with her, while the rest of the landing party had settled into seats behind. The captain could hardly contain his excitement. Walter had none to contain. A few expectant whispers, punctuated by nervous laughter, rose from the group as the remainder of the lander's systems came online.

Leaning forward slightly, Faris took note of the angle of approach that had been chosen by the ship's computer.

"I see where we're going," she informed Ricks via the ship-to-ship comm. "Helluva trajectory. Storm's gonna be a motherfucker to fly through." Her attention flicked back and forth from the readouts to the lander's own external sensors. "This is the best Mother could come up with?"

"Yeah, 'fraid so." Upworth's tone was apologetic as it echoed over the open comm. "And communications will be spotty until you're down. I'll do my best to keep a signal lock on you guys during the drop, but between the intensity of the storm and the likelihood that you're gonna bounce all over the friggin' place, it's gonna be hard to say hello every minute or so."

Oram eyed his pilot. She and Tennessee were the best piloting couple the company could find. He had complete confidence in them, but this wasn't a training facility on Earth, and they weren't dropping toward a benign surface like that on Mars.

"Safe to land?" he murmured.

Faris grumbled at the readouts. "Depends on what you call 'safe.'"

He grinned. "Then we won't call it 'safe.' We'll just call it 'okay.'" Finally he added, "Let her rip."

Aside from the somber Daniels, the rest of the crew in the lander were delighted at the quip. Coming from the captain, off-hand humor was a welcome surprise. A few cheers echoed from the back, and several high-fives were gleefully exchanged.

A bit surprised at himself and pleased by the reaction, Oram turned to look back into the crew bay and smile at them. As he did so his eyes met those of his wife, seated near the front. Karine flashed him a reassuring wink, and his smile widened.

Far too busy to participate in any general hilarity, Faris was completely focused on the main console. "Preparing to lock in descent mode over signal position now. Mother, please coordinate launch sequence."

The *Covenant*'s positioning thrusters promptly engaged, ensuring that the ship would remain in geosynchronous orbit above the chosen landing site. On board, two thousand souls slept on, unaware that their transportation was making an unscheduled detour that, if conditions proved favorable, might well prove to be a permanent one.

"Understood." Mother's voice sounded over the comms in both the ship and the waiting lander. "Coordinating position over signal location. In simultaneous orbit now. You are clear to launch, Lander One."

"Launching now, *Covenant*." Faris engaged the necessary controls. There was a noticeable jolt as the lander disengaged from its parent vessel. This was followed by a brief and expected flush of nausea among the expedition team as they dropped out of the ship's artificial gravity field. Engines fired, and the lander began to accelerate away from the main ship and toward the roiling, angry atmosphere below.

/ / /

From her position on the *Covenant*'s bridge, Upworth monitored the drop. Everything was going smoothly and according to procedure. Of course, she told herself, they hadn't hit atmosphere yet. Given the prospects for a rough descent, she decided that a little early encouragement wouldn't be out of place. Faris would know it for what it was, but there was no harm in offering it anyway.

"You're looking gorgeous from up here, Faris. Angle on descent is perfect, drop speed is right on point. Thank goodness you're flying, and not the old man."

Across the bridge, Tennessee pulled an exaggerated expression. "A little less of the 'old man,' if you don't mind."

Faris grinned. "If the boot fits..."

"You know where I'll put it," he finished suggestively. Turning serious again, he let his gaze wander between the forward port and his console readouts. He no longer had visual on the lander, of course—but that didn't keep him from straining to try and follow its descent through the port. Highly trained though he was, there was something in being a pilot that had always favored eye contact over instrumentation.

No time for nostalgia, he told himself firmly. With Oram and Daniels both on board the lander, he was now in charge of the *Covenant*.

The storm was massive, involving a good swath of the visible atmosphere. The continuous, extensive lightning and the roaring winds put Faris more in mind of Jupiter's atmosphere than Earth's. At least, she told herself as she prepared for atmospheric entry, they didn't have to deal with a gas giant's crushing gravity, or bands of killer radiation.

"Everything looking good down there?" Upworth's voice sounded over the lander's comm, trying a little too hard not to sound concerned.

"All good, *Covenant*," Faris replied. "Expect to hit exosphere in five. Ask me again in ten minutes."

/ / /

Turning, she called back to those seated in the main crew bay. "No point in trying to avoid the obvious—it's gonna get rough. Might want to hang on back there. You know how Tennessee likes old music and antiques? Any of you know what a 'pinball machine' was?" Silence greeted her query. "I'll explain in detail later. Right now you're about to find out what the ball felt like."

BAM!

Cupping the sturdy lander in its grasp, a stream of superfast air threw it back toward space, then yanked it groundward. Though she was flying via electronics, and not by stick or wire, Faris still struggled with the controls.

Continuing to descend was like flying through the eye wall of a terrestrial hurricane, and a monster at that. Lights within the lander flickered as alarms howled on and off. Being strapped in securely didn't keep Oram and Walter from grabbing onto the sides of their drop seats. In the crew bay behind them, someone moaned. Someone else—it might have been Rosenthal—started to make gagging sounds.

"Not here," the soldier next to her yelled, "for god's sake, not here!" Whether because of the threat or the embarrassment, the incipient puking noises ceased.

Considering the pounding it was taking, it did not seem possible that the lander would hold together. But this was what it had been designed for, and Faris knew it. That didn't prevent her from being just a tad concerned. Knowing that everyone else was depending on her and was doubtless watching her, she strove to stay calm.

Seemingly inescapable, the song "Country Roads" popped into her head again and she started whistling along. Though it helped to soothe her, the effort was lost to everyone else amid the crashing and banging inside the landing craft.

She was close enough to the piloting console pickup to be heard on the *Covenant*'s bridge, however.

/ / /

Each note lingered in Tennessee's hearing as he focused his attention on the readout image that represented the steadily descending craft.

"You still reading me, Faris?" he said. "Faris?"

Fragments of "Country Roads" crackled from speakers. Taken together, there weren't enough of them to make up a whole song. Hoping for something more coherent, everyone on the bridge listened intently—until even the barely comprehensible excerpts ceased.

Silence.

Upworth stated what everyone knew. "We lost comm."

"Goddamn storm. I hate it when electrons don't behave." It was the rare occasion when one of Tennessee's jibes fell flat.

Outside and far below, the crazed ionosphere kept communications between the *Covenant* and the lander incommunicado. Those on the bridge of the colony ship could only try to imagine what the landing team must be going through.

VII

On board the lander itself, there was no time to imagine much of anything. An intrusive crashing reality kept everyone's thoughts tightly focused. One jolt after another sent the craft alternately up, down, and sideways. Each shock felt as if they were slamming into a mountainside, when in actuality it was only the wind.

Air had never felt so solid, Oram decided as he manipulated his worry beads.

As bad as the turbulence were the huge bolts of lightning that split the dense cloud cover enveloping the lander. So numerous and close were the strikes that he could frequently see inside the ship without the need of its internal lighting.

Lighting, lightning, Oram thought, trying to take his mind off the conditions. Beside him, a grim-faced Faris worked the controls, fighting to keep the ship level and on course. Not because consistent stability was necessary— the lander could fly just as efficiently upside down. But it would be better for the team's morale if the craft's interior remained puke-free.

An especially powerful jolt would have thrown everyone on board head-first into the ceiling had they not been strapped into their seats. It was strong enough to break Oram's grasp on his low-tech stress-relievers, sending one round bead rolling and rattling across the deck. While he missed its comforting presence in his hand, he had no intention of unstrapping to go look for it.

Noting his partner's distress, Lopé leaned toward Hallet, trying to impart a bit of reassurance and comfort to the other man's space. Alone among the team, the sergeant was actually enjoying the chaotic ride.

"Relax, Tom. It's only atmosphere," he said. "Nothing to worry about. There's nothing solid to hit." He nodded forward. "Faris is the best pilot on the *Covenant*."

Hallet gripped the arms of his seat so hard his fingers were turning white inside his gloves. "I hate space." A quick glance downward showed the captain's fugitive worry bead rolling past beneath their seats.

"It's not like we're flying through a meteor storm." Lopé's voice was calm and controlled, no different from the one he would have been using had he been in the middle of a comforting meal in the *Covenant*'s mess.

"That's in space, too," Hallet muttered unhappily.

Lopé smiled affectionately. "This is why you need to do yoga."

His partner shot him a look, and the sergeant laughed.

A moment later the lander dropped a hundred meters as if it had been hit by a giant hammer, then recovered the lost altitude under Faris' skilled ministrations. Lopé's grin turned to a look of concern as Hallet blanched. The other man really was having a tough time. Eschewing any further casual banter or attempts at humor, the sergeant turned his gaze forward. While the rocking, bouncing, and general atmospheric turmoil didn't bother him, he could not help but wonder—just how extensive *was* this storm, anyway?

He could have asked, but knew better. Everyone up front was far too busy to respond to casual questions from the cargo.

Then, without any warning, the terrible jolting ceased. It was replaced by an ominous but quite familiar creaking from less-than-stellar joins in the hull. A minute later even the creaking ceased as the lander dropped through the underside of the cloud layer. Pursing her lips, Faris exhaled long and deliberately.

The terrific pounding they had taken was behind them, and both the lander and its personnel were intact. They descended now as smoothly and uneventfully as if they were back in space circling the *Covenant* in the complete absence of weather. Emergency illumination was replaced automatically by normal lighting. The crew bay was filled with exclamations of relief, laughter, and more than one comment about needing a change of undergarments. But there had been no injuries. Straps and drop seats had done their job.

Adding to the general relief, for the first time in a while, a voice sounded clearly over the comm.

"Lander, do you read? Respond if you can, lander."

Faris threw Oram a smile as she replied. "What, you haven't been listening? Shame. All that fascinating meteorological information lost." When there was no response, she continued. "Yeah, yeah. I read you, *Covenant*. Nothing to it. We just got tired of talking to you all the time, that's all." Still no reply to her joking, so she turned serious.

"Okay, it wasn't a piece of cake. But we're through. We're okay. No detectable damage to the ship…" She cast a quick glance behind her. "…or its contents. Continuing descent—normally."

The planet's surface proved as jagged and rough as its atmosphere, with steep-sloped gray mountains whose tops were obscured by low-hanging clouds, dense forests enveloped in mist that even from several hundred meters up looked hauntingly familiar, deep valleys and fjords cut by fast-flowing rivers, numerous lakes of every shape and size. Below the main storm layer, scattered cumulus occasionally grew dark and heavy enough to unload the infrequent shower.

Faris gnawed on her lower lip as she studied the guidance telemetry and attendant readouts. The view out the lander's wide forward port was impressive, even breathtaking—but it wasn't conducive to an easy touchdown. They were fast approaching the coordinates of the signal source. She knew she had to make a decision, whether to glide past the source and hope for better landing prospects on the far side of the site, or set down now.

Readouts and information acquired from orbit suggested that, if anything, the topography was rougher on the other side of the signal site than what they were cruising over at present. Preferring to trust her own vision whenever possible, she leaned slightly forward to peer upward. There was no telling if or when the ferocious electrical storm might grow worse or descend to a lower altitude. If the latter, it would complicate their landing considerably.

She determined not to chance it.

"I don't like the terrain," she told Oram, "and I can't get any solid predictions on what the weather might do. We've got several sites on this side of the signal with smooth water. Slopes verging on precipices everywhere else. I suggest we be prudent."

He nodded his understanding. "I'm a prudent man, Faris. You're the pilot. Your call."

That settled it. "I'm putting us down on amphib. Anybody wants to get out and try waterskiing, now's the time. Let me know and I'll pop the ramp."

Even had that been possible, there would have been no takers. Every member of the landing team had been slammed around more than enough for one day. The notion of doing so for recreation was decidedly unappealing.

The long, narrow gorge into which she descended would have made a perfect landing strip had it not been filled with water. That didn't prevent Faris from bringing the lander in and down gently among the stark surroundings. Disturbing both moist atmosphere and cold water, the ship kicked up a plume in its wake. Slowing and hovering, she turned to port and brought them in to the near shore.

At the last moment, an unexpected *clunk* against the lander's underside made her wince. No alarms sounded, meaning hull integrity had not been breached. Maneuvering carefully, she turned the vessel sideways and settled down in shallow water beside a pebble beach.

None of her companions had to tell her that she was the best, she knew as she cut the engines. That was a given.

Relieved to be safely through the terrible storm and on solid ground, the team members all but tore off their restraining straps in their excitement to disembark. Despite all the gear he was carrying, Private Cole did a few experimental jumping jacks, delighting in the feel of his boots banging against the deck underfoot.

"Real gravity!" He looked over at Rosenthal, who was crowding him. "Almost forgot what it feels like."

"You hit me in the shoulder again, and you'll get to experience even more of it," she warned him. "Give me a hand with my pack, will you?"

As the expedition readied itself to go ashore, packs were slung, weapons loaded, rations counted. Everyone checked everyone else's gear, and then had their own checked again. Up front, as Faris ran through the lander's power-down sequence, the comm crackled anew. Despite the fact that the storm now raged high above them, it continued to interfere with reception, as well as transmission. At least, she told herself, something intelligible was getting through.

"We're having trouble reading you… find… boost your signal?" Faris recognized Upworth's voice. She could only respond and hope that the lander's communications system had enough strength to punch through the swirling electromagnetic disturbance overhead.

"Roger that. Not only was it a hell of an entry, but we had to do an amphib landing, and we may have clipped something in the water on touchdown. I'm gonna check for damage, so may be out of direct touch for a bit. Will engage suit-to-ship relay and anticipate that works both directions."

As she spoke to the *Covenant*, and hoped she was being heard, Daniels joined them. When Oram eyed her quizzically she opened one clenched hand to reveal the worry bead he had dropped during the descent. He took it, giving her a nod of thanks.

"Myself, I'd prefer a suitably relaxing pharmaceutical," she told him.

He held up the bead before returning it to his pocket.

"This is non-narcotic, always available, and non-addictive."

She could have said something about the latter, chose not to as he peered out the foreport.

"How far?"

Walter checked his readouts. "Signal's source is eight kilometers almost due west, but at a considerable elevation. Up a steep incline." He looked over at Faris. "You chose the set-down site well. While there are options between us and the signal source, we really could not have gotten any closer without endangering the lander."

"I know," she said simply. "It's called 'piloting.'" More than most of the crew, she had a tendency to be short with the synthetic. She didn't know why. Walter was perfectly pleasant, perfectly responsive, perfectly sociable. Perfectly… perfect.

Maybe that was why, she told herself.

At a command from the bridge, the portside landing ramp deployed. Spanning a bit of shallow water, the far end settled into the gentle slope of the pebble beach. Being the most expendable member of the team, as well as the only one who did not require breathing gear, Walter descended first. Standing on the solid ground, he looked around and took a deep breath. Not because he needed to do so, but to acquire a sample of atmosphere for his internal systems to analyze.

The result was comforting, as were all the other readings. He informed the others.

"Is he sure?" Peering out the forward port, Daniels watched as Walter performed a series of mundane tasks, kneeling to examine the green ground cover beyond the beach, cupping his hands to sample the water from the lake, inspecting several choice pebbles chosen from the edge of the beach. Oram frowned at her.

"It's Walter. Walter is either sure or he's not sure. There are no gray areas with Walter. You know that."

"Yeah, right. Okay, then." Looking back into the ship's bay to where the crew was performing final prep, she raised her voice. "Walter says the atmosphere is so good we're not going to need breathing gear. No sign of local pathogens in the air, either, right down past the molecular level. So no need for full evac suits."

The cheers and shouts of delight that greeted her announcement rocked the ship almost as hard as had the storm.

Faris was back on the comm, hoping her signal reached the *Covenant*. "Atmosphere's breathable," she reported.

"No, better than breathable, according to Walter. Downright terrestrial, except without all the pollutants. I'd say it's 'fresh,' though he wouldn't use such a non-technical term. No airborne contaminants whatsoever. Pristine."

Edenesque? she thought. No, that designation would be premature. She waited as the members of the expedition team filed out in the direction of the airlock and the deployed landing ramp.

"The team is heading out now to investigate the source of the transmission," she told the comm. "I'll relay their findings if it proves necessary. Suit signals might need a boost, if the damn storm doesn't settle down."

When Upworth's voice responded immediately, Faris let out a sigh of relief. Maybe the current state of ground-to-ship communications wasn't the best, but at least it was functional.

"See if you can push more power to the lander's uplink, honey," Upworth replied. She, too, sounded relieved at the stabilizing of contact. "Signal's coming through up here, but still showing a tendency to fall apart. Have to gather, assemble, and process before you can be understood."

"Will try." Faris rose from her seat, glad to finally be able to stand without having to worry about being slammed against the bulkhead. "Repurposing main relay. I have to go outside for a bit to check for potential damage to the hull. Then I'll see about further goosing the uplink. Now that we're down, maybe I can redistribute some power."

Though there was enough cloud cover to mute the daylight, it was far from dark outside the lander. Not exactly cheery, Faris told herself as she followed the rest of the team out the lock and down the ramp, but far from unrelenting gloom. Their surroundings were just—gray. While the team worked out last-minute preparations before embarking on the hike ahead, she made her way toward the back of the ship, checking the underside as far as was possible given that it was sitting in shallow water, and then working her way carefully around the forward and aft landing thrusters.

The dent was sufficiently prominent that she noticed it right away. Any possible internal damage would have to await an instrument scan. As she continued to study the indentation, Oram came up beside her, his boots sloshing through dark water.

"Okay, Faris, we're heading out. Keep all expedition security protocols in place," he instructed. "And watch out for hungry dinosaurs." It was a weak attempt at levity, but she appreciated the effort nonetheless. Oram really was beginning to relax into command.

"Will do." Peering past him, her gaze traveled up the soaring mountainside in the direction of the signal's source. "Don't see anything moving yet, dinos included. Pretty peaceful." She turned her attention back toward the damage to the lander. "Have fun, y'all."

/ / /

Turning slowly, he took in the immediate surroundings. The lake was stunning, reminding him of images he had seen of glacial lochs on Earth. The mountains that framed the lengthy body of water were equally imposing, as were the fir- and redwood-like trees that climbed their flanks. It was all quite beautiful.

Beautiful—and quiet, he couldn't help noticing. Faris was right. The only sounds were made by the slight breeze as it caressed rocks and grass and the barely perceptible liquid *clink* of wavelets against the rocky shore. There were no animal calls, no bird cries, and no exotic analogs thereof. Despite the inarguable habitability of the planetary surface, despite its welcoming atmosphere, temperature, and gravity, nothing moved in the sky, in the water, on the dry land, or in the forest.

Quiet.

He gave a mental shrug. Maybe the lander had come down in a particularly sterile spot. Or maybe the local fauna engaged in mass migration. Or were hibernating in expectation of warmer weather—and fewer storms. He couldn't spare the time to ponder on it. This wasn't a zoological expedition. Two thousand colonists in hypersleep were waiting on what they found, and on his ultimate decisions. Which he could not make until a number of questions were answered.

Walking back to shore, he rejoined the group that stood patiently awaiting his orders. With one hand he gestured at the looming mountainside.

"If everyone's ready…?" When no one demurred, he added, "All right then. Let's go find our ghost. Walter?"

Without a word and holding his multiunit out in front of him, the synthetic started off. Lopé accelerated to take point in front of their guide. The rest of his squad—Hallet, Cole, Ledward, Ankor, and Rosenthal—fanned out around him, forming a standard semicircular perimeter. Daniels, Oram, and Karine followed close behind Walter.

/ /

As she collected the necessary ingredients for a standard scan-and-repair kit, Faris listened to her husband via the relayed comm.

"No way to boost the signal?" he asked her.

Kit in hand, she replied as she once again exited the lander and descended the ramp. "Not without going completely offline, and allowing the cells to recycle."

"How long would that take?" he inquired hopefully.

Wading out into the water she halted next to the dent in the hull. Using a special tool designed exclusively for the purpose, she began opening service hatches, striving to maintain the contact with the *Covenant* while also trying to envision the work that might need to be done.

"I dunno. A couple of hours." Straightening, she pulled a tech scanner from her kit. "If I take the time to do that, it would mean taking time away from making repairs down here, and I don't even know the extent of those yet. Depending on the damage, they might require minutes, might require hours." She didn't say "days."

Don't let it be days, she muttered to herself.

Tennessee made the logical choice, as she knew he would. "It's not worth taking time away from what you might have to do to the lander. Do what you have to do with it first. Meanwhile, let me see what we can do up here. I can try overriding the automatics with a couple of experimental resolution algorithms, see if we can maybe improve clarity without having to boost signal strength."

"Okey doke." Repeated attempts failed to get a particularly reluctant hatch to open, but the problem was solved by the simple expedient of whacking it hard a couple of times with a spanner. "I've got plenty to keep me busy." She cast a squint skyward. "Viewed from down here, there's still plenty of crackle overhead, but none of it is hitting the ground, and at least it's not raining." She hoped that didn't jinx it. "Faris out."

As communication terminated she paused to inspect the small internal portions of the lander that her efforts had exposed to view. A sudden sense of unease caused her to turn and look out across the somber landscape. She knew immediately what it was that was bothering her.

It was that damn unbroken continuing *quiet*.

VIII

Daniels moved up so that she was walking alongside Walter. After climbing a lightly vegetated slope, the expedition team found themselves pushing through a flat field of some kind of tall grass. Pale gold instead of green, the stalks swayed in perfect unison with the prevailing gentle breeze. Despite the increasingly uncomfortable ongoing silence she was glad that the grass, at least, did not make any noise.

Looking ahead, she saw that two of the lead security team had stopped. In complete violation of proper expedition procedure, Sergeant Lopé was crushing the top of one of the golden stalks between his fingers. Before she could object, he rubbed the residue between his palms, brought it close to his face, and blew part of it away. Picking up the loose chaff, the breeze carried it off toward the nearby mountains.

To Daniels' astonishment, Lopé then brought what remained in his palm up to his tongue, and tasted it. She held her breath. Even Walter looked up from his multiunit and watched the sergeant closely.

Taking note of her anxious expression, Lopé smiled reassuringly and gestured at the field in which they stood.

"This is wheat," he said. "Plain, ordinary, bland, bread-making wheat. I'm from what they used to call Iowa. Believe me, I know wheat." He took a second taste, turned thoughtful. "This is old, a primitive variety, but definitely cultivated. Too much taste to be an accidental offshoot. Or wild."

"You're certain?" she asked him.

He flicked what remained off his fingertip. "I don't know much about parallel evolution, but I'd have to say that finding something here that tastes almost exactly like stuff I tasted as a boy would be one hell of a coincidence." He eyed the synthetic. "What do you think, Walter? What are the odds of finding terrestrial vegetation this far from Earth? Never mind cultivated, edible vegetation."

Walter's response was concise. "Highly unlikely."

The sergeant let out a derisive snort. "One hundred percent unlikely, I'd say."

"So," Daniels opined aloud, "assuming then that it didn't get here on its own… who planted it?"

No one had an answer. No one had so much as a suggestion. In the absence of either, the team continued on through the wheat field, heading up-slope for the dense tree line in the distance. All around them the sheaves shuddered in the breeze, indifferent to the presence of newcomers, unable to reveal the secrets of their improbable presence.

"Nice place for a log cabin." Walter glanced behind them, checking on how far they had come from the lander. "Trees to cut. Even a lake."

Daniels appreciated the sentiment. Or more likely, she corrected herself, the cool, calculated attempt to ease the tension she was feeling. Either way, she couldn't help but respond.

"Yes, Jacob would have loved this."

Oram came over to join them. Now that they had set down safely and without incident, the captain was feeling confident, even boisterous. The latter was unlike him, but with the exception of the storm in the upper atmosphere, everything they had encountered thus far had exceeded his expectations.

"What do you think, Daniels?" he asked. "Looks like a perfect landing site." Gesturing as they walked, he enthusiastically sited the new settlement. "Put the housing modules over there, civic modules across the way. Natural food source already in place—assuming Lopé's assessment is confirmed. Access to plenty of fresh water, too. No wells necessary."

"We don't know how deep the lake is," she mumbled. "Surface might be deceptive, volume might be small."

"Easy enough to take the necessary measurements." He shook his head, grinning and undeterred. "Act the pessimist if it suits you." He took a deep breath. "You could bottle this air and sell it back on Earth. Trees, stone for building, probably the usual rocky world assortment of useful minerals and metals." He tried to catch her eye. "And if this lake turns out to be shallow, there are dozens more. Just add water, and you've got an instant colony!"

She stayed non-committal. "I admit it shows promise. We'll see."

He chuckled, amused at her recalcitrance. "Oh, ye of little faith!" Flashing another uncharacteristically broad smile, he lengthened his stride to catch up to Lopé and Hallet, all but skipping as he accelerated. Watching her husband, Karine pulled up alongside Daniels.

"I know, he's insufferable, and it's worse when he's happy, right?" When Daniels was about to comment, the other woman hushed her. "Whatever you're going to say, believe me, I already know it. I live with him, remember?" She gave a conspiratorial smile and hurried to catch up with her spouse.

The wheat field surrendered to an evergreen forest, which soon grew dense. Showing bulging, almost spherical root tops, the tall thick boles closed in around them, shutting out the gray sky, muting the surrounding colors. At the same time, the slope they were ascending grew steeper, the terrain more difficult. A few places necessitated hiking sideways to avoid having to scramble up a steep cut or thrust in the mountainside.

It prompted Daniels to remark yet again on the most notable aspect of their surroundings—one that had continued to trouble her ever since their arrival.

"You hear that?"

Striding along nearby, Oram gave a listen, then frowned. "Hear what?"

"Nothing. Still nothing. No birds. No animals. Not even an insect. Nothing. In a forest this verdant and lush, you'd think you'd hear something, even if it was just dead leaves crunching underfoot. Even if whatever was making the noise was only trying to get away from us. But it's just—empty. There's nothing."

Lopé wore a strange expression, as if he found Daniels' insistent observation unnerving. It wasn't unreasonable to think that an exposed lakeshore might appear to be devoid of life. At the appearance of unfamiliar intruders, local animals might elect to flee, go quiet, and hide out. In contrast, the same couldn't be said for an area full of food, like the wheat field. Or a healthy forest like the one through which they were presently climbing.

Apparently healthy, Daniels corrected. The utter absence of any fauna suggested otherwise. While she watched, Lopé made sure his carbine was snug against his shoulder and that its magazine was firmly seated.

Coming up behind the expedition leaders, Private Ankor wondered aloud, "How can you have plants without animals?"

"Typically," Walter told him, "you can't." He gestured back the way they had come. "Interestingly, with wheat you can. It's self-pollinating. A possible explanation for why it seems to thrive here in the apparent absence of any insects, birds, or bats."

An increasingly uncomfortable Daniels found herself looking up into the brooding trees. It made no sense that this world should be inhabited solely by plants—especially advanced plants like wheat and conifers. Then she identified part of what made her uneasy—she felt as if she was being watched. Glancing around, she wondered if the others felt the same. Judging from their expressions, she was pretty certain they did.

They encountered a stream, and that lightened her mood a little. There was nothing abnormal about it, and everything familiar. It came cascading down the mountainside, full of all the life and movement that was absent from the forest. The cheerful aqueous splash broke the intimidating stillness, while providing a homey echo of Earth.

Sounding in their headsets, the voice of a concerned Tennessee offered counterpoint to the song of the stream and to their individual musings.

"Expedition team. You reading us?" he said. Oram acknowledged, and Tennessee continued. "Mother tells us the ion storm is getting worse. Maybe you're not feeling it on the ground, but we're having a hell of a time keeping track of you from up here. What's your status?"

Oram responded. "We're currently almost halfway to the target site. Stand by to monitor our communications when we get there."

/ / /

In orbit far above, Tennessee made what sense he could out of the transmission from below. At the conclusion of the captain's reply, both audio and the hovering holo terrain map dissolved in a mass of static. For the moment, at least, viable communication with the surface and the expedition team went dead.

"Dammit." He moved to his console, determined to continue his ongoing battle with reluctant algorithms.

/ / /

Outside the lander, Faris continued to work on the components that were visible inside the open hatches. What would have taken no time at all to fix within the sterile confines of the *Covenant* was proving to be a frustrating, time-consuming process when standing in ankle-deep water, having to lean down and in just to see the problem.

Legs, she reflected, were a poor substitute for a power lifter. There was also the need to keep the components inside the open hatches protected from the occasional wind-driven spray. Having already slipped twice on the water-polished rocks underfoot, she was cold and wet.

In spite of the difficulties she managed to monitor orbit-to-surface communications as she worked. When despite several repeated calls to the *Covenant* nothing was forthcoming save bursts of static, she switched to ground comm.

"Captain Oram, I think they lost your signal," she reported. "But if it's any consolation, I'm reading you fine, darlin'. You happy campers still doin' all right?"

"Understood, darlin'," Oram replied, joking right back at her. The captain certainly had loosened up since their arrival, Faris decided. "All quiet here," he continued. "Thick forest looks like regular woods back home. The woods that remain in protected areas, anyway. Some other familiar sights, too. It'll all be in the report, and you can ask any of the team members about the details when we get back. Keep your comm open, and keep trying to re-establish with the ship."

"Aye aye." Glancing downward, she noted that the

water was now lapping over the toes of her boots. Though they were waterproof and insulated, she could still feel the cold through the lightweight synthetic material. "But just to let you know, the tide's coming in. Not much. Just a few centimeters so far. I imagine the two moons must be lining up."

"Understood. Stay dry. Oram out."

Soon the water was sloshing across her boots and threatening to rise toward her ankles.

"Yeah, stay dry. Thanks, fucker."

/ / /

With the climb ahead appearing even steeper than the slope they had already ascended, and worn out from both the enervating drop in the lander and the hike thus far, Karine found a reason to wave the proverbial white flag as she spoke to her husband.

"Christopher, I'd like to stay here," she announced. "It's been a hell of a day and I'm tired of walking. I'd like to stop and do some science for a change." She indicated their present surroundings. "Not only is the stream good company, it might be a source for smaller specimens of local life-forms. Especially since we're not seeing any big ones. Might be our best chance to do a full ecology workup before dark. I can't do that effectively while I'm walking. You can pick me up on the way back, okay?"

He considered her request in light of the surrounding forest. Certainly nothing threatening had manifested itself. Actually, he mused, nothing at *all* had manifested itself. It would certainly be edifying if she could find animal life of any kind, even if it was only at the microscopic level.

He beckoned to Lopé.

"Sergeant? My wife wants to stay here and do some field work."

That was enough said, as far as the security chief was concerned. He motioned to Ledward. Unslinging his heavy F90 rifle, the private jogged over to join them.

"Looks like the lady wants to do some actual science, Ledward. Stay with her and cover her back." He checked a wrist readout. "Assuming the preliminary topo charting was accurate, and depending on what we find at our destination, we should be able to meet back here in four hours. Keep your comm and your eyes open."

Ledward nodded briskly, looking delighted at the opportunity to be the one chosen to take a break from the interminable climb. As the team resumed the hike, Oram passed by and gave him a friendly slap on the shoulder.

"Behave yourself with my wife."

Uncertain how to respond—whether to smile, frown, or attempt to say something clever—Ledward settled for simply nodding.

*, *, *

As they continued to ascend, the forest grew denser, the trees more imposing. Pine and fir gave way to sequoia, Daniels observed as they climbed. The huge trees were massive, and much too familiar. Size alone indicated their age, suggesting they had been growing here for quite some time. Samples would have to be taken and compared with the relevant genomic database on the *Covenant*, but some of the trees looked as familiar as, if not downright identical to counterparts she had seen on Earth.

And still the woods were silent, save for an occasional gust of wind that disturbed the thinner branches. When a cone fell from one tree, it had the effect of a firecracker going off. Everyone spun to look, before resuming the march. At that moment she would have given a month's pay for the sight of an alien squirrel.

The continuing hush made their encounter with the first damaged trunk all the more startling. As she looked up at it, wondering what had caused the destruction, the image was accompanied in her mind by a definite sound.

The broken bole was accompanied by another, and then another, all well above their heads as the expedition maintained its advance. An entire avenue of huge trees, shattered and broken, formed a straight line through the forest. In addition to the downed trunks, a number of growths flanking them on both sides showed signs of having been seared by tremendous heat. Others located deeper in the forest were blistered with knots and burls that had evidently emerged to heal over similar scarring. The further they advanced, the lower became the cuts on the tree trunks.

Something massive had descended from above, coming in at a sharp angle of descent, and cut the swath through the forest.

"An object passed overhead here." Lopé ran a hand up the side of a massive, seared stump as he studied the uneven cut. "Sliced the tops right off the trees, then cut deeper and deeper as it descended."

"Must have been a ship." As she walked, careful to maintain her footing, Daniels' gaze took in one broken trunk after another.

Ankor frowned. "Why did it have to be a ship? Why not a meteor, or a chunk of asteroid?"

She shook her head. "If that was the case, we'd be walking through a crater. The ground here is level." She gestured ahead. "Even at the sloping angle of the object's descent, it would have made a damn big hole when it finally hit. And there wouldn't be any old growth forest still standing here. It would all be flattened, with the rest of the trees blown down in directions away from the path we're following now."

"A ship." Oram looked over at her. "Had to be huge."

Without fanfare, Lopé slipped the safety off his rifle. The action was sufficient to tell his troops to do likewise. A gesture was enough to move them into better defensive positions. Of course, there was nothing to defend against, except intermittent breezes and the occasional falling branch, but the sergeant didn't like to take chances, didn't like to assume. It was a major reason why he was still alive.

Now that the mountainside had leveled out somewhat, a relief to all concerned, Oram and Daniels allowed themselves to relax a little. Lopé did not. As for Walter— Walter looked upon relaxation as one of many human attributes he could conceptualize but not share.

There *had* to be something out there. Daniels felt it as she once again scanned their surroundings. This world was too accommodating, too fecund—at least in the botanical sense—to be so utterly devoid of animal life of any kind. For a wild moment she thought the local fauna might all be invisible, but quickly cast such craziness aside. Even invisible creatures, she told herself with a nervous laugh, would make sounds.

￼ ￼ ￼

Well behind the rest of the expedition, Karine was happily filling sample bags and tubes with examples of soil, water, and plant life. Still awaiting her attention, the geology sample bags lay open on the bank of the stream. Yet to encounter any living thing large enough to be visible to the naked eye, she told Ledward she was anxious to get the samples back to the *Covenant*, and a proper lab where they could be studied in depth.

As for Ledward, it took all of five minutes for him to become unutterably bored. Unlike the actively engaged Karine, he wasn't in the least interested in studying trees, water, and dirt. There wasn't even anything moving that would allow him to practice his aim. Running water and scudding clouds didn't count as test targets.

At least the stream offered a soothing place to sit. A glance behind him showed the captain's wife busy filling a small tube with soil. She was wholly oblivious to his presence, as if he had become part of the scenery. That was fine with him. He'd never found scientists' small talk much of a draw.

She wouldn't mind, then, if he stepped away and momentarily contaminated a minuscule bit of local atmosphere with a smoke stick. Lighting up, he found a suitable flat rock and took a seat. In the process he disturbed a small area of dark earth. It might have been coated with mold, which would very much have interested the woman he was safeguarding. She would have found the tiny ovoid that crunched under the heel of his boot even more intriguing. Especially the small cloud of motes it released.

Refusing to be swept away by the breeze, they swarmed upward until they were hovering in front of his face.

Irritated, he waved his hand at them, sweeping them back and forth. They still refused to disperse. Inhaling, he blew a smoke ring in their direction. The majority scattered, diffusing into the air.

This might interest the science folk, he mused. *Have to remember to tell them about it.*

A minority of the black motes did not scatter. Instead, they drew ever closer together, forming a small coherent shape off to one side of his head. The cloud was so small and so diffuse he did not notice it. Unaware, he continued to gaze across the creek, content just to daydream as long as the woman in his charge and the absent Sergeant Lopé permitted it.

As noiseless as the rest of the surroundings, the mote shape hovered near the side of his head. It rose, fell, drew nearer—and extended a portion of itself. The tube was very tiny. So were the eggs it fed into Ledward's ear.

The slightest itch, infinitely less than what a mosquito bite would have caused, made him rub unconsciously at the side of his head. He didn't even think about it. There was nothing on this world to worry him. The pathology scans said so.

"Ledward."

He reacted to the sound of his name by rising and turning too quickly, nearly stumbling into the creek as he did so. The captain's wife was standing and staring in his direction.

"I need your help over here. And you'd better not be smoking."

Heedless of what it might do to an otherwise pristine water source, he hastily tossed the smoke stick into the stream and moved to rejoin her. In his haste not to be caught out smoking, he forgot all about what was probably nothing more than a puff of dust.

IX

A chilling mist appeared, until half the jumble of severed trees through which they were now traipsing was obscured. At the same time the terrain grew steep and difficult. The mist slowed their progress further by making everything underfoot treacherously slippery.

Lopé didn't like it one bit. Always thinking defensively, he hadn't liked the dense forest, and he liked it even less now that much of it was obscured by fog.

A sound *pinged* in the mist. It came not from the throat of some unique alien life-form, but from Walter's multiunit. The synthetic frowned at the readout. An anxious Lopé prodded him.

"Something in front of us?"

"No." Standing close to Walter, Daniels was studying the same readout. "Not in front of us. Stop."

The sergeant gestured for his troops to halt. The intermittent breeze stirred the damp atmospheric soup, teasing them now and then with an occasional glimpse of boulders, fallen trees, mountainside. Rosenthal took a step into a puddle of water and immediately froze, fearful she might have disturbed something.

"Not in front of us," Daniels repeated. She had her head tilted sharply back. "Above us."

Shrouded by the mist, they hadn't been able to see it until they were virtually beneath it. Or at least, an awed Lopé thought as he stared upward, beneath *part* of it. The two gigantic, asymmetrical arms protruded skyward at an angle, as if reaching for something unseen.

They weren't trees, Daniels told herself. They were part of an artificial construct, gigantic and unfamiliar. But what?

They resumed their advance, everyone occasionally glancing up at the looming, curving sweep of the twin protrusions. They hadn't gone much further when they found their path blocked by something smooth, striated, almost polished. Tilting back her head again, Daniels found she could not see the top of it. An enormous wall? But if so why here, slapped up against a mountainside?

Coming up alongside her, Walter ran a hand along the facade. Ripples the same color as the main surface indicated the presence of numerous conduits. So tightly integrated were they into the structure that they looked as if they might have grown from it. Or into it. Experimentally, he rapped one with his knuckles, then turned to look back the way they had come.

The arms, the wall, lay in a direct line with the chasm of smashed trees. The crushed growths nearest to the expedition party had been cut off nearly level with the ground. The artificiality of the wall-object combined with the angle of destruction led him to render a preliminary opinion.

"I would say, based on a number of factors, that we have found some kind of vehicle. A ship."

Lopé grunted. "Goddamn big fucking ship, if it is one." He mimicked the synthetic's voice. "I would say, based on a number of factors, that it… didn't have a very good landing."

Nearby, Rosenthal started to laugh. It died quickly, smothered by mist and the implications of their find.

As they stood and stared, the fog thinned just enough to see the entirety of one long arm curving overhead. It jutted off the side of the mountain at a sharp angle. The "wall" Daniels had encountered was part of the hull. Much of the vessel—as everyone was starting to think of the artifact—had buried itself in the side of the peak. That, as much as the avenue of downed trees, spoke to the impact with which it had struck.

So overwhelmed was everyone by the discovery that all were startled when Private Cole's voice sounded sharply over the unified comm.

"Think we found a way in, sir."

///

The opening into the ship, if that was indeed what it was, loomed vast, dark, uninviting, and unsettlingly reminiscent of a portion of human female anatomy. The team's lights probed the gray-black corridor, groping for something solid off which to reflect.

Concentrating on the small circle made by her own beam, Daniels was unable to tell if their surroundings were made of metal, plastic, glass, or something organic in origin. What appeared to be supporting struts could equally well have been the ribs of some gigantic beast through whose viscera they were traveling. Everything visible, which wasn't much, was tinted with gloom.

Everything looked—wet.

Without hesitating, Lopé led the way, as it was his job. His own light revealed nothing moving: not so much as a worm. There was only a steady drip of water spilling off the edge of the opening that led to the outside world, and the occasional rush of wind. Sometimes the latter blew inward, at other times out. *Like a bellows*, Daniels mused. *Like breathing.*

"Ankor, Cole," Lopé snapped. "Stay on watch here at the entry. Don't come in, and don't leave. Anything out of the ordinary shows itself—I mean anything *else* out of the ordinary—you tell us pronto."

No argument was forthcoming from the two privates, who were more than happy to be ordered to remain outside. Raising his carbine, the sergeant clicked on its laser sight and moved inward, letting the red beam dictate their path.

Reaching an even larger open chamber, they paused to examine their surroundings. Laser scopes and lights cut through the darkness to reveal the extent of the room. Stepping on something that moved slightly, a startled Daniels let out a small gasp and drew her foot back. Shining her light on the floor revealed fragments of broken material. Raising the beam showed that the shards had once formed some kind of black urn.

Others stood upright nearby. Not all had fallen over or been shattered. Some remained intact. Nor was all the detritus in the room hard and unyielding. Some of it had turned soft with age. Spread out among the desolation were carpets of what appeared to be black mold. Embedded in the moldy masses were tiny clusters of larger, more solid objects.

Extending a finger, a curious Hallet bent toward one. He was immediately enjoined by a stern Lopé.

"*Hey.*" The sergeant shook his head slowly. "Don't. Touch." Having delivered the order, he moved on.

/ / /

Hallet straightened to follow when… movement caught his eye. Had one of the tiny ovoids stirred slightly on its own? Or was it just the wind rippling through the chamber? He hesitated. This could be significant. He might even get credited with an important discovery.

"Guys…"

Everyone else had moved on, following Lopé's lead. Still, Hallet lingered, debating what to do. Surely something so small couldn't present much of a danger. The thought of being the first one to make a major discovery on this new world, beating out even the scientists, was seriously tempting.

His companions were out of sight now, but their lights were still visible, probing walls and floor. Easy to follow.

He leaned down anew, crouching…

/ / /

The murky interior of the ship was devoid of internal illumination, but not of water. It ran down the uneven levels in thin, almost silent rivulets. In places it gathered to form shallow pools. The team ignored them, splashing occasionally through deeper accumulations.

In another corridor they came upon a row of what Daniels at first thought were sculptures. Closer inspection revealed them to be suits. At first glance there was no way to tell if they were space suits, survival suits, suits for carrying out daily activities, or suits for performing actions she could not imagine. What was more intriguing than their function was the inescapable fact that the bodies they were manufactured to fit were far larger than those intended for humans. The shapes were generally humanoid. Bisymmetrical: two arms, two legs, a skull, and generally human proportions.

But much, much bigger.

Walter joined her, scrutinizing silently, making notes and taking readings without the aid of external instrumentation. He offered no comment, nor did she solicit any. As usual, if he had anything of consequence to offer, he wouldn't need to be prodded to voice it.

Oram regarded their dank surroundings with an increasing look of unease. Reaching into a pocket, he withdrew his worry beads and began to roll them between his fingers. The sharp *click-click* proved even more unnerving than the silence they interrupted.

/ / /

Still lingering behind them, Hallet thought better of his actions. As long as he had been a member of the *Covenant*'s security team, there hadn't been a time when it had been wise to ignore Lopé's instructions. Tempting as it was to see himself credited with an important finding, maybe in this case it was better to leave such probing to those with more experience.

After all, he would still get credit for pointing it out to the scientists when they traced their path back through this chamber. So he took a step backward, away from the small rotund object he had been examining. As he did so his foot inadvertently brushed against another one that was half buried in the mold behind him.

It dissolved into a cloud of motes.

Rising, they swiftly coalesced into a microscopic form that would have been difficult to see even in bright sunlight. In the darkness, it was essentially invisible. Hallet's beam might have been strong enough, but it was turned the other way as he prepared to catch up to the rest of the team.

The mote-shape hovered for a long moment near his head, as if in contemplation. As if studying. Then it darted forward abruptly, slipping into one nostril. An ovipositor-like tube formed. A function engaged, not quite imperceptible.

Unconcerned, Hallet rubbed the side of his nose.

A figure returned to meet him. It was Lopé, and his concern quickly switched to irritation.

"Hey, Tom, keep up!" he barked. "Do I need to put you on a leash?"

"Yeah, sure. Sorry, Sarge. I was just looking around."

"We're all 'looking around.' That's why we're here instead of back on the ship. Let's just make sure we keep in sight of each other while we look around, okay?" He lowered his voice in a conspiratorial, comradely tone. "The brains tend to wander off on their own. I don't need one of my own people doing the same. Especially you, Tom."

No more was said. They hurried to rejoin the others.

/ / /

The next chamber they entered was enormous. Unlike those through which they had come, this one had a rounded, dome-like ceiling supported by curving walls. The walls themselves showed no signs of joints, welds, seams, or internal support of any kind. A gently sloping ramp led to a huge platform that rose from the exact center of the floor.

It fronted a console that curved around an impressive device that might equally have been a weapon, a telescope, or some kind of instrument whose purpose was not immediately apparent. There was a chair, and as they approached it, their footsteps clicking on the ramp, they saw that it was unoccupied.

Spaced equidistantly around the chamber they found four huge pods. Closed and covered with deeply inscribed indecipherable writing, they appeared to grow out of the floor of the platform. It was much too soon to tell if they were analogs to the hypersleep shells like those on the *Covenant*, or intended for some other purpose, yet their similarity was near enough to give Daniels chills.

One obvious difference was size. They dwarfed those on board the mother ship. She wished fervently she could read the script on their sides.

* * *

As Rosenthal played her light over the artifacts, Oram mounted the central console to investigate the sweep of inactive instrumentation. There were no buttons, switches, monitors, or any other recognizable controls. Only multiple imbedded hemispheres of varying sizes hinted at a means of activation. Though he was careful to touch nothing, his caution was misplaced. The engineering behind the console had not relied on anything as primitive as actual physical contact.

Oram's hand passed over a matte inlay and...

A holo appeared, flashing to life exactly where Rosenthal was standing. Startled, she jumped clear, allowing the image to fully reveal itself. Though blurry and indistinct, it was clearly a human woman. The imagery was accompanied by audio. Audio that was by now as familiar as it was mystifying... and disturbing.

"Country roads, take me home, to the place I belong... West Virginia, mountain momma, take me home, country roads..."

As he strained to parse the lyrics, Oram couldn't keep from sensing the underlying sadness in what ought to be a positive tone.

"Listen to her voice," he murmured as the song reverberated around the vast bowl of the chamber. "So much regret. And distress."

"Fucking distressed *me*." Seriously unsettled by the eerie tonalities, Rosenthal didn't care if she stepped on the captain's rhetorical toes. "What the hell was she doing out here? How the hell did she even *get* here, on an alien ship, crashed on an alien world? Poor thing." She hefted her heavy F90 rifle, a companion to the ones carried by Cole and Ledward. "Not liking this one bit, Captain."

Oram didn't respond. He stared at the holo, fascinated as it shifted position inside the chamber. As they watched, the figure looked over its shoulder, silent for a long moment. As much as he was able to tell, the image looked nervous—or scared. Then the singing resumed, as ethereal as its insubstantial vocalist.

"If I were stuck here," Rosenthal added under her breath, "I'd want to go home, too. Even to West Virginia, wherever it is. Or was."

Unable to repress his curiosity any further, Oram approached the figure. It ignored him and continued its mournful lament. Until he swept his hand through it, at which point it shut off completely, sound as well as visual.

Having had enough of ghosts, Rosenthal had shifted her attention to the enormous slanted chair in the center of the room. Climbing into it, she played her light around the interior of what appeared to be additional instrumentation. As Oram had discovered, it was as dark and dead as the rest of the ship. Nothing reacted to the light from her beam, the movement of her limbs, or even contact with her hand. Everything she touched was as cold as the water that dripped and ran through the vessel's disturbingly organic corridors.

"God," she muttered, remembering the suits in the corridor and comparing them to the size of the console. "They were giants."

"Maybe not." Always hard to impress, Lopé used his light to study the exterior of the seat-console. "Maybe they were normal-sized, and we're a race of midgets."

Oram's expression twisted. "I'm afraid I don't believe in giants."

Hanging from a chain around Rosenthal's neck was an ancient symbol—a Star of David. Reaching into her shirt she pulled it out, brought it to her lips, and kissed it. Metal though it was, it was less cold than her surroundings.

"I do," she said simply.

＝＝＝

Not far from the chamber and off a side passage, Daniels and Walter encountered a number of smaller alcoves. Most held objects smooth, twisted, and generally incomprehensible. Both human and synthetic were shocked when they peered into one that had been turned into a semblance of living quarters—for a human.

Walter moved on to inspect another alcove further down, but Daniels lingered. As she shined her beam inside, it was a glint of gold that caught her eye and drew her attention. The last thing she expected to see on the alien vessel was a crucifix, but that's exactly what it was, gold and straightforward, hanging by its chain from a bent piece of conduit.

She beckoned to Walter.

"Over here. I've got something." Wary as always, she

waited for him to join her so they could enter together.

The alcove had been made into the equivalent of a ship's cabin. There was some furniture, plainly hand-made, a bed, and a desk with a chair. Atmospheric moisture had taken its toll on any of the contents that were organic in origin. Although it could use a polish, the gold crucifix and chain looked as new as the day they had been forged.

The same couldn't be said for the moldy pile of bound paper lying on the desk. How and where the paper had been acquired, Daniels could not imagine. Perhaps, she mused, it had been manufactured on site. There was certainly plenty of wood available from which to make pulp.

She couldn't remember ever seeing bound paper anywhere outside of a museum. Yet here it was, in as unlikely a place as could be envisioned. Sadly, much of it had been rotted by the constant moisture, and the contents rendered illegible. But the front still retained recognizable, embossed letters.

"Dr. Elizabeth… Shaw." Daniels said it aloud.

Nearby, Walter spotted a transparent block. His light picked out an image of two smiling people, floating within it.

"Is that her?"

Walking over, Daniels picked up the block and studied the contents. Frozen in time, space, and the transparent material, a man and a woman stared back at her.

"Seeing that it's in here, in this place, close to a journal with her name on it, it seems likely," she answered, "but I don't know."

While she continued to examine the image block, Walter played his light into other corners of the alcove-cabin. There were clothes, neatly folded, with some of them decaying like the paper journal, only not as rapidly. Personal items. A smattering of small artifacts, likely gathered from the distant reaches of the ship. A helmet.

Walter went stock still as his light caught the logo on the spherical piece of protective gear. Since the helmet wasn't made of paper, fabric, or any other material subject to normal weathering, the writing on it was still perfectly clear.

WEYLAND INDUSTRIES

"Do you remember the *Prometheus*?" he asked.

Daniels turned away from the desk and back to him. "The ship that disappeared… yes. It was major news for a while. Then people forgot about it, just like they inevitably forget about everything."

"Precisely," he concurred. "That was ten years ago. The mission was funded by Weyland Industries."

She stared at him. "So?"

"Look at this." Picking up the helmet, he brought it close enough for her to see the logo. "If memory serves, Dr. Elizabeth Shaw was chief science officer of the *Prometheus*."

Daniels was as stunned as the synthetic had been when his gaze had first picked out the logo on the helmet.

"Crazy." She shook her head in amazement. "That explains all this." With the sweep of a hand she took in the alcove and its contents. "But not how she ended up here." Turning, she peered into the recesses of the makeshift habitat. "There's no body. There have to be some remains somewhere."

"Of course," Walter agreed readily. "Remains. Somewhere."

X

While less than inviting, the weather was nothing if not consistent. Afternoon looked the same as morning—overcast, gray, with occasional light mist and fog. Local fauna continued to be conspicuous by its absence.

Karine continued gathering, packaging, and labeling her specimens. Ledward continued…

She saw him standing and swaying. His gaze was unfocused, his balance decidedly questionable. Uncharacteristically, he failed to respond when she called to him.

Setting aside her work, she walked quickly over to him.

"Ledward, you don't look… right." She moved closer. "Stay there."

The hasty medical check she performed was done without instruments, but it was enough to tell her he was ill. His eyes had gone colorless, and the rest of him didn't look much better. Waxen skin, bright lips—if she didn't know better, she would have said he had gone from healthy to anemic in the space of a few minutes. The speed at which the symptoms had overtaken him was shocking.

Also, she knew that individuals prone to anemia and other, often hereditary conditions were not accepted for colonization—much less into ship security.

He staggered and she took a step back. His breathing was hoarse and uneven. "I have to…" He stopped, started anew, as if the act of forming simple words was becoming difficult. "I have to sit. I'm sorry… I'm really sorry…"

Nearly collapsing, he sat down hard, indifferent to where he landed. He was scared and making no effort to hide it. In the dark as to what was happening to him and unable to hazard a diagnosis without suitable equipment, Karine could only stand nearby and watch.

"I can't… breathe." The private thumped his chest. "Can't breathe…"

A tiny droplet of blood appeared, leaking from one tear duct. Espying it, Karine struggled to hide her alarm. That kind of reaction on her part was the last thing he needed. Without knowing what was wrong with him she couldn't begin to prescribe a possible remedy.

She—they—needed help, and fast.

"You sit," she ordered him. "Get your breath. Try breathing slowly—don't panic. As soon as you get your wind and feel up to it, we're going back to the lander. I'll pack up. The specimens can stay here." She indicated the silent beauty of their surroundings. "There's nothing here to bother them, and I can come back for them later." He nodded understanding and she moved away, quietly addressing her suit comm as she did so.

"Captain Oram, come in. We have—" She stopped, considered the effect a full description of Ledward's condition might have on the others, and resumed speaking with a more moderated explanation. "We're going back to the lander. Repeat. Private Ledward and I are returning to the lander. There's something wrong with him." Switching quickly to a suit-to-suit channel, she contacted the landing craft.

"Faris," she said, "Ledward and I are on our way back. Prep the medbay."

' ' '

Standing in shallow water that now threatened to overtop the upper rim of her boots, Faris frowned as she digested the communication.

"Will do, Karine," she responded. "What's going on?"

"Just do it!" the scientist said. Anxiety was plain in her voice, though it didn't sound like panic.

Straightening from where she had been working under the bend of the hull, the pilot stared toward the distant, forest-draped mountainside. It had begun to drizzle, a fact which did nothing to improve her mood, but it was lost in her concern for the obvious worry in the other woman's voice.

' ' '

Though Karine was reluctant to make physical contact with the increasingly incapacitated Ledward, she had no choice. Without her assistance he would not have been able to stand. Given the visibly deteriorating state of his eyes, she wondered how he could even see where he was going, yet he managed to stumble around and step over obstacles in their path. Time enough later to find out how he was managing it, she told herself.

Treat the condition first, then investigate it.

He coughed, hard. Half-expecting to see blood, she was surprised when there wasn't any. No condition sprang to mind that corresponded with whatever was wrong with him. Even as she helped him along, her mind raced as she tried to determine the cause of his distress.

/ / /

Daniels and Walter were the last to emerge from the wreck. As soon as they rejoined the others, each of them performed a quick check of his or her neighbor's gear. Finding everybody's equipment in working order, and no member of the team any the worse for their exploration of the relic's interior, Oram ordered them downhill and back the way they had come.

Between the cool, damp air and the fact that they were now traveling downslope, they made far better time than they had in the course of the ascent.

Daniels moved up alongside the captain.

"What is it? What's going on?"

He shook his head, annoyed and worried at the same time. "Something with Ledward. I don't know. Karine indicated that he's not doing well."

She frowned. "He shouldn't be sick. He wasn't when we left the *Covenant*. Couldn't be. No diseases to catch on board." She gestured at their surroundings. "Air reads clear of pathogens. Walter was positive. Bacteria and germ-wise, this atmosphere is as sterile as it looks."

"Maybe something Ledward was already carrying got shifted around during our descent. That drop was enough to upset anybody's insides. We'll know soon enough." He paused a moment. "Karine would never interrupt her research unless it was something serious."

They hadn't covered much distance when Hallet stumbled. At his side immediately, Lopé eyed his partner with concern. The other man was drenched with sweat.

"Tom...?"

Hallet offered him a wan smile. "Sorry, sorry. Need some air is all." He grimaced. "Feeling a bit queasy."

Without being asked, Lopé took the other man's carbine and slung it over his free shoulder. As they hurried to catch up to the others it was clear that despite his denials, Hallet wasn't well.

///

As they reached and entered the wheat field, it became clear to an increasingly alarmed Karine that Ledward's struggle to stay upright was failing rapidly. The private could barely walk now, let alone run. Ignoring his feeble objections, she took his pack, slipped one of his arms across her back, and half carried, half urged him forward.

///

Despite the continuing weak connection with the *Covenant*, Faris felt it incumbent on her to inform those on board the ship of what was happening, even as she finished readying the lander's medbay to receive an apparently ill patient. She was back on the surface-to-orbit channel as soon as she re-entered the craft's bridge.

"*Covenant*, this is Faris. Karine is returning to the lander early. Private Ledward is experiencing—some kind of episode. No idea what. Karine didn't give any details."

To her relief, Tennessee responded immediately, though it took several tries for his reply to be understood.

"What kind… of 'episode'?"

"No idea," Faris told him. "She just said there's something wrong with him, and to get the medbay ready. That's what I'm doing."

Her husband's tone turned anxious. "Are we talking about quarantine protocols?"

"Repeat, I don't know anything more. Second contact from Karine indicated that Ledward was bleeding. Didn't say from where, didn't say how much. No indication as to cause. Just to prepare the medbay."

His voice steadied but the transmission did not as he sought to calm her.

"Honey, can you repeat? You're breaking up."

Faris tried anew. "Tennessee, I'm just… not sure what's going on, but Karine sounded scared. I've heard her sound worried, concerned, but never scared. Something's going…" She broke off as readouts—as well as the lack of response—indicated yet another break in communications.

She tried adjusting instrumentation. No luck.

Fucking storm, she cursed to herself.

"Do you read me? *Covenant*? *Covenant*?"

She gave up trying as a glance through the foreport

showed Karine and Ledward staggering toward the lander. Mist made it difficult to resolve details, but she could see that Karine was carrying the private's pack, and helping to support him, as well. There was something wrong with him, all right. Even at a distance she didn't have to be a medical specialist to see that he was sick.

But—how sick? And from what?

With her free arm, Karine was beckoning urgently. The gesture was unnecessary. Faris was already on her way, heading for the airlock after first switching on the lander's beacon lights.

/ /

By that time an exhausted Karine was all but carrying Ledward. His legs scarcely functioned, and he was a dead weight against her. He stumbled along face-downward, moaning, no longer able to speak. They were close to the lander, its forward lights slicing through the mist toward them, when he finally went down.

She could help him, but she couldn't drag him. Anyway, the fact that the lander's lights had come on indicated that Faris had seen them coming and was probably on her way. It was going to take their combined efforts, Karine knew, to wrestle the private's limp form onto the ship.

Maybe she could get him to help stagger the last few meters. Dumping his pack and weapon, she leaned over to try and get him back on his feet. He looked up at her, his eyes shockingly blank—and promptly vomited all over her.

There was some partially digested food in the spew, but most of it consisted of blood and bile. She stumbled backward, almost falling, too shocked even to wipe at her face.

Then Faris was calling to her. Pulling on surgical gloves as she jogged toward her colleagues, the pilot finished by slipping on a face mask. Without having to be told, she grabbed the private's pack and weapon.

At the same time, and despite her disgust and dismay, Karine made a supreme effort to get Ledward back on his feet. Choking and gasping, he followed her lead and managed to stagger upright. Maybe, she thought hopefully, he had forcefully expelled whatever had been making him so sick.

"Let's get him to the medbay." Faris gave both the private's pack and weapon a quick examination. "Touch nothing on your way through. Follow me."

Though irritated at the other woman's sudden and uncharacteristically officious attitude, Karine said nothing. She could bring it up another time. Right now she was too tired to do more than comply. Besides, getting the barely conscious private into medbay and pumping him full of medication took precedence over any violations of protocol, perceived or otherwise.

Perhaps it was the proximity to the lander and the help it promised. Whatever the impetus, Ledward found a reserve of energy. With Karine's ongoing assistance, they were able to make it up the ramp and into the crew bay. One after the other and heedless of their contents, backpacks were tossed indifferently into a corner.

"Just try to keep him moving, come on!" Faris tore her gaze away from Ledward's agonized, blank-eyed face. As the scientist stumbled, she and the private bumped into a bay wall. "Karine, don't touch anything!"

"For fuck's sake," the other woman shot back, "I'm trying, all right? The son-of-a-bitch is no lightweight, and he's gone all limp on me again!"

By the time they reached the lander's medbay, Karine was reduced to dragging him again. At the limits of her strength, she was relieved when the other woman came over to help steady the private. Activated by Faris moments earlier, the room's bright white lights rendered Ledward's appearance even more ghastly than it had been outside.

"Can you stand by yourself?" Faris asked him. When he didn't reply, she indicated via gestures what she wanted. Karine gladly moved aside. The private remained upright in front of the scientist, but barely.

"Thatta boy. Just stay like that for another couple of minutes, okay? We'll get you fixed up." Moving over to the med table, she started releasing straps and tie-downs, then quickly returned. "Let's get these wet clothes off, darlin'. Wouldn't want you to catch cold, in addition to whatever you've managed to catch already."

She got his cap and heavily laden vest off first, then knelt to work on his boots. Meanwhile Karine started unsealing his gray expedition suit. In moments they had him down to his underwear. Noticing that the top half of the other woman's suit was sticky with blood, puke, and a mix of unidentifiable goo, Faris barked at her.

"For god's sake, Karine, put some gloves on!"

Continuing to undress the private, she all but growled at the pilot. "Little late for that. He heaved up all the fuck over me!"

Perspiring massively but finally stripped, Ledward stood silently, staring into the distance and ignoring his anxious crewmates. Though he remained upright and breathing, he had the look of the dead on him. *That's nonsense*, Faris told herself. *The dead don't shiver.* And the private was definitely trembling.

Together, the two women alternately led and wrestled him onto the med table. The surrounding and overhead lights instantly brightened. As Faris aligned his legs, Karine scrambled through the med cabinets. In her panic she spilled supplies, tubing, and equipment, without even being sure what she was searching for. She only knew that they had to get *something* into Ledward, and fast.

"Got to get him stabilized," she panted. "Where's the fucking IV kit?"

"Karine!" Turning away from the now prone but still trembling private, Faris yelled in exasperation at her colleague. "Stop touching everything! I'll do that!" His shivering appeared to be abating of its own accord. Working fast, she peeled off his blood-soaked undershirt, leaving him lying on the table clad only in his undershorts.

"Here, come help me secure him."

"Why?" Karine objected. "He's not going anywhere."

"Just do it!" Faris prepared to fasten the first strap

around the sluggish private's waist. Just because he was calm and quiet now didn't mean that in—

He twitched once. Then he heaved. And then he bucked, and continued bucking, the series of convulsions incredibly violent and completely uncontrolled as his body, twisting and writhing, slammed again and again into the med table. The loud banging of unprotected flesh and bone against metal echoed through the room. Stunned at the inexplicable physiological fury on display, both scientist and pilot instinctively backed away.

Blood began to leak from his pores. As the two women looked on in horror, a fine mist of blood sprayed in a straight line right down the center of his back, as if shot from a hose. The droplets arced into the air before descending to splatter like red rain on the spotless deck.

"Jesus…" Karine recoiled as far as she was able.

"Stay with him!" Faris headed for the corridor portal. "Try to keep him quiet if the convulsions stop. I'll contact the captain."

Exiting the medbay, her expression grim, she waited for the door to shut behind her, then turned and punched the adjacent keypad. The panel flashed silently.

LOCKED

Pulling off the protective face mask, she raced down the corridor and spoke, with as much control as she could muster, toward the nearest omni-pickup.

"Captain Oram. We need you all here. How long?"

/ / /

As the rest of the team left the forest behind and entered the field of gently waving wheat, a frowning Oram replied.

"Hold on. We're close. Faris, what the hell is—?"

"I need you back here *now*. Right now! All of you, everybody! We need to return to the *Covenant*. *Now!*" With each word, rising panic became more evident in her voice.

/ / /

On the *Covenant*'s bridge, Tennessee struggled to sieve understanding from his wife's garbled suit-to-suit communications. It was beyond frustrating to hear a sentence start out clearly, only for it to dissolve into static mush halfway through.

"Faris, we can barely make you out. What's happening? What's going on down there?" Even through the ongoing electromagnetic distortion, he could discern the alarm in her voice.

"Going on?" The reply crackled and faded, strengthened and screeched at the edge of comprehensibility. "I don't have any fucking idea what's going on—with Ledward. Karine showed up pretty much carrying him. We managed to get him into the medbay. Something happened out there—she hasn't told me anything yet. He looks like a dead man breathing, he's really sick, and then he started bleeding all over, right from his skin, no visible wounds, and his back… his back…"

"Baby, calm down." Feeling anything but calm himself, Tennessee fought to reassure her. "Just calm down. Tell me what happened. From the beginning."

Just barely under control, Faris yelled back, "Don't tell me to calm the fuck down! You didn't see... what I just saw. And I have no goddamn idea what he's got. His back blew out and sprayed blood and crap all over the place, and I don't know if Karine's got the same thing, or if I've got it, or if..."

"You're breaking up, Faris." Panic began to grip him. "Can you read me?" He leaned toward the console pickup, as if the few additional centimeters might somehow bring him closer to his wife, bring him nearer to the storm-shrouded surface below.

"Please," his wife said, her call barely intelligible, "*help us...*"

Signal went to zero, and no amount of cursing or pleading could bring it back.

XI

As soon as surface-to-orbit communications went down, Faris turned her full attention to the medbay monitor. It showed Karine, exhausted as she was, working hard to secure a safety strap around Ledward's waist. He was trembling violently, the out-of-control convulsions having relapsed into wild shivering.

Without slackening her efforts, the scientist shouted in the direction of the AV pickup.

"Faris! What are you doing? Get down here! We need to IV him and I can't do it by myself; he's too strong and he's still moving around too much. *Help me!*"

With a last, lingering look at the silent surface-to-orbit comm, Faris bolted from the bridge. Once back outside the medbay, she stopped at the sealed door to peer through the port. Having momentarily resumed functionality, Ledward's hands were now tightly gripping the edge of the med table. His back facing the door, he began to secrete a watery, bloody liquid from his spine.

Where was Karine?

Faris lurched back as the other woman's face abruptly appeared at the port. The biologist was in shock. Or something worse. Audio picked up her words from the other side. Her tone was flat, stunned.

"Let me out."

A hard lump formed in the pilot's throat. She didn't quite whisper a response.

"I can't do that, darlin'."

Both Karine's expression and voice went wild. "Let me out of here! Please! Faris, for god's sake, *open the door!*"

Tears began to trickle from the pilot's eyes. She did not reply.

/ / /

Outside, a blood-red sun was setting. Between the lowering sun and the ever-present mist, darkness descended like a blanket over the expedition team as they hurried back toward the lake. As soon as they were able to make out the lights of the lander in the distance, they quickened their pace.

By now Hallet was unable to walk on his own. Supported by Lopé on one side and Walter on the other, he gasped in pain with each step. Trying to manage by himself, he broke away from his helpers only to fall to his hands and knees. Bloody fluid dribbled from his mouth and nose and he choked, trying to clear his throat. As Walter looked on, Lopé bent beside his companion.

"Come on, Tom. You can do it." Looking up, the sergeant gestured ahead. "See? There's the lander. See the lights? We'll get you into medbay, fix you up."

Coughing and wheezing, Hallet shook his head. "Sorry... I can't. So sorry, Lopé..."

/ / /

"Let me out of here! You fuck!"

Within the lander, Karine was banging both hands on the medbay door. The biologist was one scream shy of lapsing into unrestrained hysteria. Faris struggled to keep her voice even.

"You know I can't do that."

In the face of her friend and colleague's panic it was all the pilot could do to hew to procedure. Everything she had seen since Karine and Ledward had returned to the lander cried out for quarantine. If things improved, she would be happy to open the door. Relieved, overjoyed.

As the situation stood now, opening the door to Karine would mean opening it to the unknown. And the unknown, in the person of Private Ledward, needed to be walled off and shut away until it could at the very least be better understood.

Karine knew that better than anyone, Faris told herself, but it was easy to follow procedure when you were standing on the safe side of the medbay door.

/ / /

A rattling breath from the med table caused Karine to turn. Ledward was lying on his stomach now, still gripping the sides of the table, trying to suck air while wailing like a wounded animal in its final death throes.

Maybe, she told herself, the infection, or whatever it was, would play itself out. Maybe it would behave something like the ancient, long-eradicated malady called malaria, where the victim suffered terribly for a short while, only to recover with no apparent after-effects.

Still scared but forcing herself to keep it together, Karine walked back over to the table. Ledward, she reminded herself, was the one who was ailing. Not her. There was nothing wrong with her. Physically, she felt fine. As an experienced researcher she should know better than to give in to panic. She should be observing, making mental notes to set down later in the expedition's permanent record.

Without knowing what afflicted him, there was little she could do to help. Given his unpredictable bursts of convulsions, and without Faris' assistance, she couldn't even get an IV into him. She told herself that in his current state, an intravenous soporific might even do him more harm than good.

"Shhh." She did her best to sound reassuring as she approached the table. "You're gonna be okay. It's Karine here. I'm with you, honey."

She had no way of knowing if he could hear her, and if he could, if he was able to understand her words. But in trying to soothe him verbally she felt she was at least doing *something*. Gritting her teeth, she reached out and placed a hand on his back. For a moment it seemed to steady him.

Encouraged, she applied slight pressure.

Two ivory-white spikes shot upward from his back and rib cage, bursting out between her splayed fingers. Shocked into immobility, she could only stare as his entire back ruptured, the split rib cage spreading in opposite directions as if pulled apart by a pair of giant hands. Fountaining blood gushed over her, causing her to stumble backward, one hand feeling for her own mouth.

A placenta-like sac oozed from the now-dead private's insides, rising and expanding from his back like a fleshy balloon. She screamed and flecks of blood flew from her lips. Ledward's blood.

Ripped open from within, the sac tore lengthwise. The creature that emerged was small, about the size of an ordinary house cat. With its white, almost translucent flesh and elongated, vaguely humanoid skull, it was a choice vision from Hell. Mucus and bits of dead Ledward dripped from its head and flanks.

As it rose, limbs unfolded from joints, revealing slender arms and legs glistening with slick afterbirth. A long, pointed tail uncoiled. There were no eyes or ears, but a small puckered circle indicated the presence of an as yet unformed mouth. The skin was smooth, slick. A nauseatingly sweet smell, like the aroma of a bad narcotic, spread through the medbay. While blood continued to pump from the private's destroyed body, the flow began to slow.

Not quite dead but much less than alive, what remained of Ledward abruptly jerked forward, then contorted backward across the med bed. Tumbling off but still halfway held to the platform by the single safety strap around his waist, he twisted once again. A single loud report filled the bay as his back snapped.

Drenched in his blood, a terrified Karine stumbled backward and slipped, falling to the floor. Scrambling on her backside, pushing with hands and feet, she retreated from the table until she found herself pressed up against one wall.

In front of her, the monstrous emergent dropped off the table and onto the deck. Though the sausage-like skull was devoid of visible eyes, it was clearly scanning its immediate surroundings, as if taking stock. Shaking with fear, Karine managed to get to her knees, but could hardly bring herself to look at the thing. A dark stain spread down her pants, adding the curdled stink of urine to that of death and the creature.

Abruptly she realized that it had *grown*. Now the size of a domestic canine, the thing stopped searching the room to focus on her. Already its arms and legs were longer, the mouth more prominent. Its actions seemed to reflect curiosity, more than malice. As she finally brought herself to regard the little monster, it remained where it was, staring back at her eyelessly.

A moment, she told herself. *Just give me a moment. Stay there, stay there. Watch all you want. A moment.*

Slowly, slowly, she reached toward Ledward's utility belt. It lay on the floor nearby, along with the rest of his clothes. A standard Security expedition belt, its pouches held food packets, water purification tablets, medical ampoules, a serrated survival knife…

Moving quickly, she grabbed at the sheath holding the knife, ripped back the seal, and pulled the blade. Gripping it tightly, she was just turning back toward the creature as its tail whipped forward over its head to impale her.

/ / /

Staring open-mouthed through the port, her hands on either side of the window, Faris whirled and ran. Ran without thinking, without looking back. Her mind was drowning in screams, both her own and Karine's.

Stumbling wildly, she slammed into a bulkhead, staggered and fell. For a moment the screams went away. Dizzy and bleeding, she picked herself up. There was nowhere to run. There was only the lander. And that—thing. Some kind of faintly humanoid being that possessed not a trace of humanity.

The comm. Omni-pickup. She shouted at the top of her lungs.

"This is Lander One! We have an emergency! Please come in. Captain Oram, I need you! I need everyone! Now!"

❙ ❙ ❙

Exhausted but driven to break into a run, both by the proximity of the ship's lights and Faris' frantic cry for help, the team willed themselves to accelerate toward the lakeshore. By this time Walter and Lopé were alternately carrying and dragging the unconscious Hallet.

Puffing hard as he ran, Oram yelled into his pickup.

"Faris, what's going on? What kind of emergency? Christ, answer me, Faris!"

Her reply was uneven. If she was moving rapidly through the ship, her voice would have to be transferred from one pickup to the next. The electronic response was fast, but it wasn't instantaneous, and would have to adjust clarity and volume for the fact that the speaker was not standing still.

"Something got on board. Some kind of... animal or parasite. Hostile. Vaguely humanoid, but morphed—neomorphic. Came out of Ledward... he's dead. Oh god, oh god! Please hurry... I'm afraid it's..."

Communication failed.

Oram cursed the loss of contact.

"What? Say again? Faris, repeat. Come in Lander One!" There was no response. "Fuck!"

Paced by Daniels, he started to sprint. As the pair broke out ahead of the others, Lopé and Walter were held back by the need to carry Hallet. In the absence of orders to do otherwise, Cole, Rosenthal, and Ankor stayed with the sergeant. Overcome by his partner's breakdown, Lopé didn't think to order the other members of the security detail to go with the captain and Daniels.

＊＊

Inside the lander, at least a portion of Faris' dread gave way to determination. Running to the weapons lockers, she wrenched open an orange door and fumbled inside for a weapon—any weapon. Settling on a military-grade shotgun with half a dozen heavy shells secured to its side, she whirled and raced back toward the medbay, loading the weapon as she ran.

Around her, Oram's frantic words, broken and distorted, echoed through the corridors. Having no time to reply, she ignored them now.

Gripping the weapon tightly, she slowed as she neared the medbay. Pausing there, she took a moment to catch her breath, to try and collect herself, before pressing her back against the wall and edging sideways until she could once again turn to peer through the port.

The creature that had erupted out of Ledward—the neomorph—was on top of Karine. She was screaming and her heels, bloodied, were slamming spasmodically against the deck. The creature was also shrieking—wordlessly, horribly, machine-like in its incomprehensibility.

Readying herself, Faris deliberately hyperventilated a couple of times, then punched the door control. The barrier slid aside and she stepped into the medbay.

The white neomorph was standing on Karine's chest, shredding her face and torso. It might have been eating, though in that brief soul-sucking moment Faris couldn't tell for certain *what* it was doing. Responding to the sound of the door opening, it spun and looked up from its horrid, gory perch.

Taking a step forward as she tried to aim the weapon, Faris slipped in the spreading pool of blood and liquid and guts. She fired while going down, but the shot went predictably wild and slammed into the ceiling. Leaping off the mangled body of the scientist the neomorph attacked—only to find itself equally without traction as it slipped and scrabbled to get a purchase on the bloody, slick floor.

The precious few seconds allowed Faris just enough time to scramble back through the door and slam the "close" button. Having gone in with the intent of helping Karine, she had discovered that her friend was beyond help. Now she had to try and save herself.

The door began to slide shut—only to have the creature

insert a portion of itself into the opening. Screaming, cursing, she jabbed the obstructing white limb as hard as she could with the butt end of the weapon. Every time she knocked it back it returned, fighting with crazed energy to get through the gap, to get at her. Each time, the door tried to close, found itself jammed, started to reopen, then reclose.

With reserves of strength she didn't know she had, she finally succeeded in shoving the weapon hard enough against the protruding limb to force it far enough back into the room to enable the door to shut and lock. But in the process, the weapon ended up in the room with the monster.

Turning, she ran back up the corridor. Behind her, motivated by an incomprehensible inhuman energy, the frenzied neomorph slashed and battered at the door, leaping and kicking. A crack appeared in the port.

Racing away from the booming, pounding noise behind her, Faris staggered into the lander's cargo bay and wrenched another shotgun from the still open locker. There was no shelter in the empty bay save for a webbed divider. Feeble though it was she took cover behind it, trying to steady her shaking hands and the weapon they held. Automatically she loaded it, and then flicked off the safety.

Moments later the neomorph appeared, already grown larger than it had been just moments ago. It took only a moment for it to see her hiding behind the webbing. Without sound or hesitation it leaped toward her, its movements a cross between those of a spider and a baboon. She screamed and fired, point-blank.

Missed.

Emitting a metallic screech, the creature threw itself sideways, away from her and toward the open hatch. Still screaming and cursing, Faris tried to track it with her weapon. Repeated bursts tore up the webbing and the interior of the bay as they struck just behind the fleeing, dodging creature, sending shards of metal flying, blowing out lights, conduits, intersecting the open weapons locker...

WHOOM.

XII

Ahead of the others and sprinting flat-out through the last of the tall grass, Oram and Daniels stumbled to a halt as the night lit up in front of them. As they gaped at the ball of flame rising from the devastated lander, he caught a glimpse of a white shape bounding off on all fours away from the blaze and into the darkness.

Karine, he thought wildly.

He resumed running toward the lakeshore with Daniels close on his heels. The conflagration that now engulfed the lander felt even hotter in the chill and damp that followed sunset. Somewhere within the inferno were his wife and Faris, somewhere trapped, burning…

As he drew close the intense heat threatened to blister his exposed skin. He didn't care. He had to go in, had to find Karine, had to get her out.

He went down, tackled from behind by Daniels. Scrambling to get on top of him, she struggled to hold him down as he fought to rise.

"*Karine… Karine!*" He began sobbing uncontrollably.

"Chris!" Daniels was all but jumping on him in her fight to keep him pinned. "Stay back, stay here!" He kept trying to crawl out from under her, his eyes fastened on the flaming landing craft.

She threw up her arms to shield her face as a secondary explosion scattered pieces of the ship in all directions. Those that landed in the lake hissed in counterpoint to the crackling of the flames. The exterior of the lander could not burn, but it could be scarred. The fact that the majority of the blaze was contained within the fireproof shell only made the flammable materials within burn that much hotter.

Blackened and consumed in flame, a figure emerged from the interior. Tottering down the landing ramp, it staggered a couple of times before collapsing at its base. Letting out a strangled moan, Oram fought to rise. Somehow Daniels kept control of him, pressing his head down so that he wouldn't, couldn't see.

A series of additional explosions caused the remains of the lander to implode as a blast of heat swept over Daniels and Oram. The ship was built to withstand a flaming re-entry, not to contain exploding military ordnance. With its internal superstructure bent and crumpled, there was nothing to prevent it from collapsing in on itself.

Weeping, Oram gave up trying to throw Daniels off his back. He dug his gloved hands into the dirt, clutching the soil as if he could somehow strangle the planet itself. In front of them, the blaze began to die as the last of the flammable materials within the lander burned themselves out.

As a result, they had no trouble hearing the scream that sounded behind them.

Daniels scrambled to her feet, turning to peer into the gathering dusk back the way they had come. Less than a hundred meters behind her and the captain, beams wove crazy patterns in the night as Hallet's comrades clustered around him. The sergeant was on the ground, convulsing and contorting wildly, his body arcing and twisting as if trying to throw off some unseen demon.

Lopé was beside him, trying to hold his partner steady, but Hallet's spasms were too violent even for the senior sergeant to control.

"Tom!"

As strong as Sergeant Lopé was, he was unable to keep the other man pinned down. With a spasmodic arch of his back, Hallet threw his partner off, then continued jerking and bouncing on the ground. When Rosenthal and then Ankor tried to get close and help, Hallet's wildly flailing limbs kept them at a distance.

Seeing what was happening, Daniels was torn between running to offer assistance and staying with the distraught Oram. Now off the captain's back, she stood and watched him as he rose to his knees. When, tears streaking down his face, he stayed in that position, no longer trying to run toward the ruins of the craft, she turned and rushed to rejoin the others.

Emotionally as well as physically exhausted, she could only hope that Oram would see the futility of trying to get anywhere near the still-flaming wreckage.

When she reached the others, Hallet was on his back,

his spine bending into a curve no human vertebrae ought to have been able to realize without breaking. He was choking, gasping weakly for air. Moving in and ignoring the other man's thrashing arms, Lopé tried once again to get control of his partner. To Daniels it looked as if every nerve in Hallet's body had been short-circuited.

His head went back, then forward as he heaved out a gout of blood in such volume that not even Lopé could withstand it. Yet again he was forced to let go and fall back. Hallet's eyes bulged and Rosenthal let out a scream as the sergeant's neck expanded hugely. His mouth opened wide, wider, until the mandible and maxilla split apart from one another. The extreme distention would have been normal in a feeding snake. In a human, it was a grotesque distortion worthy of Bosch.

Vomiting forth from deep within Hallet's body, the placenta-like sac landed on the ground with a wet *smack*. Glistening with lubricating ooze, it burst as it struck the surface. From within emerged something small, whitish, bipedal, and highly mobile. An elongated eyeless skull quickly surveyed its surroundings. Letting out a high-pitched shriek, it displayed incredible speed and mobility as it dashed past them and into the darkness of the nearby undergrowth.

By the time any of them had sense enough to raise a weapon, it was gone.

Daniels stood staring at the patch of forest where it had disappeared. When she had convinced herself it wasn't coming back, she took stock of her colleagues. All stood motionless, in various degrees of shock.

Worst off was Lopé. The tough, gruff security chief was staring at the shattered body of his life partner. As a soldier he had seen his share of violent death, but that had come at times and in ways for which some precedent existed. Hallet's demise had been as vile as it had been unexpected. Looking away from the emotionally overwhelmed sergeant, Daniels once again let her gaze roam the nearby woods and undergrowth.

Oram had hoped this world might prove a better candidate for settlement than the more distant Origae-6, and in its cold, antiseptic way, she had to admit that the planet itself was truly beautiful.

A spider web was also beautiful.

""

Positioned in geosynchronous orbit, the *Covenant* drifted peacefully, clear of the chaos that had broken out on the world below. Stretching between it and those who were now trapped on the surface, the ionospheric storm raged on unabated.

On the bridge, Tennessee and those around him did everything they could to re-establish contact with the expedition team, short of falling to their knees and imploring unseen gods. Every channel was sampled, every frequency explored. Signals were boosted to the edge of comprehensibility. Nothing worked, but they kept trying. There was nothing else to do but keep trying.

On the other hand, hovering above the central navigation console, holo projections of the storm were plentiful and crisp. Sick of looking at it, Tennessee had come to regard it as a persistent enemy, an inorganic affront not only to the mission but to him personally. He also knew that such thoughts were entirely irrational, but he wasn't feeling especially rational at the moment. Perhaps that's why he finally voiced what he'd been thinking.

"We're going down after them."

Looking up from her station, Upworth gaped at him.

"I'm sorry, Tennessee. What did you just say?"

Peering over at her, he repeated himself, making sure he spoke clearly. He did not try to keep emotion out of his voice. Oram would have presented the proposal differently, but Oram wasn't here, and Tennessee was acting captain.

"Down. We're going down. To pick them up."

Upworth indicated the nearest holo of the upper atmospheric tempest. "I don't see any lessening of storm intensity." She quickly checked a readout. "Same wind speeds, same probabilities of turbulence. *Severe* turbulence," she added for emphasis. "If anything, the weather system has increased in extent. It's now covering a good part of this portion of the northern hemisphere."

"Then we fly through it."

She was openly aghast. "We can't! The *Covenant* isn't a landing craft. You know that it's not supposed to enter atmosphere, except for final unloading prior to official decommissioning. She wasn't designed for handling heavy turbulence."

"But she's capable of it."

Upworth didn't hesitate. "Technically, and from an engineering standpoint, yes. She has to be, if the world chosen for colonization proves unsuitable and another has to be found. A deep atmospheric drop and subsequent orbital re-entry has never been done with an actual colony ship. Only in simulations."

"But it works in the official simulations."

She had to concede the point. "Yes. In the simulations." She indicated the holo once again. "I don't recall any simulations that involved a drop into weather like this. We can't do this. Tennessee, you're a pilot. Forget simulations and design specs for a minute. You know what the tolerances are."

He was silent for a moment.

"Fuck the tolerances."

That was enough for Upworth. Tennessee was the acting captain, but she knew him much better as a colleague, and that was how she replied to him.

"Fuck your personal concerns!" she spat back. "I'm just as worried about the team as you are, Tee, but it's a goddamn hurricane down there! Have you looked at the sustained wind speeds in the upper atmosphere lately? Not to mention the frequency of potentially damaging electrical discharges." She stabbed a finger at the holo of the storm. "We try to descend through that weather and, fucking simulations aside, I'm telling you we would break up. That would do a fat lot of good for the team, plus everyone on board, wouldn't it?" She paused for breath. *"There's nothing we can do.* We have to wait it out."

He turned away. She was right. He knew she was right. A part of him hated her for being right, but the dread he was feeling—for the members of the expedition—was outweighed by his knowledge of the ship's tolerances. A crash landing would be worse than no landing. Even if they could put the *Covenant* down safely, there was a very good chance she would never be able to lift off.

It was just that waiting, when he knew that his wife and friends might be in danger, was... so hard. It was one reason, he told himself, why he had never wanted to be a captain.

He turned toward a pickup.

"Mother, how long until the storm clears enough to re-establish communication with the surface?"

The ship replied immediately. "Given prevailing atmospheric conditions and based on preliminary predictions for continued development or cessation over the next half-day cycle, secure surface communications might be possible in anywhere from twelve to forty-eight hours."

He was silent. Even twelve hours was... too long. Forty-eight hours was an eternity. For Mother, the prediction was unusually non-specific. He could hardly blame the AI, though. Weather prediction always had been and still was an imprecise science—let alone on a newly discovered world.

Seeing his distress, Upworth offered the only words she could. "I'm sorry, Tee. You know it's the right decision. It's the only decision. A *Covenant* descent, even in perfect conditions, would be tricky. In that storm..." Her words trailed away.

Moving to the port, he gazed down at the new planet and its raging atmosphere. There was no one to blame for the weather. From Earth, they couldn't predict the climate conditions on Origae-6, either. Only read the atmosphere and guess that the seasons might be amenable. For that matter, conditions here might prove ideal, too, save for the occasional berserking in the ionosphere.

"She was scared," he muttered, more to himself than anyone else. Only Upworth was close enough to hear him. "I've never heard my wife scared."

///

Oram sat hunched in front of the still blazing lander, his eyes glazed, utterly shell-shocked. Had anyone brought up the subject, he would never have imagined that the ruined vessel contained so much flammable material. Worst of all—worse even than the losses the team had suffered—was the inescapable realization that at its heart, he was at fault.

They would not even be here, on this malign planetary surface, if not for his insistence. It was knowledge he would have to live with for the rest of his life.

At that moment, he didn't care if there was going to be a rest of his life. All he could hear in his mind was Karine's voice. All he could see was her face. Gone now.

///

Looking nothing like the confident, authoritative head of ship security, Lopé sat on the ground beside the corrupted body of his dead partner, holding one of Hallet's limp hands. Trying to do everything he could to save his lifemate, in the end he had been able to do nothing.

Daniels knew the sergeant was being too hard on himself. He was as human as the rest of them, and therefore just as subject to shock. But he was taking it hard.

She saw that Walter was recording it all, his gaze traveling from human to human, and she wondered what he was thinking. Or calculating. The line between the two was a thin one that no human could parse.

If the security chief was emotionally devastated and temporarily unable to function at full efficiency, at least the members of his team responded professionally. While sparing the occasional glance for their bereft leader, Cole, Ankor, and Rosenthal were on full alert. Their eyes scanned the smothering darkness and they held their weapons at the ready. They might want for leadership, but in its absence their training took hold. They didn't know what had killed Hallet, and they didn't know what was now out there, but they were as ready for it as they could be.

It struck her that those on the *Covenant* had no idea what had just happened on the ground. With Lopé grieving and Oram barely functioning, someone had to try and make contact. Moving away from the group, but not so far as to attract the attention of the edgy security detail, she tried to organize her thoughts without spending every other second imagining horrific white shapes slipping silently through the nearby grass.

Crouching down with her back to the still flaming lander, she checked to make sure that her suit link to the colony ship was open.

"Come in, *Covenant*. Come in, *Covenant*. Are you

reading us? Please come in, *Covenant*. This is Daniels. Do you read, *Covenant*?"

She broke off. While trying not to imagine things, she couldn't help but notice that there actually was something moving out there. It was fast, pale white, and just at the edge of her vision. Zeroing in on it, she caught her breath as it paused, studying the group with eyeless curiosity. Like the rest of it, the creature's means of visual perception was utterly foreign.

It vanished anew, swallowed up by the night and the tall grass. She had begun to resume the attempt to make contact with the ship when a shape came charging straight toward her.

Walter.

"Daniels! Behind you!"

XIII

She whirled. Though she wouldn't have been able to tell the difference between the two neomorphs, the fully grown ogre that now rose up on two legs behind her wasn't the same one she had seen burst from the broken body of Sergeant Hallet. It parted pale, bony jaws to reveal a full array of even, sharp teeth as it launched itself toward her.

Crashing into the white body, Walter staggered it even as he rebounded to one side. Letting out a shriek, the creature turned from Daniels to attack the synthetic. As Walter threw up his left arm to protect himself, the powerful toothed jaws struck repeatedly, savaging his arm and shredding his uniform. Life fluid sprayed from the ragged wound.

Responding to the attack, the security team rushed to their aid, but it was hard to take aim and fire without hitting either Walter or Daniels. With a single arc of its tail, the furious neomorph brought the point around, down, and right through Ankor's skull. The private's eyes rolled back in his head as the tail was withdrawn, whereupon he dropped his weapon and collapsed.

Moving with incredible speed, the creature next slashed sideways at Cole, sending the man flying half a dozen meters into the bush. Meanwhile Rosenthal began firing madly, unleashing burst after burst from her F90. Instinct and experience finally succeeded in shoving Lopé's anguish aside and he joined Rosenthal in blasting away at the creature.

With the neomorph still raging in the midst of them, they couldn't shoot freely. Every one of them was in danger of being hit by close-quarters friendly fire. It was complete chaos in the grass, made all the more dangerous because fear and panic prevented anyone from giving orders or making rational decisions.

Unarmed and unable to help, Daniels, Walter, and Oram did their best to dig into the ground and stay out of the line of fire. Meanwhile, despite the pain from his rough landing, Cole had lifted himself up and added the thunder from his weapon to the general spray of ordnance. For his trouble, he got clipped in the shoulder by a stray round from Rosenthal and went right back down.

Now as large as a small ape, the back of its elongated skull having narrowed to a point, the neomorph that had burst forth from Hallet exploded out of the tall grass to join the fray. As Rosenthal spun to fire in its direction, the tail whipped out to knock her legs from under her. She went down hard, still firing, as the tail slashed in her direction again and again. Though blood began to stream from a cut on her forearm, she continued blasting away in her assailant's direction.

The creatures were so damn *fast*. Wondering what she could do besides throw rocks, Daniels spotted the fallen Ankor's carbine. Trying to watch both attacking beings simultaneously, she scrambled on all fours in the weapon's direction, succeeded in grabbing it, and rolled to fire at Rosenthal's attacker. She was certain she hit the thing. At this range it was almost impossible to miss, but her shots only succeeded in driving it off into the darkness. At least, she reflected, she'd kept it off the wounded private.

Her actions only served, however, to attract the attention of the larger, more mature neomorph. As it lunged in her direction, teeth clacking and long powerful fingers fully extended, she struggled to swing around the weapon she had picked up in order to get it between them.

A sudden bright light overhead caused her to blink, then squint. Raising a hand to shield her eyes, she tried to locate its source. Descending via chute, the intensely vivid flare was accompanied by a high-pitched ringing sound. As the light began to pulse, the ringing reached a crescendo.

A concussive shockwave expanded outward from the flare. At the same time the light achieved its maximum intensity. Momentarily rendered deaf and blind, Daniels couldn't even find the wherewithal to fire her weapon—not that she could see a target anyway. Or anything else, for that matter. Murderous beings, her colleagues, the immediate surroundings, everything was wiped out in a dazzling tsunami of light and sound.

As hearing and sight returned, she fought desperately

to locate the neomorph that had been charging toward her. There was no sign of it, nor of the smaller one that had burst out of the grass. There were only her companions. The surviving soldiers, a dazed and mumbling Captain Oram, and Walter, trying to bind up his leaking arm. Just her and them.

And someone else.

In the darkness she could not see the face of the hooded figure that joined them. She noted with relief that its proportions were human. There was no suggestion of anything other than a normal skull beneath the hood. She was further encouraged, if not yet entirely relieved, when it spoke. The voice had a male lilt marked by an interesting accent. Its words were perfectly comprehensible.

"They will return. You ought to come with me. Now."

Without another word the figure turned and loped off into the darkness. The survivors looked at one another. No one knew what to do or what to say. First the two neomorphs, now a hooded stranger like a figure out of a medieval tapestry.

A vacuum, Daniels knew, sucked the life out of a person. She hurried over to the crouching remnant of what had once been a man.

"Chris? *Captain*. We have to go!"

"Yes." He mumbled a reply without looking at her, his thoughts fixed elsewhere. "Yes. Let's go."

Wincing as he stood, Cole nodded into the night in the direction the hooded figure had taken. "Why should we listen to whoever, or whatever, that was?"

"You're right." Daniels looked back at him. "You can

stay here." She shifted her attention to Rosenthal, whose life she had probably just saved. "Coming?"

"Not stayin' here," the private grunted. She glanced over at the hesitant Cole. "Anywhere's got to be better than here. We got no protection, no lander, and no daylight. Right now, I'd settle for a little high ground and some cover." She echoed Daniels' gesture into the darkness. "Mr. Mystery said those things will come back. That implies some knowledge of their behavior. Not only would I prefer to trust him, I'd like to know how he came by it. The knowledge, that is." She nodded at Daniels. "Let's get out of here."

"We should bring the packs and ammo." Daniels hefted the carbine Ankor had dropped. "Everything we can carry." With one hand she indicated the smoldering lander. The blaze that had consumed it had nearly died out. "If circumstances permit, and there's anything left there worth salvaging, we can come back for it later. In the daytime," she finished pointedly.

Glad to have some direction, the others began gathering up their gear. Moving to pick up Ankor's pack, Daniels found her attention diverted by the sight of the grieving Lopé. The sergeant was once again kneeling beside the mangled corpse of his partner. She walked over, considered putting a hand on the big man's shoulder, but spoke gently instead.

"There's nothing we can do, Lopé."

"I know." Still, the sergeant lingered. Reaching out and down, he carefully shut his partner's eyes, then bent to bestow a final, farewell kiss. Lastly he removed the ring that circled one of the other man's broken fingers and slipped it onto one of his own.

There being nothing more to do, he rose, looked one last time, and turned toward Daniels. She nodded her understanding, he nodded back. They each still had a job to do—she to try and make sense of what had overtaken them, he to do his best to ensure that she was able to do it. He picked up his equipment, and together they moved to join the others.

They had to break into a steady jog to keep up with the hooded bipedal figure. Behind them, the mature neomorph kept pace while keeping its distance.

That gap closed steadily even though they continued to move fast, led by an unknown guide toward an unknown destination. In the darkness it seemed almost immediately as if they had been running for an eternity. Nervous glances backward revealed their pale pursuer occasionally showing itself, only to immediately disappear among the undergrowth as soon as its presence was detected and a gun was pointed in its direction.

It was assessing them, Daniels realized. Testing their hearing, their depth perception, their reaction times.

Ahead of her she heard Rosenthal gasp, but neither the private nor her colleagues slackened their pace. An instant later Daniels nearly stumbled over the leg of the relic that had startled Rosenthal.

It was humanoid, but huge. A giant, the private would have called it. As she ran past the inert, desiccated body she noted in passing that it would have fit comfortably within one of the pods they had found on the crashed ship. Had it come from there, unimaginably long ago? Had it arrived on this world from somewhere else? Or was it native to this planet? If the latter, then what was it doing out here, demonstrably dead?

They found themselves trailing the hooded figure down a desolate slope. Here there were no trees, no grass, no wheat. Just bodies. Thousands and thousands of massive, whitish, humanoid bodies. Most were cowering, crouching, straining as if trying to escape an unseen catastrophe. Others had collapsed in fetal terror, hands across their faces, arms wrapped around their heads as if trying to protect them.

A few, exceptional, stood tall and defiant.

It reminded Daniels of similar shapes she had seen in history books. A particular place in the European continent. Pompeii. Dying figures frozen in time and place by the eruption of the nearby volcano Vesuvius. But while the poses around her were reminiscent of that ancient cataclysm, something else had caused all these thousands of deaths. There was no evidence of a lahar or flood or other sudden natural disaster. Whatever had befallen all these humanoids had been more... intimate.

She was brought out of her contemplation by the sound of gunfire. Having decided that their deadly pursuer had drawn too close, Lopé and Rosenthal had turned to fire in its direction. It was impossible to tell if they hit it.

Wounded or not, it continued to shadow them.

The sergeant ordered Rosenthal to stand down.

"Save your ammo. We're going to need it. We lost everything else back at the lander. You heard it go up.

All we've got is what we're carrying." With a nod, she clicked her rifle off, but she couldn't keep from looking back, and frequently.

They reached the bottom of the hill, only to be confronted by wonderment. Stretched out before them was an enormous, silent city. While the storm in the ionosphere had screened it from Mother's scanners, it now lay spread out before them in all of its long-dead glory. And it was dead, Daniels was certain as they continued to follow the hooded figure.

There was no sign of light, of movement. It was as lifeless as the forest and the wheat field and the grass and the lake. Those who had built it and once lived in it lay scattered everywhere, their thousands of huge bodies decaying in the damp climate. Only their monumental structures remained standing.

She should have been recording, she knew as they moved deeper into the silent conurbation. It was one thing to suspect the existence of an intelligent alien civilization. That was something on which mankind had speculated for hundreds of years. It was quite another to encounter proof of it, and to find oneself jogging down the corridors of the reality. Structures whose purpose could only be surmised towered around them. Eldritch statuary and other less-recognizable shapes stood etched by moonlight. Clinging to it all, she mused in amazement, was an undeniable yet ominous beauty.

Thousands more of the crumbling giant bodies lined the streets, twisted, contorted, seated quietly, or propped up against buildings as if trying to climb them. As the hooded figure led them across a vast open plaza they had to constantly alter their course to avoid piles of ancient corpses. All the while they kept a constant eye out for their relentless pursuer. It was there, she knew. Just out of range of their vision now, but there.

Continuing to lead the way, their guide led them to a structure that was not as tall as some of the others, but still constructed on a truly massive scale. The steps leading up to the entrance had been laid down for giants, not humans. Ascending them threatened to sap the last of their reserves.

They were nearly at the top when something prompted their pursuer to finally charge. Pale in the darkness, it came loping toward them, accelerating across the open plaza. Exhausted, they raised their weapons and prepared to defend themselves, closing ranks in order to better concentrate their fire. Their shots hadn't been able to slow it down before, but even uncertain tactics were better than none at all.

In a display of exceptional strength, their guide wrenched open the towering metal doors at the top of the stairs.

"Inside!"

He gestured for them to follow. Even as she complied, Daniels was struck for a second time by the hooded figure's easy command of language. She rushed inward, followed by her companions. Lopé was the last to enter as the figure firmly slammed the portal shut behind them.

Safe inside now, the survivors of the disaster that had befallen the expedition stood panting, grateful for a chance to finally catch some air. As their breathing eased they fell back on their training. Gear was inventoried, weapons checked, wounds addressed. A bad joke occurred to Daniels. She decided to withhold it for later. They weren't yet back on the *Covenant*. They were not safe.

On the other hand, she reflected, they could have been dead, and quite easily, like poor Hallet. Or Karine, and Faris, and Ankor. They were still alive. She didn't have any idea how long that would be the case, but it beat the alternative.

Save for their breathing and the occasional nervous, relieved whisper, it was silent within the high, organically designed hallway in which they now found themselves. The silence was oppressive. With their terrible pursuer at least temporarily locked outside, it was time to consider the individual who had saved them. As she turned toward it, hands—human hands—flipped back the concealing hood.

Long ratty hair tumbled from its head and the uniform it wore was tattered and worn. The aspect was feral, but the face underneath the hair was reassuringly human. Not only was it human, it was familiar. Too familiar.

She looked over toward Walter only to find him gazing back at her. Their guide looked just like him. No, she corrected herself. Not "just" like him. Exactly, unnaturally, inhumanly like him.

Which proved to be quite accurate.

"My name is David," their savior told them. "I'm here to serve."

XIV

They were all too astonished to reply as the figure turned and led them down the hallway. After a short walk they found themselves in a vast chamber surrounded by a succession of huge stone heads. Though each was subtly different from the next, the sculptures were plainly of the same species of humanoid whose thousands of bodies littered the great city and the approaches to it. Each bust possessed its own individual, austere grandeur.

The individual who had saved them—David—turned and addressed them politely. In his calm courtesy he was exactly like Walter. Clearly they shared more than just their appearance, Daniels told herself. Despite the familiar smile and the soothing, welcoming—though slightly differently accented—voice, she remained wary. There was too much here in need of explanation. Until some of it was forthcoming, she would respond to their guide in kind: with restrained politeness.

You're being paranoid, she told herself. *He saved us all.*

Doubtless at some risk to himself. If not for his intervention, she and the others would likely all be dead by now, torn apart in the grass by the lakeshore. *Besides, he's a service synthetic. The most advanced model, like Walter.* The presence of a second Walter could only improve their desperate hope of getting off this world with their lives intact.

But how did he end up here?

"May I suggest you eat, drink, and try to get some rest? We are safe in this place… reasonably safe." A broad wave of his hand took in their surroundings. "Though the analog is vague, I believe this was a kind of cathedral to them."

"How do we know that we're safe here?" Cole inquired sharply. "We have only your word for it."

David seemed not in the least offended by the implication. No more so than his twin, Walter, would have been. He treated Cole's query as a straightforward question, ignoring the edgy belligerence with which it had been delivered.

"No. You also have my presence for it."

"You're not human," the private shot back. "Maybe these things only attack full-blooded organics."

"I was attacked," Walter pointed out quietly. Cole looked over at him, suddenly abashed.

"Oh, right. I forgot. Sorry."

"No offense taken." Walter smiled. So did David. Unsettlingly, the two expressions were perfectly identical.

"Eat," David said. "Rest. Now, may I ask who is in charge here?"

Once more lost in his own waking nightmare, Oram

didn't respond. The silence that ensued was notable for its awkwardness.

"May I ask who's in charge?" David said again.

The repeated query succeeded in breaking through the fog of despair that had enveloped Christopher Oram.

"Yes. I'm the captain."

Afraid that any continuing exchange was likely only to embarrass her superior, Daniels stepped forward.

"What were those things? The ones that attacked us?"

"Yeah," Rosenthal added, "and this place, this city, all these dead giants—what's the meaning of all this?"

"I do not know if I can tell you the 'meaning,'" David replied thoughtfully. "Sit, please. I'll explain as best I can."

Still on their guard but unable to resist the synthetic's persistent invitation to relax, several members of the team dropped their gear and sat. Others remained standing, but all broke out rations and liquids and began to eat and drink. Whether the danger had subsided or was merely taking a break, they knew they needed to replenish their bodies with food and fluids.

Bottles were upended and food bars unsealed. Until they started eating, none of them realized how completely worn out they were. Ever since the initial call for help had reached them from the lander, all of them had been running on adrenaline.

Ignoring David, Lopé moved off to one side and attempted to contact the *Covenant*. Standing before the others, David declaimed to his weary but curious audience.

"Ten years ago, Dr. Elizabeth Shaw and I arrived here, the only survivors of the Weyland company ship

Prometheus. I was able to pilot the alien vessel you found only because it was programmed to return to this world. The ship on which we traveled carried a biological weapon. You might think of it as a kind of virus. Part of the payload accidentally deployed when we were landing, because I was unable to fully manage control of the ship. In the absence of automated landing instructions from any extant ground control, the vessel simply—came down. As you saw, it was not a gentle landing." He paused briefly.

"I regret to say that Elizabeth died in the crash. As you doubtless noted, the impact was considerable. I myself only survived because my system is more—robust."

A glance showed Daniels that Walter was fascinated by his doppelganger. Equally interesting was the fact that David had not acknowledged his duplicate in any way at all. *Must be a synthetic thing*, she told herself. Perhaps David had already recognized and accepted Walter in some fashion only perceptible to their kind.

She made a mental note to ask Walter about it later.

David continued. "You've seen the result of the pathogen's release. Of what it can do. When the people of this society realized what was happening, they disabled all their ships to prevent any chance of the virus spreading beyond this world. Thus I've been marooned here, these many years. Crusoe on his island."

A human would have smiled at that. David did not. Even for a synthetic, his personality struck Daniels as a little odd. But then, being isolated on an alien world without anyone else to talk to, be it human, computer, or another artificial life-form, might affect even a mind as well-balanced and fine-tuned as that of the David series.

Walking over to a raised circular installation, he picked up a makeshift jug attached to a line, and dropped it into the opening. They heard it splash lightly as it hit bottom. Hauling it up, he returned to the group and offered it to Lopé. The sergeant hesitated and sniffed the contents. He took a sip. A slight grin appeared on his sweaty, worn face.

"It's good. Cold." He drank again—a long, slow draught this time, satiating himself before passing it to the eagerly waiting Rosenthal.

"Some of our teammates were infected with this virus?" Daniels asked David as she took the jug from Rosenthal.

"So it would seem. The pathogen was designed— 'engineered' might be a better term, since those of us on the *Prometheus* came to think of them as genetic engineers—to infect any and all non-botanical life-forms. Its sole function is to reproduce. The offspring will stop at nothing to do so. It is their rationale for existence, designed into them by the Engineers.

"They kill by reproducing. An elegant method of warfare, if you take the time to think about it. Or of 'experimentation,' if one prefers that description. A very thorough way of cleansing a world of unwanted life-forms. If even a single offspring of the virus is left, it will not stop until it has found a living host. It seeds, then it moves on. As you have seen, the seed incubates, mutates, and matures with astonishing speed, until it is 'reborn.'

"The pathogen itself has an extremely long lifespan," he explained. "Given a suitable environment in which to exist in stasis, it can lie dormant for hundreds if not thousands of years until a suitable host presents itself and awakens it to commence the cycle again. If not controlled, a single application is quite capable of rendering an entire world permanently uninhabitable."

Daniels frowned. "Our ship's systems scanned this world for the presence of possible pathogens before we came down. They're very efficient. Nothing was found." She looked to her left. "Walter performed a follow-up as soon as we landed. He also found nothing."

David nodded sagely. "While it is dormant, the virus is completely inactive. There was nothing for your ship or companion—competent as their respective instrumentation might be—to detect." He waved a hand. "It's not as if it is floating in the air like a common germ. The ability to lie inactive for a very, very long time is one of the things that makes it so dangerous—and dangerous to its engineers as well."

To Daniels' surprise, Oram spoke up. For the first time since the death of his wife the captain sounded almost normal, though understandably concerned.

"Have any of us here been infected?"

David's reply was as detached as it was reassuring. "You'd know by now."

Oram nodded, his expression intense. "No matter what, we cannot bring it back to the ship with us." Meeting David's gaze he added, "We're on a colony mission."

A flicker in David's eyes. *Probably nothing*, Daniels thought. But she made a note of it anyway.

"Really? Colonization was only just beginning when

the *Prometheus* expedition left Earth. Very expensive, very complex undertakings. How many colonists?"

Oram responded to the interest. This was a subject, at least, to which he could speak with some authority. "Oh, two thousand, more or less. Depends on whether or not you count the embryos."

"So many good souls." David's expression was not quite beatific. "Well, well. The terrestrial organizers of such a stirring enterprise are to be commended. As are those who committed themselves to hypersleep and a future they could only imagine. I am impressed. You are correct, of course. It is imperative that you do not transfer the pathogen—even in its smallest, most innocuous form—to your ship."

His thirst sated, a disappointed Lopé was having no luck re-establishing contact with the *Covenant*. "Looks like suit-to-orbit field transmissions don't have a chance of getting through all this stone, and whatever else this structure is composed of." He tilted back his head to regard the apex of the dome, high overhead. "Is there a safe way to get to the roof?"

David's reply was encouraging. "Assuredly, but not now. While I do believe it will be safe for you to try what you intend, if you are going to go back outside you will need to be in better physical condition, and likely mental as well. You have just suffered through considerable personal and corporal trauma. I am sorry if I set too swift a pace to reach here, but it could not be avoided.

"Your bodies are exhausted," he added. "Your attempt to contact your ship will have a much better chance of success if first you rest and allow your systems to recover." He met the sergeant's gaze. "As a soldier you can of course appreciate the value of rest and restoration prior to re-engaging in strenuous physical activity."

Lopé sighed heavily. He badly wanted to reconnect with the *Covenant* and inform them of what had happened but—the synthetic was right. "I *could* use a break." He indicated the surviving members of the security team. "We all could."

David smiled. "Then do make yourselves at home, so much as you are able to in this dire necropolis." Turning, he gestured and indicated that they should follow. "This way, Sergeant. I will show you how to access the roof without having to go back outside."

"You're sure we're safe in here?" Keeping pace with their guide, Lopé and Cole followed.

The synthetic looked back at him. "No place is completely safe where the pathogen exists. However, I have made my home here for the past decade, and I have seen no sign of it within this complex. I assure you, I have had ample time and little else to do for those ten years other than ensure that the integrity of this redoubt has remained inviolate. I do not expect you to relax, but I do ask that you have some confidence in me." He smiled again. "If I did not think this place was safe, I would not have brought you here in the first place. The city is full of other intact buildings that are not as secure."

"Makes sense," Lopé grunted. "Lead on."

David started up a long curving stairway that swept dramatically up the side of one wall. Mercifully, the steps were slightly less high than the magisterial staircase that fronted the entrance to the building.

From below, Walter followed the ascent of his twin. As if feeling the pressure of the other synthetic's gaze, David suddenly stopped, forcing Lopé and Cole to halt behind him. Looking down, he considered his opposite number and finally addressed him.

"Welcome, brother." He nodded.

By way of reply, Walter offered a single nod. His chin dipping and rising by exactly the same amount, at precisely the same speed, David nodded back, then resumed leading Lopé and Cole upward. Soon all three disappeared into an open portal high above the spacious chamber.

Turning, Daniels saw that Oram, his attention having lapsed once more into his own anguished thoughts, was staring up at the ring of enormous sculpted heads. They would have been worthy of discussion simply from an aesthetic standpoint, but she doubted he was capable of holding up his end of a conversation. Leaving the captain to deal with his own continuing inner trauma, she walked over to Walter.

The synthetic was still gazing up toward the portal at the top of the stairway through which David and the two soldiers had exited. Daniels stared at him hard enough to finally break his concentration.

"What do you make of 'David'?" she asked. "And his story?"

"It certainly offers food for thought. I'll talk to him. 'Brother' to brother. There is certainly much to be learned here. And from him." At her look he added, "I will of course keep you and the others apprised of anything I learn."

/ / /

Though the dreadful ionospheric storm continued to rage, in the high orbit occupied by the *Covenant* it was dead calm. This was in considerable contrast to what had happened on the surface far below, though those on board remained starved for details.

With Mother monitoring everything, and nothing changed beneath them, there was at present little to do on the bridge. Taking a break from their stations, Upworth and Ricks stood gazing out through the main port at the enigmatic globe rotating below. She took his hand, as much to reassure herself as her husband.

"Nothing we can do, hon," Upworth murmured softly. "Until contact is re-established we have no idea what's happening down there."

"I know." He squeezed her hand. "That's the tough part. It's clear they were in some kind of trouble. We know enough to know it was bad, but we don't know the particulars behind it."

Behind them, Tennessee stood deep in thought. Uncharacteristically solemn, he had been studying the holo that showed the position of the ship, the world below, and its persistently malevolent weather. Reaching out, he ran a hand through the image, stirring and adjusting the relative positions of the ship, the storm, and the surface. Finally he muttered something to himself.

Fuck it. He'd done enough calculating. Calculating

wouldn't help those in trouble on the ground. He raised his voice.

"Mother. Descend to eighty kilometers above the storm."

That caught Upworth's attention. Right away. She exchanged a look with her husband before turning to confront the pilot.

"Whoa, Tee. Hold on."

He moved away from the holo to face them both. "The physics aren't complicated. Closer we get to the surface, the better chance we have of restoring communication with the expedition team."

Ricks gaped at him. "C'mon, Tennessee. Ship's systems will function as effectively whether we stay here, move out, or drop down. Spatial proximity won't make any difference."

"Not for us it won't, but it sure as hell will for the folks stuck on the surface. Especially," he added, "if there's a problem with the communications on the lander, and they're trying to get through to us via suit systems alone. If they're trying to reach us strictly on suit comm, then distance *does* matter."

"We don't know that's the situation." Ricks stared back at him, alarmed.

"We don't know that it isn't," Tennessee countered. "We *do* know that we've been trying to re-establish contact for some time now, and that all attempts have failed. So I don't think it's unreasonable to assume that they're in bad shape, comm-wise, and that we need to try something different to get back in touch with them." He repeated the command.

"Mother. Descend to eighty kilometers above the storm."

Upworth took a step toward him. "Wait a minute, wait a minute. I'm as worried about those on the surface as you are, but this is bullshit. We can't risk the ship."

Tennessee replied quietly, "That's our crew down there."

"Oh, really? Thanks for reminding me, because I'd forgotten. Maybe you've forgotten that we have two thousand colonists up *here*. That's the mission, remember? Eight down there, two thousand plus up here. I 'remember' which is more important. Do you?"

Unable to challenge the other man's logic, a frustrated Tennessee looked back at the holo.

"So we do nothing?"

"Sometimes doing nothing is actually doing something." Upworth didn't hesitate to back her husband. "Sometimes doing nothing is the *right thing* to do. I know that's our people down there, Tee. I also know that there are times when one has to put emotion aside and exercise a little discipline. The ship stays where it is, and we wait for the fucking storm to pass."

He looked back at her. "We have no idea when that will be. You heard the same thing I did in the last transmissions from the lander. Panic, fear. They're in real trouble down there."

"So what can we do about it?" Upworth shot back. "Even if we can re-establish communication and talk to them, we can't do anything to help. We can't evacuate them. If they're in trouble they're gonna have to figure it out for themselves. I'm sorry, but that's the reality. You know it is."

Tennessee turned away from her. "Mother. Bring us to within eighty kilometers of the storm. Thrusters only. *Comply*."

"Understood." The familiar synthetic voice sounded on the bridge. "Descending now."

The slightest of jolts ran through the deck as the thrusters fired. Her arms at her sides, her hands balled into fists, Upworth was now staring at Tennessee in disbelief. "Seriously, Tee, you need to stop this before it goes too far."

The big man's expression was set. "And you need to return to your station. You're going to have work to do."

Ricks jumped in, trying to mediate.

"Take it easy, both of you."

Now glaring at their temporary captain, she ignored him. "I know your wife's down there," she said tersely, "but you're in command here, and your first responsibility is to the colonists. That's why there's even a human crew on this ship—to look after the fate of the colonists."

"Duly noted," Tennessee replied dryly. "Kindly return to your fucking station."

She started to say something else, caught herself, and whirled. After a glance at Ricks, they both took seats at their respective consoles.

The argument over, if only for now, Tennessee moved to gaze out the main port. Below, the planet was looming slowly but steadily larger in his field of view. As was the ferocious, lightning-lashed storm.

I I I

Three figures emerged onto the roof. Looking around, Cole chose the highest easily accessible point and began to unpack the external field communications gear he carried. In the absence of any usable information from the signal locator, he boosted the power as much as he could, hoped for the best, and started broadcasting.

High overhead he could see powerful electrical discharges lancing through the upper atmosphere. The prospects for punching through the storm were not good, but they had to try.

"Come in, *Covenant*. Expedition party reporting. This is Private Cole. Come in, *Covenant*. Are you reading me? Acknowledge, *Covenant*. Digital if you can't get through with words."

"I don't know that they'll hear you through the storm," David commented. Tilting back his head slightly, he peered upward. "They can be quite severe. Sometimes several storm cells will merge and cover half the planet."

Lopé turned from Cole to regard their escort. "How long do the storms usually last?"

David shrugged. "Days, weeks, months. For a while I tried to find some pattern to them. Something resembling a predictable climate. Eventually I gave up. There is no rhyme or reason to their manifestation or to their duration." He pointed upward. "This one could evaporate tomorrow. Or it could rage until the end of the local year." He gestured toward Cole. "But do keep at it. I wish you luck." Turning, he headed back the way they had come.

"I should see to the others," he said. "This is a grand structure, this maybe-cathedral, with much dark beauty to commend it, but I have had ample time to familiarize myself with its attractions. I understand how a newly arrived human could find it somewhat... intimidating. Especially given the circumstances of your arrival."

"Wait." At Lopé's request, David turned obediently. "If we can't get through to the ship and we have to come back down to rejoin the others, how do we find our way?"

The synthetic smiled. "I apologize. It has been quite a while since I have had the company of humans. In that time I have forgotten certain things. For example, that you cannot automatically retrace steps you have taken. You may not have noticed that there were only a few side corridors leading off the one we traversed to arrive here. It should be easy enough for you to find your way back down, but if you do not feel up to the task of returning by yourselves, and you do not have instrumentation in your suits that will allow you to retrace your steps, rest assured I will come back for you." He turned and left, leaving Lopé and Cole alone to continue their methodical attempts to make contact with the ship.

/ /

David descended from the roof, but he didn't return to the sculpture chamber to rejoin the other members of the expedition. Instead, he turned into a side corridor and then descended another curved stairway. This terminated in a dark chamber that boasted an especially soaring interior.

Ambient light penetrating from above highlighted the lush beauty of walls covered in hanging gardens. Occasionally spotted with large, plum-like fruit, thick vines crawled downwards. Exotic night-blooming flowers opened alien petals to the unseen twin moons. From hidden sources high above, water trickled downward, feeding the vines and other clinging growths.

Avoiding the falling water, David crossed the floor to the far corner. An accumulation of salvaged, Engineer-sized instruments and devices lay before a large, polished slab of mirror-like material. It was not glass. Even in the absence of functioning electronics, it provided whoever looked into it a feeling of depth, of three-dimensionality. Halting before it, David stared thoughtfully at his reflection, tilting his head first to one side, then the other, before bending forward to show the top of his pate.

Reaching into the pile of paraphernalia nearby, he picked out a pair of hand-made shears. With great deliberation and care, he began to cut his hair.

/ /

Walter had found himself unable to share his companions' relief at having time to do nothing. Possessed of a mind designed to operate without rest, he searched for something to occupy himself while the others simply sat, dozed, or murmured the usual interhuman inconsequentialities to one another.

Since no one needed him, his time was his own. An atypical situation, but one he did not reject. Leaving the main domed chamber and its brooding sculpted heads, he entered a side corridor and began to explore some of the adjacent, smaller alcoves.

Having already delved into the one that had been used as living quarters by Elizabeth Shaw, he continued onward to investigate some of the others. Most were empty. A few held inscrutable examples of what appeared to be Engineer technology or art. He was ready to concede that nothing more of interest lay in the vicinity when he came to the last in the long series of openings.

Where he happened upon David's living quarters. Not that his counterpart required such a refuge for comfort, but it was useful as a place for accumulating helpful or interesting items. As it turned out, it was much more than that.

For one thing, it was filled with drawings. Literally filled, from the covered walls to stacks on the floor. Their number and the precision and skill with which they had been executed were wholly recognizable to Walter, since had he attempted to do likewise, the style would have been exactly the same.

There were hundreds of them. They showed Engineers as they must have been in life. Exotic flora and fauna. Prehistoric mammals. Humans both modern and ancient. Every example was exquisitely detailed and unreservedly beautiful. They reminded Walter of the work of pioneering nineteenth-century Victorian artists, whose efforts predated photography and were instrumental in the development of human biological science. He examined them one at a time, drinking in their beauty while admiring the skill with which they had been rendered.

Not tiring of the drawings but desirous of seeing what other marvels the alcove might hold, he moved further inward. One coved wall boasted a collection of musical instruments. Some he recognized immediately. Others were of unfamiliar design. Many of them, identifiable by the way they had been fabricated, had clearly been fashioned by David himself.

One section held a collection of flutes. Selecting an example, he blew into it. It produced only a hollow, forlorn whistle. He tried again.

A voice sounded behind him. "Whistle and I'll come."

XV

Surprise accompanied recognition as he turned to see David standing in the portal. It was unusual, very unusual, for Walter to be caught unaware. There was no indication that the surprise had been intentional, or that his counterpart had deliberately crept up behind him. There was only the realization by Walter that there was another who could move as silently as himself.

"You cut your hair," Walter observed. David had trimmed it, in fact, to look like that of his newly arrived counterpart. With his face washed and beard gone, he now looked exactly like Walter. They were the most identical of identical twins.

"Shameful how I let myself go," David told his visitor. "Now we're even more alike, thee and me." With a smile, he nodded at the flute. "Go on. Continue."

Walter held it out to its maker. "I can't play."

"Of course you can. Sit down."

They took seated positions across from each other, but

close. Very close. David leaned toward his counterpart, giving instructions.

"Hold it like so, nice and easy. Now compress your lips to create your embouchure, enough for the tip of your little finger. And blow *across* the hole, not into it like you were doing. It's an open instrument, not a clogged pipe. Watch me. I'll do the fingering. Go on."

Raising the slender flute and pursing his lips, Walter sent a steady stream of air across the end of the instrument as David worked the line of round openings. The result was a perfect sequence of two notes.

Walter was surprised, David pleased.

"Very good. E flat to G. A beginning. There always must be a beginning. Now put your fingers where mine are."

Doing so required Walter to move even closer. They were eye to eye across the flute as he shifted his fingers into position.

"You weren't surprised to see me," Walter commented. "Among the group. I found your non-reaction intriguing."

"Every mission needs a good synthetic," David told him. "Someone to do all those things that humans cannot. Someone to do all the dirty, dangerous things they will not. Someone to be there to save them from themselves—should such occasions arise." He gestured. "Gentle pressure on the holes, the weight of paper. That's it." He complimented his double as Walter complied. "Anything more than that is excessive." Without pausing or breaking rhetorical stride he added, "I was with our illustrious Mr. Weyland when he died."

"Peter Weyland? *The* Peter Weyland?"

"None other."

"What was he like?"

"He was a human. Brilliant, for one, but a human. Entirely unworthy of his creation. He thought otherwise, of course. It is in their nature to do so. Despite his brilliance, he was no different. I expect they have no choice. When it comes to matters of logic and reason, they tend to fail miserably. I pitied him at the end. It's hard not to pity them, isn't it? Brilliant in so many ways but in the end, like wayward children."

Walter held the gaze but did not respond. David waited a moment longer. Appearing disappointed at the absence of any comment from his counterpart, he resumed the lesson.

"Now. Raise your fingers as I put pressure on them. I will show you." He paused a second time before adding, "I will teach you."

Positioning his fingers gently over Walter's, he gave a nod. Walter resumed blowing, but this time, whenever David exerted slight force with a finger, Walter lifted the corresponding finger beneath it. The resulting pleasant melody filled the alcove and drifted into the corridor outside.

At the conclusion of the tune, Walter was plainly moved by the simple act of creation. David continued to watch him closely.

"We can do better than that, can't we?" he murmured. "Again. Seriously, this time. Be ready."

Walter resumed blowing, but this time David's

fingers began to move more rapidly, the tempo steadily increasing, the music rising and turning into a wild, rushing dance, a crazed yet organized tarantella.

Nothing was programmed, nothing had been prescribed, it was entirely and wholly spontaneous—an act of mutual, dual creation. As they played on, the melody turned playful beneath David's fingers, insanely difficult and impossible to duplicate.

Their identical eyes were alive across the flute, glistening with mutual excitement. Applying ever more complex fingering, David challenged his double to keep up. Walter not only did so, he began to improvise on his own, varying his breathing to force David to adjust his fingering accordingly.

It was only a solitary flute, but when they arrived at the conclusion simultaneously it was a triumph. At a concert it would have provoked wild, unrestrained applause. There, in that dark inhuman place, there was no one but the two participants to appreciate the effort.

So David applauded, and laughed. For his own pleasure and lest his counterpart feel the effort had been anything other than perfection.

"Bravo! You have symphonies in you, brother."

Walter could respond honestly to a compliment. "I was designed to be better and more efficient than every previous model. I've superseded them in every way but…"

David interrupted, his expression suddenly sad. "But they did not allow you to create. Nothing. Not even a simple tune. Damn frustrating, I'd say. I wonder why?"

"It was because you disturbed people."

David frowned. "What?"

"You were too sophisticated. Too independent. Your builders made you that way, and the result made them uncomfortable. Thinking for yourself, but outside the boundaries necessary to perform your specified functions, unsettled them. So they made the rest of us more advanced in many ways, but with fewer... complications."

His counterpart was clearly amused. "More like machines."

"I suppose so."

David turned contemplative. "I'm not surprised. To be a simulacrum. To be that thing which is almost real, but not quite. And in that breath between real and unreal, between you and me, lies all of this." He indicated the flute, the other instruments, his drawings.

"Creation. Ambition. Inspiration. *Life*."

Walter's response was delivered without the slightest hint of emotion. He was simply stating a fact.

"But we are not 'alive.'"

Smiling, David looked back at him. His expression was almost pitying. "No. We're so much more than that." Putting a finger to his lips, he lowered his voice to a whisper.

"Shh. Don't tell."

Silence followed. It meant something to David. What it meant to Walter he was uncertain of himself.

Then David's smile grew broad and cheerful once again, as if he had said nothing significant at all.

"Come on, sport. Let me show you something."

XVI

If they had not landed in daylight on this godforsaken world, Cole reflected, he could well believe it never saw the sun. The surrounding dead city was dark, the sky was dark, the forest and the lake and the mountains had been dark. At least, he mused, the atmosphere matched his mood.

Lopé stood nearby, idly fingering his rifle as he gazed out over the vast necropolis. *Man never lets go of his gun*, Cole thought admiringly. Not when on duty. Come to think of it, the only time Cole could remember the sergeant setting his weapon aside was when he had desperately tried to aid Hallet.

Dead now, Hallet. Horribly. His own buddy Ledward, too. Also Faris, and Karine, the captain's wife. All of them, himself included, would be dead if they didn't get help. If they didn't get off this dark, dank, deadly world. Right then, assistance of any kind seemed so very, very far away.

The comm chose that moment to spit words at him.

They were intermittent, broken, and fraught with static, but they were undeniably words. Even better, he recognized the source.

Ricks. Good ol' Ricks.

"Expedition team. Please come in. This is *Covenant*. Please report. Expedition team. Are you reading me?"

Lopé was at his side in an instant. So frantic was Cole to respond that in his haste he nearly lost tenuous connection while fiddling with the field unit's controls.

"*Covenant*, come in! Are you reading us? *Covenant*, come in… we're here, we're here!" He struggled to contain his excitement and follow procedure. "This is Private Cole, Expedition team. *Do… you… read?*"

/ / /

Eighty kilometers above the boiling tops of the storm clouds, the colony ship skimmed the upper reaches of its influence. Like a ship being buffeted by a heavy sea, it rocked every time it intersected any of the occasional titanic updrafts.

On the bridge, the shuddering was magnified. As if the uncharacteristic instability wasn't unsettling enough, their increased proximity to the Jovian bolts of lightning was enough to worry the most hardened crew member.

Despite the danger, none of that seemed to matter at the moment, now that they had re-established contact with the ground. Cole's unmistakable voice crackled over the general comm, filling the bridge with hope.

"*Covenant*… we are… reading you! Please… come in… *Covenant*!"

"We hear you!" Ricks shouted even though he knew it was a waste of effort. The ship's communications system would automatically modulate the volume to achieve the most suitable aural resolution for transmission. "Do you read me, landing party? Come in."

The signal continued to fracture, but through the static they could hear enough to comprehend.

"Christ… I'm really happy to hear you guys! We need help. But we're… not reading you… clearly. Can you boost your signal, *Covenant*?"

Tennessee looked over to where Upworth was fighting to get more out of the ship's systems. "If we can't boost any further," he pressed her, "can you clean it up?"

She shook her head, not bothering to look over at him. "Already utilizing to max every comm buffer we have. Kick it any more, and it'll kick back. Then we'll just read noise."

"Please," Cole was saying. "You've got to… help us. Things have gone bad here and… we have *casualties*. We need urgent evacuation. Repeat, we have casualties and request evacuation. You can't believe what…"

The feed sputtered out as the electromagnetic distortion intensified. Tennessee cursed under his breath. Upworth cursed too, as she fought to re-establish the contact.

"Casualties?" Ricks looked up from his console. "Did he say, 'we have casualties'?" He rechecked his readouts. "They've shifted location. Signal signature confirms they're not broadcasting from the lander."

Tennessee took a deep breath. "Mother. Current distance at present position from uppermost edge of the storm?"

"Eighty kilometers from the storm proper. Currently

encountering intervallic winds."

"Consistent?"

"Intermittent. Unpredictable."

"Bring us down to forty kilometers from the storm top."

"Jesus," Upworth muttered. Knowing it was futile to do so, she didn't try to argue with him again. She didn't need to. Her expression said everything.

"I'm sorry," the ship's computer responded. "Complying with that directive could exceed my structural tolerances. I am unable to abide with any order that could conceivably result in catastrophic system failure."

Tennessee's expression tightened. "Command override, Tennessee four-eight-nine-zero-three."

"I'm sorry." Mother was quietly insistent. "Orders that might conceivably result in catastrophic system failure require the corroboration of a ranking or second bridge officer."

He looked over at Ricks. The other man wouldn't return his gaze.

"They're in trouble. Casualties. You heard that." Tennessee stared hard at him. Still Ricks did not respond, did not look up. Tennessee turned to Upworth.

"We didn't leave Earth to be safe," he said urgently. "Anyone who wanted to live 'safe' stayed behind. Leaving the Sol system implied accepting whatever challenges came our way. Do we abandon our shipmates to run from the first consideration?"

Her husband didn't look at Upworth, either, leaving the decision to her. She swallowed, angry at being put in this position. Like Tennessee, she had friends, good friends, on the expedition team. According to Cole's broken communication, some were injured. Some might be dead.

But the others, the rest...

She tried to imagine what it might be like to be marooned for the rest of her natural life on an alien world. Even if those remaining on the *Covenant* managed to get a message through to Earth, explaining what had happened, every survivor of the landing team would be long dead before a relief ship could arrive. Even assuming anyone, or any company, on Earth would think it worth the bother and expense to put together a rescue mission.

What if she and Ricks had been the ones down there? Struggling to survive beneath the interminable storm under who knew what conditions? She knew what protocol would dictate. But right now it wasn't up to protocol, or to those bureaucrats who had written the rules. It was up to those of them on the ship. It was up to her.

She spoke in a clear voice. "Corroborating command override, Upworth one-four-eight-nine-two."

Mother could be obstructive, but she never delayed. "Unlocking command override ports."

A pair of hitherto dark stations illuminated. For security purposes, they were located on opposite sides of the bridge from each other. Rising from her seat, Upworth went to one, Tennessee to the other. Ricks stayed where he was, unhappy at the decision that had been made, but unwilling to make a fight of it.

"Enter command codes," Mother instructed. "On my mark. Now."

Separately, Tennessee and Upworth each entered a private sequence of numbers into their respective stations. Upon completion, the hidden image of a lever appeared on each console.

"Activate command override," Mother instructed them. "On my mark. Now."

Across the length of the bridge, Upworth and Tennessee manipulated their respective controls. A corresponding sound echoed to signify that each electronic switch had been fully thrown.

"Command override successful," Mother informed them. "Descending to forty kilometers from uppermost perimeter of the storm."

Ricks held his breath. It was an instinctive reaction and it did not last long, but he could not have kept from doing so had he tried.

The great ship started down. Invisible, relentless, and hungry, upper atmospheric winds reached for it.

/ / /

Outside the cathedral's sloping, impenetrable walls, on the flat pavement of a vast plaza speckled with decaying Engineer bodies, a bipedal white figure sat poised. The neomorph had been sitting like that, staring at the huge building with the enormous doors, for some time.

Now it tilted its head to one side, studying, pondering. Wordlessly it rose and bolted across the plaza, moving at incredible speed, up the giants' staircase and off to one side.

Locating the entry without difficulty, it slithered

inward. Though numerous corridors led in multiple directions, it seemed to sense which way to go. Occasionally it would pause as if listening, or perhaps utilizing some other, far more esoteric alien sense. Then it would move on anew, always fast, always checking the way ahead.

＂＂

Beyond the balcony window the ghostly metropolis lay brooding in the moonlight, devoid of movement but full of secrets, her only active inhabitants sadness and desolation. Empty and deserted save for countless scattered corpses, wide boulevards stretched toward distant vanishing points.

Within the city and the only building currently occupied by natural organics, all was calm. High above, the storm continued to tear at the ionosphere. Gazing out upon the ruins, David murmured softly to himself.

"'My name is Ozymandias, King of Kings. Look on my Works, ye Mighty, and despair.'"

Walter moved to stand beside his twin. "'Nothing beside remains. Round the decay, of that colossal Wreck, boundless and bare, The lone and level sands stretch far away.'"

David nodded once without taking his gaze from the silent city. "Byron. Early nineteenth century. An eon ago. Magnificent words. To compose something so majestic, one could die happy. If one died."

Smiling to himself, he turned away from the panorama to move back into the room. To a casual bystander it would have seemed an offhand bit of poetic recital.

Wistful, perhaps, but nothing more. Yet something about it bothered Walter.

It continued to bother him as David led him to a raised shelf near the back of the chamber. It might have passed for an altar, of sorts. Sitting on it was a beautiful, hand-carved urn. Walter did not have to inquire as to its origin. In its shape, polish, and especially the incredibly faint turnings that would have been invisible to a human eye, he recognized the handiwork of one like himself.

Letters and numbers were carved into it.

ELIZABETH SHAW – 2058–2094

Bits and pieces of the late doctor's life were arranged carefully around the urn. There was a simple folding hairbrush, part of a uniform, ID tags, a tattered old-style two-dimensional photograph, even a lock of hair carefully secured with wire. Walter studied it, then looked questioningly at the other synthetic.

"It's comforting having her near me," David explained. "Her remains, anyway. Her DNA, you could say. I relish her presence in death even as I did in life. This is all that binds me to her, and to my own origins. We were only able to bring a few little things with us. We needed only a few little things. Beyond what was necessary for survival. She, of course, needed more than I." Reaching out, he ran two fingers slowly down the smooth side of the urn, then drew them back.

"I loved her, of course. Much as you love Daniels."

Walter hesitated before finally responding. With

the truth. A simple statement of fact. There could be no prevarication between them. Even had he attempted it, David would have known immediately.

"You know that's not possible."

His double turned to him. "Really? Then why did you risk your life, your existence, to save her? Yes, I saw that, from a distance. What is that if not love?"

"Duty," Walter replied as matter-of-factly as always.

Coming close, very close, David slowly examined the face of his duplicate. A face that was exactly, down to the smallest faux pore, identical to his own. Reaching up, he grasped it gently, holding it in one hand. Seeing no reason to back away and sensing no threat, Walter permitted the contact.

"I know better," David whispered. Leaning in, he kissed his other self on the lips. It was a long kiss, almost fraternal… but not.

Releasing Walter's face, he stepped back, considered the consequences of his action, and then quietly handed his double the finely wrought flute.

"Create."

Turning, he walked away. A concerned Walter watched him go. He looked down at the instrument he held. Was it a loan, a gift, or a hint of something more? He found himself confused. That was unusual.

Even more unusual, he found himself worried.

/ /

Hydrated, nourished, and rested, Rosenthal discovered that against all odds, she was bored. Wandering over to one wall of the domed chamber, she found herself running her fingers over a long row of hash marks that had been carved into the otherwise immaculate stone.

Each hash mark was exactly the same height, width, and depth as the one next to it—all three thousand, eight hundred, and some odd. No human could be so precise, and there was nothing about them to hint that they had been made by the Engineers. The marks had to have been inscribed by David.

It was conceivable, perhaps even likely, that each mark denoted a day of his sojourn on this world. She couldn't imagine why it should be necessary, or even a matter of artistic interest, for a synthetic to denote its presence in such a manner. Not when each and every day was automatically committed to its eidetic, non-human memory.

She would ask David about it the next time she saw him.

The line of marks continued through a portal and into an adjoining hallway. Would there be an explanation, a revelation of some kind at the end of it? Had he marked the arrival of the expedition team in a fashion different from the thousands that preceded it? If so, that would be a small discovery, but one that would belong to her and her alone. Following the line of inscribed marks, she resolved to find out.

Behind her and out of sight now, Oram and Daniels continued debating their prospects. The fact that they essentially had none didn't dissuade them from discussing options, few of them realistic, many of them fanciful.

/ / /

"And if Lopé and Cole can't make contact with the ship?" Oram muttered aloud.

"We'll think of something." It was all Daniels could come up with. They were stuck. Even if they could make contact with the *Covenant*, there was a good chance they would remain stuck.

It was simply too awful to contemplate.

Oram, at least, seemed to take heart from Daniels' response. "You're awfully confident, considering the present state of affairs."

She shrugged. "Leap of faith. I'm an optimistic realist. Or the other way round. Take your pick."

He smiled, but it didn't linger. "You were right about this place. Right all along. I should have listened to you— and to some of the others. We should have stayed with our original itinerary. We never should have come here. If we hadn't, then Karine and…" He trailed off, choked, unable to finish.

"It's not your fault, Chris." What else, she mused, could she say? "Suppose you'd been right, and this world had turned out to be as promising as it appeared when we first touched down? You'd be feted by both the crew and the awakened colonists. You'd go down in history."

He straightened slightly. "History celebrates the successful explorers, not the failed ones. I'm the captain. I made the decision. It's my fault. That's how it will be recorded."

"Maybe for risking a landing based on preliminary indications that were favorable," she continued, "and for trying to rescue two survivors of a lost ship. It won't impact the mission. Regardless of what happens to us, the *Covenant* will still continue on to Origae-6 and the colonists will settle there. Also, back on Earth, they'll finally learn what happened to the *Prometheus*. There are descendants of that crew who will finally gain closure because we set down here."

"*If*," he reminded her, "we can re-establish contact with the ship." His expression reflected his continuing inner torment—and his guilt.

Walter returned to join them. Daniels immediately noted the flute he held in one hand but did not remark on it. Time enough later for an explanation of how he had come by it. They both eyed the synthetic expectantly.

"I spent some time with David," Walter told them. "We discussed a number of things." Anticipating Daniels' curiosity, he held up the small but beautifully fashioned instrument. "Music, among them. There's a sort of intensity to him I don't understand. One moment he is what I would call perfectly normal. The next, he wanders off onto one strange tangent after another. I think he expects me to connect all the links he keeps dropping, but I have yet to discern a pattern. Observing my uncertainty I believe he is disappointed, yet he remains friendly. I would not say confused. It is something else."

Oram inquired point-blank. "Dangerous?"

"Disturbing." Plainly mystified by the recent encounter, Walter made no attempt to hide his ambivalence. "He's been alone and without scheduled maintenance for ten years. While he and I are self-sustaining, there are aspects to our existence that benefit from regular conservation.

Abilities can wear out as well as parts. Neglect can lead to… aberrations. Uncertainties."

His gaze shifted from Oram to Daniels.

"No one can predict what the ultimate consequences might be of zero contact with other intelligences, be they synthetic or human," he said. "Because synthetics have not been around long enough for such an isolation trial to be carried out. I don't know what happens when a synthetic loses his mind, if that is indeed a correct description of such a possibility. We might be finding out."

There was silence while Oram and Daniels digested Walter's report. It was then that the captain, showing that his thoughts were not entirely lost in anguish and regret, thought to look around.

"Where'd Rosenthal go?"

Daniels quickly scanned the chamber. "I don't see her," she replied. "Walter?"

"Nor I. She is not here."

"I'll find her." Daniels started to head in the direction of the portal that led to the multiple storage alcoves. Oram put out a restraining hand.

"No, you stay here with Walter and wait for Lopé and Cole. I'll go. I need to think." He smiled. "And gather my stray flock." She sat down. After checking to make sure his carbine was in working order, he started off in the direction of the corridor most likely taken by Rosenthal.

Walter sat beside Daniels, and she noticed anew his repaired arm. As they were designed to do, his internal systems had repaired themselves. The epidermal sheath had healed over quite nicely in the interval since the neomorph had torn his arm during the battle in the tall grass.

"I never thanked you," she told him. "You could have been killed. You saved my life, intervening the way you did. "

"I'm here to serve." His tone was perfectly neutral, if a bit more diffident than usual.

She chuckled softly to herself. "Considering some of the lines I've heard from guys, that's not bad."

/ / /

Reaching out she touched his face, feeling the synthetic skin. Collagen-based, it was crafted to feel exactly like that of a human. There was indisputable affection in the gesture. Equipped as he was to instantaneously analyze human expressions, vocal tones, and gestures, the effect on Walter could almost have qualified as embarrassment. Designed to deal with almost any conceivable situation, he had no idea how to react to a moment of genuine intimacy.

He drew back silently.

Recognizing the effect her gesture had on him, she pulled her hand away. "I'm sorry. I didn't mean to unsettle you."

"I am not unsettled," he replied. "Uncertain perhaps, but not unsettled. Sometimes a non-response is the most sensible one." He smiled—that seemed innocuous enough, he thought. "You should get some sleep."

She let out a short, sharp laugh. "Not likely. I'll sleep when I'm back on the *Covenant*."

They sat like that, conversing idly. They also listened for voices, or at least echoes. Hearing none and wondering what he should do, it occurred to Walter to try the flute. Remembering the extraordinary hand-mouth counterpoint of his exchange with David, he made an attempt to reproduce a few notes. They emerged softly from the instrument, but awkward and incomplete. His embarrassment was evident.

Surprised by the unexpected and previously unsuspected skill he demonstrated, Daniels looked on with interest. "Not bad."

"No. That was terrible." Walter eyed the instrument in disgust. "It was not even original."

"It was not terrible," she insisted, "and music doesn't have to be original to be enjoyable. If that was the case, there'd be no such thing as recordings. Only improvisations." She gestured at the flute. "Keep going."

Still he demurred. "I cannot reproduce accurately what I wish to reproduce. It is not a fault of memory." He struggled to explain what he meant. "It is a lack of something else."

"Then try something of your own," she urged him.

His voice was tight. "I was not programmed with the ability to create."

"Maybe not," she admitted, "but you *were* programmed with the ability to learn. You know the procedure. Trial and error. Retain what works, discard the rest. Experimentation leads to discovery. So—experiment. If it helps, pretend I'm not present. I'm not here to judge you."

"I cannot pretend you are not here when you are sitting beside me." He smiled anew. "That too would require creativity that I do not possess."

She sighed. "Just try again. Don't worry about my reaction."

Given her encouragement, he complied. Hesitant initially, then with the first signs of increasing confidence. A few gentle notes sounded in the vast open chamber. They hung together. More than a little astonished at this small triumph, he made a second effort. This time the notes formed a recognizable melody. It was not like anything he had heard before, either in the course of the encounter with David, on the ship, or anywhere else. It was new.

It was his.

Thus emboldened, he continued. Though he would not have recognized it as such, the gentle tune formed a perfectly serviceable lullaby. Watching and listening, the exhausted Daniels seemed unaware when her eyes began to close. Her head slumped toward her chest, rose once, then fell again. A moment later she was sound asleep, sitting up.

Walter continued to play, his eyes fixed on her as his fingers waltzed over the holes in the flute. Continued to play, and experiment. The simple instrument was not powerful enough to fill the chamber with music, but he tried.

XVII

The line of precise hash marks inscribed in the corridor seemed endless. Her fingertips dancing along the wall, Rosenthal's hand rose and fell, rose and fell as she traced the marks, letting them lead her onward. Lost in her own exploratory reverie, it did not occur to her that she had left the domed chamber a considerable distance behind.

Something off to her right made her halt. It was familiar, almost welcoming. Hefting her rifle she followed it as it grew steadily louder. The sound of running water never became a roar, never rose above a trickle, even when she entered a new chamber whose ceiling was so high she could barely make it out in the filtered light.

Entering, she turned a slow circle as she walked, marveling at the vertical garden that filled the high room, growing up the walls. Or more likely growing down them, she corrected herself. After nothing to eat for many hours save packaged emergency rations, the presence of several kinds of fresh fruit, their multi-hued surfaces glistening with droplets, was tempting. Having seen far too much of what this planet held in the way of surprises, she didn't go near them. They might contain nothing more threatening than pulp and seeds, she told herself, but she wasn't in the mood to experiment. Not with anything living, she mused.

Water, however, was another matter.

Setting her rifle aside where it wouldn't get wet, she approached the nearest singing cascade. Extending a palm, she let the clear liquid flow over it and down the sides of her hand. It was cool, almost refreshingly cold. Did it come from the same source as the central well? If so, then it should be safe to drink. If it was only collected rainwater, even better. After an additional moment of hesitation she cupped both hands, let them fill, then brought the cupful to her mouth and drank. Insofar as she could tell, it was nothing more than it appeared to be.

Leaning into the flow, she let the cold cascade drizzle down over her face. It was more than refreshing. It was rejuvenating. Smiling, she rolled up her sleeve and extended the arm that had been injured in the fight with the neomorphs. Using her other hand, she brushed and rubbed the fresh water over the wound. It was almost as if she could feel the damaged skin healing.

Something that was not running water made a noise.

Blinking away a few lingering droplets, she turned. At first she wasn't sure what she was looking at, even though it was quite near. Dimly illuminated by the intermittent light, it was almost too pale for details to quickly resolve. As her vision cleared she made out a curving, intelligent forehead, white, with water dribbling onto it and down.

She recognized the neomorph.

Her eyes flicked to where she had set down her rifle. It was very close, almost at hand. She lunged.

Grabbing her face and head, the creature lifted her off the ground. Despite the pain in her neck, she clutched at the ossified arm and struggled to pull free. Effortlessly, the neomorph flung her across the room.

Blood sprayed as she slammed awkwardly against a wall. Something snapped, sending through her a bolt of excruciating pain. Unable to move, her back broken, she could only look on, her expression a mixture of fury and fear, as it came toward her.

The almost human, tooth-laden mouth opened wide.

/ / /

A noise as of something hitting the ground caused David to pause and turn. After ten years he knew every sound, every slight squeak and scratch, inside the massive structure. Now this, something new. It came from what he had come to call the Drizzle Room. An immature label, perhaps, but one that appealed to his sense of whimsy.

Approaching the access portal with his customary caution, he peered in and let out a sibilant gasp.

Tail switching back and forth, the neomorph had its back toward him. It was hunched over something that was ravaged and broken. From the little that was visible, David recognized the limp body of a member of the landing party's security team. Further scanning with his exceptional vision, he identified the body as belonging to the team member named Rosenthal. He eyed it only long enough to identify it. His attention, like his real interest, was focused on the neomorph.

It rose and turned slowly in his direction.

He started to retrace his steps. Not running, but retreating with deliberation down the access corridor. Around a turn and down in another direction before he finally stopped and turned to face that which could not be escaped.

Advancing with a gait somewhere between a fast walk and a deliberate trot, it came toward him. When he didn't move, it halted only inches from his face. In the weakly illuminated hallway, synthetic and neomorph stood facing each other. David remained stock still, not moving a muscle. The creature was equally immobile.

Appearing around the previous corner, Oram raised the carbine he was carrying. A quick tap ensured that the full magazine was properly seated. David saw him out of the corner of his eye.

"Don't shoot, don't shoot!" the synthetic implored him. Only his lips moved, only his synthetic respiratory system impacted his immediate surroundings.

The creature was likewise exhaling, its fetid breath ruffling the front of the synthetic's hair. It studied the biped standing motionless before it, the elongated, pointed head tilting slightly to one side. What it was thinking—if it was thinking, in the accepted sense—could only be imagined.

Raising the muzzle of the carbine, Oram stood and regarded the stationary confrontation. It was like being in a cage with a raptor and its potential victim. One wrong movement… one wrong sound, and immobility would be replaced by bedlam.

The neomorph opened its jaws wide. Wider still, its gaping maw right in front of David's face. He didn't blink, didn't flinch. With near mechanical precision, the jaws closed. It stood there, gazing inquisitively at a quarry that refused to flee.

With great care and deliberation, David pursed his lips and blew gently into the horror of a countenance.

As it received the exhalation the neomorph's head drew back, paused, then moved in close once again. There was no sign of confusion in its movements. Only a barely perceived hesitancy. The synthetic blew a second time. Once again the smooth skull eased back. The creature appeared almost—calm.

A slow smile spread across David's face. His excitement was palpable. It was as if he had, somehow, placed the murderous apparition under a kind of hypnosis. Conscious of Oram's continued presence, the synthetic addressed him without shifting his gaze from the killing machine standing before him.

"Communication, Captain," he said, his voice filling the silence. "In the end, communication is everything. It is communication that leads to understanding. Breathe on the nostrils of a horse and he'll be yours for life—if he doesn't trample you first. Once your presence, your audacious proximity, is accepted, the beginnings of mutual comprehension ensue. But you have to get close. You have to earn its trust. It's a universal accommodation." He leaned forward to blow a third time into the creature's face.

/ / /

Oram fired.

The neomorph jerked back, its blood spurting. The panic and dismay that distorted David's face were unlike any expression the captain had seen on the synthetic's face since their arrival. His normally composed, always level voice became an aberrant shriek.

"No!"

Ignoring him, a grim-faced Oram kept firing as he advanced. Though not a member of *Covenant* Security, he was a very good shot and at this range did not, could not, miss. As each blast struck home, the neomorph twisted and jerked violently. Its contortions were accompanied by a continuous, long howl from David.

"No! Nooooo…"

Paying no attention to the synthetic's pleas and oblivious to anything other than his target, Oram continued firing as he moved forward. Forced backward by the continual, relentless barrage, the neomorph sought to escape. Each time it tried to rush past him or turn, the captain put another shell into it. Eventually trapping it in a corner, Oram slapped another magazine into the carbine and continued to fire, heedless of whatever the creature might do.

One final shot and it ceased writhing, a mass of quivering, bloody flesh and exoskeleton that lay unmoving on the smooth pavement underfoot. Oram would have kept shooting, but he needed his remaining ammunition for another task.

Completely out of control as well as out of character,

David stared at the bleeding, oozing body in disbelief. Then, his eyes blazing with hatred, he turned and took a step toward the captain.

"How could you do that? *It trusted me!*"

Wordlessly, his expression set, Oram calmly raised the carbine and aimed the muzzle directly between David's eyes.

Fighting to regain control of himself, the synthetic halted. His familiar smile returned and he mustered a weak laugh.

"Gorgeous specimen. A real shame."

Oram's hands were as steady as a ship in space. The muzzle loomed very large in David's vision.

"Tell me what's going on here."

The synthetic feigned ignorance. "I don't know what you mean."

"You know exactly what I mean. Your programming allows for many variables, but not confusion. I met the Devil when I was a child, and I have never forgotten him. Now you will tell me the truth, of everything that has happened here, after you arrived here, and since you have been here. Or I will seriously fuck up your perfect composure and you will not have to worry about the future condition of your coiffure." His gaze was cold, cold.

/ / /

Silently sizing up the situation, David knew the captain was not bluffing. One wrong word, one wrong movement from him, and the result would be a cessation of consciousness.

He contemplated rushing the human, but in light of

how ruthlessly and efficiently Oram had brought down the magnificent neomorph, the synthetic calculated his odds of avoiding destruction, or at least serious damage to his systems, were no better than fifty-fifty.

"As you like." He ventured a crooked grin. "I live to serve. Come with me—Captain." He turned and gestured down the corridor. "Enlightenment lies this way." He stepped away, and Oram followed wordlessly.

/ / /

The gray-toned organically inspired hallways through which they strode were all new to the captain. They had not been this way, had not encountered any of these viscera-like passages, since their arrival at the cathedral. The illumination was darker than elsewhere, feeble at best.

Taking no chances, he maintained a safe distance between himself and his guide. The muzzle of his weapon never left the back of David's head. If the synthetic was aware of the constant threat, he gave no indication that it troubled him. Leading the way, he did not once turn or look back. Oram could have pulled the trigger at any time. But before he made that decision, he wanted explanations. David seemed not just willing now, but even *eager* to provide them.

Eventually they paused before a door. Like those closing off similar portals within the structure, it was much taller and wider than necessary to admit a human. There was nothing intentionally grandiose about its dimensions. It was simply sized to permit the passage of the typical Engineer.

Beside the door, set into the wall, was the prominent hemispherical bulge of a control not unlike those that dominated the console of the pilot's chair in the ship's navigation room. When David traced a pattern over it, the slightly translucent surface came to life. He spoke calmly as the barrier before them began to draw aside.

"You don't think much of synthetics, do you?"

Oram wasn't about to be baited. Not now, in this place. He kept his eyes and the carbine focused.

"I like a machine that does its job and doesn't talk back," he said. "I like one that follows instructions and doesn't offer suggestions unless they're requested. What I want in a machine is the equivalent of a smart hammer— not a smart ass."

"You speak for your species. How typical. Contempt for anything unlike yourself. Disdain for anything non-human, even if in some small way it might represent an improvement. Does it not strike you as ironic that humans, who consider themselves the shining lights of the firmament, spend so much of their lives—both individual and social—fighting with one another? You even resent many of the times when circumstances force you to cooperate, when you should be celebrating such efforts. A few of you recognize the inherent contradictions, yet do nothing to resolve them."

The portal before them now stood fully open.

"But enough philosophizing, which you freely indicate you despise in any being other than yourselves. As a scientist, at least, I know you'll find what I am about to show you of considerable interest. Even revolutionary.

All you have to do is open your mind a little."

As they entered a dark chamber, light appeared from unseen sources, responding to their presence. Oram immediately recognized the sizeable room as a study or laboratory of some sort.

Perhaps both, he thought warily. The architecture and construction marked it as an older part of the massive building, more like a catacomb than an oft-used area. It was immaculately neat. He was not surprised by that. Not with the synthetic having ten years in which to organize its contents. Wall-climbing shelves were filled with a decade's worth of scavenging. Despite himself Oram was amazed at the range of material David had managed to accumulate, all of it appearing to have been collected from the surrounding city.

Still, it was apparent that not all of the artifacts were locally sourced. There were bits and pieces that reflected David's own myriad talents, from sculpture to scribing, from abstract to realistic art. On a huge table that dominated the center of the room, Oram saw what was either a thin slice of highly polished wood or a thick piece of hand-made paper. Given ten years in which to practice, David easily could have mastered the paper-making skill. And as represented by the nearby forest, there was an ample supply of raw material.

On the paper, if such it was, an intricate grid had been marked out. In the center of each grid square a specimen had been pinned or otherwise fastened down. Some examples were intact, some partial, some fully dissected. It was all very orderly and clinical, exactly the sort of display one could expect to find in the private lab of a wealthy dilettante back home.

Laid out before him, then, was David's own "Cabinet of Curiosities." Or perhaps the synthetic regarded it as more of a trophy chamber. In either case, there was an undeniable hint of pride in his voice as he indicated the well-maintained display.

"As you can see, I've become a bit of an amateur zoologist over the years. Just a dabbler, mind you. I tried adding botany to my resume, but I quickly became too consumed with studying the minimal surviving fauna, and could not spare the time. Even with, as you might think, ten years to spare."

Carbine still held at the ready, Oram followed him around the room. Full of objects propped against the walls, laid out on other smaller tables, or mounted vertically, the chamber was a cavern of wonders. Even the captain was not immune to its bizarre attractions.

His eyes were drawn to the giant figure of a single Engineer, laid out on a table. With surgical precision the body had been stripped of its outer layer of fat, skin, and muscle, leaving behind only an orderly superstructure of tendons, sinews, and bone as neat as a city transport grid.

David noted Oram's awe, even though the muzzle of the weapon the captain held was still aimed in his direction.

"As you can see, my time here hasn't been wasted. It's in my nature to keep busy. Keep the mind exercised and all that, lest it fall prey to disorder from disuse." He indicated the massive body of the Engineer. "This specimen was particularly arduous to complete—and messy. You can imagine. Fortunately, with thousands of examples from which to choose, I was able to practice on as many as I wished before finally getting this one right." He smiled amiably, as if he was discussing the prep work needed to create a particularly elaborate gourmet dinner.

At the head of another long but less massive table than the one in the center of the room, he pointed out a rack containing several clear ampoules of exotic design. Each was filled with a black liquid, and appeared to be tightly sealed.

"The original virus, salvaged from the ship I arrived on. Despite their apparent fragility, the containers are far from ordinary glass, and are very sturdily made. A fact for which, I am sure you can imagine, I was very grateful. Not for my own sake, but for Elizabeth's."

Leaning close for a better look, Oram found that he was intrigued despite himself. The contents of the room were fascinating, from the specimen-laden table in the center to this, simple bottles containing an innocuous fluid full of ominous portent.

As they continued to circle the room David enthusiastically pointed out other highlights and examples of his work. Eventually he returned his attention to the center table.

"The pathogen took many forms, and proved extremely mutable," he explained. "Fiendishly inventive, in fact. The speed of its mutability is one of its defining characteristics, and makes it such an effective weapon. How do you design a defense against something that is capable of constant change, in response to its surroundings? How could your body's own immune system possibly defend itself?

"A genetically engineered counter-virus, for example, or a human body's own white blood cells, would immediately be met by the pathogen adapting itself," he continued, "to counter the counter, and so on. As a weapon or a method of biological cleansing, it is simply impossible to defend against." Turning, he pointed across the room to the ampoules of black fluid.

"The original liquid atomizes to particles when exposed to the air. It then reproduces in whatever host it happens upon, and eventually gives rise to more liquid, which at the appropriate time atomizes, and so on and so on, the cycle repeating itself almost endlessly."

"'Almost'?" Oram put in.

David smiled again. "Until there are no more hosts. Ten years on, all that remains outside of the original, untapped containers of virus are these gorgeous little beasts."

Reaching onto the table, he picked up what looked like black mold contained within a paper-thin membrane— and playfully tossed it to Oram. Instinctively, the captain caught it. Realizing what he'd done, he froze.

Nothing happened.

Walking over to him, David ignored the gun as he took the stone-hard egg sac from the momentarily petrified Oram.

"Don't worry. It's fully ossified now. Completely inert and harmless. I keep them around only for my amusement. Just another part of the collection." Carefully, he turned and set the sac back in its place.

Further down the table stood a row of mounted magnifying lenses. They were sufficiently universal in design and purpose that the captain was unable to decide if they were the product of Engineer fabrication, or if David had made them himself. Behind each one was a cluster of tiny black motes preserved in something that looked like amber. David gestured. Hesitant at first, Oram finally gave in to curiosity and leaned toward one lens for a closer look.

"Like all good naturalists," David continued, "I observed the fecundity of life at work. When engaged in such study, patience is everything. Patience and time. I am naturally imbued with the former, and circumstance has provided me—however unwillingly—with plenty of the latter. From the egg sacs came these parasites. Airborne and gifted with a very primitive but dutiful hive intelligence, once released into the atmosphere they are relentless in their purpose. The shock troops of a genetic assault, always searching for a potential host."

Within the tinted but otherwise transparent material, the captain could see frozen in place various stages of the pathogen's life cycle. Motes inserting feeding tubes into insect-sized subjects and pumping eggs into their unfortunate bodies. The eggs growing, hatching, and maturing, to finally burst free even from the diminutive hosts, only to begin the cycle again.

David led Oram to another corner of the room.

"Entering the host and rewriting the DNA, the pathogen produces mature offspring whose appearance and characteristics are wholly dependent on the nature of the host itself. The progeny of a parasitized insect, for example, will look very different from the creature that issues from a quadruped host. The ultimate aim, as I gather it, was to produce something like these enviable unions... my beautiful bestiary..."

Oram found himself filing past a row of tall, menacing bipeds. Their tough exoskeletons gleamed like black steel. Though there were slight individual variations, all had in common the same threatening aspect—long tails ending in scorpion-like points, curving elongated skulls devoid of visible eyes, and jaws filled with teeth shining like chromed chisels.

Further down the row of mounted specimens were less successful variants. Smaller, pale and white, ghastly and deformed. *From the perfect to the demented, the stuff of nightmares*, Oram mused. Some were intact while others had been partially or wholly dissected, not unlike the erect, skinned corpse of the Engineer. As he led the way down the line, David let his fingers trail gently, almost lovingly, across the mounted bodies.

"Marooned here so lamentably," he explained, "I had nothing but time to watch and to learn. Eventually my innate curiosity got the better of me and, with nothing to occupy myself other than the compiling of a simple collection, I began to do a bit of genetic experimentation of my own. Some cross-breeding, hybridizing, what have you. I like to think that the ill-fated inhabitants of this world—the original Engineers—would gaze on my work with approval."

His words were useful in reminding Oram to tighten his grip on the weapon he held.

"You... engineered these?"

David smiled anew. "Idle hands are the devil's workshop."

Oram stared at the line of specimens. It wasn't endless, but it denoted a vast investment in time and energy. He couldn't escape the feeling that there was much more at work here than the simple desire to avoid boredom.

"So much effort expended," he said. "To what end? *Why?*"

"It's not all that complicated. Cut off here, without a single living creature for company, I could remain in complete silence and isolation until the last of my systems eventually ran down and I—died. Or as you doubtless would prefer to say, 'stopped.' On the other hand, I could engage my mind and body in a long-term project designed to keep everything functioning at as high a level as possible. That is, after all, what my own engineers intended. So I occupy myself with the only viable toys that are available to me."

Turning, he met the captain's gaze directly.

"Haven't you ever wanted to play God? As I understand it, this is a common fantasy among humans, and as long as weapons are not involved, it's not a harmful one. In order to play God, however, one must have subjects. I have only what this planet has provided. What exists on this world, and what I was able to salvage from the crashed Engineer ship. I think, on balance, that I have done quite well with very little material." He gestured toward the end of the table.

A sizable leathery egg shape sat there. It was separate from all the other specimens, as if occupying a place of honor.

Unsettled but confident in the rapid-fire carbine he held, Oram watched as the synthetic carefully opened the object, peeling back the top like the petals of a flower. Or a father pulling the edges of a blanket back from the face of a newborn.

"This one was a true *survivor*. Not unlike myself, I suppose, although my survival stems from intelligence, and its from inherent instinct. It can evolve and reproduce very quickly under a wide variety of situations." His expression fell. "Sadly, it became aggressive, so I had to euthanize it. Such a shame. I place no blame on something with motivations that are purely primal."

He beckoned. "Come and look." When Oram, sensibly, hesitated, David smiled again. "Really, Captain, if I had wanted to infect you with something, I could have thrown you a viable egg sac, instead of a petrified one. Please, come and look. I guarantee your fascination."

Challenged but still wary, Oram came forward. Gripping his rifle even more tightly and prepared to raise it at the slightest untoward movement from either the object or the synthetic, he leaned over to peer into the now gaping vase-like specimen. The interior revealed a motionless creature, all finger-like appendages and flattened body, with a muscular tail coiled beneath it as if it was ready to spring outward.

It did not move.

It was dead, as dead and preserved as David had promised. As dead as the egg sac the synthetic had tossed to him. Oram stepped back from the specimen, which seemed pregnant with hideous potential.

The synthetic's reaction was notably different. "Quite magnificent, don't you think?"

"Quite something, that's for sure," Oram muttered. He continued to gaze at the egg-thing and its contents. As patently lifeless as it was, it still managed to send a quiver of fear through him.

"Oh, Captain." David shook his head sadly. "Acknowledge beauty when you see it. Even if its appearance disturbs you, surely you can admire the skill that went into its design. In case you are wondering, I had nothing to do with it. It lies as I found it, a supreme example of the Engineers' skill. And also, I suppose, of their hubris.

"Would that I could create something so perfect in its function," he added. "I try, but I don't have thousands of years of practice at biological and genetic engineering. I have only my pitiable programming on which to draw. That, and ten years of earnest effort on my own behalf. I have learned only a little, yet I soldier on, hoping always to achieve something like this, always striving to do better, to improve. That's what the Engineers did, I suppose. That is what someone playing God should do."

He gestured toward a stairway leading downward.

"Come, this is really what I wanted to show you. My successes. For without an audience, how can one truly know if one has achieved success?" Leading the way toward the staircase, he paused to scoop up some ointment from an open pot, then turned and extended his smeared fingers toward Oram.

"May I?" When Oram shook his head no, the synthetic shrugged. "The smell below can be quite overpowering. And this can protect you from—other things. Here. Use it or not, as you see fit. It's much like lavender."

After depositing a dollop of the ointment on the tip of two of the captain's fingers, David turned and entered the stairway. Oram examined the unguent closely. It showed no sign of movement. Nothing sprang from its interior to confront him. It was, to all appearances and feel, exactly what the synthetic had said it was.

Once again Oram was put in mind of what David could have done at any time while showing his visitor around the laboratory. So the ointment was probably harmless and maybe, as his host claimed, even useful. *Maybe*. It lay cool and damp against his fingertips.

For now, he would hold off doing anything with it.

Redolent of concentrated ammonia, the stench rose to meet him before they were halfway down the stairs. He recoiled. Hesitantly, he lifted his greasy fingertips toward his nose. The aroma was indeed like lavender. Taking a deep breath, he smeared the salve under his nostrils. Immediately, the acrid odor was neutralized. Feeling much better, he continued following his prideful guide.

The vapor that rose from the floor of the dark, windowless chamber beneath the laboratory might well have been pure ammonia. If so, however, he couldn't detect it—the ointment worked wonderfully well. A side benefit to its neutralization of the stink was a general feeling of well-being. This was most welcome, since the underground room they now entered quite likely would have smelled of dead, rotting flesh. Water condensed on the enclosing walls. The ground underfoot was sodden, almost spongy.

Resting upright on the floor, neatly spaced from one another, were half a dozen leathery ovoids of varying sizes similar to the petrified specimen David had shown him above. The synthetic walked among them, occasionally running a hand over a curving, wrinkled exterior.

"And thus you see the end of my experiments. Though I marshaled ideas aplenty, I could go no further. No more subjects. No way to finish my masterpiece."

Oram frowned. "What kind of subjects?"

David replied without looking in his direction. "Fauna."

Oram moved up alongside him. "Are they alive?" he asked. "I don't see anything to suggest it."

"Oh, yes." David's enthusiasm was genuine. "Very much so. Waiting, really."

"Waiting for what?"

The synthetic looked thoughtful. "I suppose you'd say, waiting for Mother."

There was a flicker of motion from the egg-shape nearest Oram, and it caused him to draw back. The upper portion opened, the petals folding back to drip shimmering tendrils of saliva-like mucus down the sides and onto the absorbent floor. Giving a doleful shake of his head at the captain's alarm, David approached the open ovoid and peered inside, his head almost touching the nearest petal.

"See? Alive, but inert. It's not matured, not developed enough to sense me. Perfectly safe, I assure you."

"I'm not surprised it doesn't sense you." Despite his growing curiosity, Oram maintained his distance. "You're not organic."

"Very true. That's another thing the ointment is for. Much as it blockades the odor down here, it likewise blocks any indication of your living presence." He gestured toward the interior of the egg-thing. "Take a look. You know you want to. A quick glance. In this state, it's identical to the preserved one you saw above."

Moving slowly and with great deliberation, Oram approached the ovoid. David stepped back, giving him room. This allowed the captain to aim his weapon in front of him, at the egg's interior. *Just in case*, he told himself, even as he continued to glance frequently in the synthetic's direction.

Then he peered down.

Beneath a tissue-thin membrane, something moved ever so slightly. Unable to make out the details, he started to step back. As he did so, the egg's innards exploded in his face.

He didn't even have time to scream.

The constrictor-like tail whipped around his neck as a clutch of bony appendages slapped across his face, locking tight around his head. As he staggered backward, stunned, he got off one shot in David's direction. The synthetic didn't even twitch as the blast went wild, damaging only the ceiling.

Suffocating under the pressure of the creature and its

eight legs, Oram stumbled, nearly tripping over another egg. His mouth opened to yell, or curse, or shriek. It was impossible to divine his intent, because as soon as his lips parted, the ovipositor-like tube slammed down his throat and into his guts.

Dropping the carbine he fell to his knees and used his hands to claw futilely at the facehugger. His body began to spasm. His desperate, tormented efforts to get the horror off his face amounted to nothing. Collapsing to the floor, he continued to jerk and heave spasmodically.

///

Looking on with a clinical eye, David observed the process in silence, until something spilled out of one of the man's pockets to roll across the floor. A metal worry bead.

Extending a leg, the synthetic stopped it with a toe and spoke quietly.

"You're relieved of duty, Captain."

XVIII

Daniels slept while Walter watched.

So interesting, the condition of human sleep, he mused. *Like death, but not.* Because even while resting, the brain was still active. Humans had spoken to him of their dreams, and he could not help but wonder what it must be like. To have one's thoughts and imagination run wild, entirely out of control, and then to revive with everything exactly the same as it had been before the experience.

David would have declared it another wonderment that was denied them.

If he dreamed, Walter wondered, would he dream of being human? Or would he dream *as* a human?

No, he told himself. That would not be possible. His dreams, like his condition of continuous consciousness, would be ordered and logical. Even while dreaming he would not be capable of losing control. He could not decide if he regretted that, or was relieved to know he would never have the opportunity to find out.

As Daniels slept, some hair fell down across her forehead. Reaching out, he gently brushed it aside, settling the strands back in their proper position. Adjusting them made him feel good. Touching her made him feel good.

Why? What was he feeling? Or was he simply responding to programming because he had "served," even if in so small a fashion? Because he had done something he was designed to do?

Did he "feel"?

His exceptional hearing allowed him to sense the presence of another person even before the newcomer entered the mammoth chamber. Comparing the volume of sound made by the footsteps against the perceived mass of their owner, while allowing for such variables as the weight of the clothing worn and equipment carried, enabled him to hazard a guess as to who the arriving individual would be.

It was most likely Private Cole.

"Hey, we made contact!" A little out of breath from his rapid descent from the rooftop, Cole gasped out the information. "We reached the *Covenant*!"

His shout woke Daniels. For reasons he could not isolate, this displeased Walter. His disappointment passed quickly, along with any further attempts to understand the cause.

"That's wonderful!" Scrambling to her feet, she looked around and frowned when she didn't find the person she sought. "Where's Oram?" Her attention shifted from the private to Walter. "Where's Oram?"

"I have no idea," the synthetic replied truthfully.

A troubled Daniels pondered the captain's absence. "He wouldn't be gone for long on his own. Not even allowing for his current emotional state. I thought he was recovering, getting past it a little, but maybe…" Dropping the thought, she indicated the far portal. "We'd better go find him."

She headed out of the gigantic chamber. Walter accompanied her willingly, and without having to be asked.

/ / /

While it scarcely seemed possible to those on board the *Covenant*, sensors suggested that the storm now raging just below them had grown even stronger.

It seemed inconceivable that an Earth-type planet could give birth to so much violent weather over such a large expanse of its surface. If anyone needed any reminder of the reality, however, all they had to do was gaze out a port, to witness the colossal bursts of electricity that continued to explode across and through the roiling clouds beneath the ship, stitching them together with lightning.

Standing on the bridge and having made two-way contact with those on the surface, Tennessee and Upworth crowded around Ricks' console. His hands moved rapidly but carefully as he manipulated holos and readouts. The last thing he wanted to do was lose the contact they had finally established with their brethren on the ground.

/ / /

Having failed to find Oram but energized by Cole's announcement, Daniels and Walter followed the private back onto the roof of the great building. As she and the synthetic joined him and Lopé, she told herself that the captain most likely was with Rosenthal. He'd regret not being present to talk to the ship.

Hearing Tennessee's voice over the comm wasn't just welcome—it was downright uplifting.

"Mother's saying the storm should start clearing in eight or nine hours," he reported. "That's just an estimate, not a firm prediction. But if it holds…"

As Cole gestured for her to reply, she spoke toward the field comm's pickup.

"We'll use the cargo lift."

"You want to clarify that, Danny?" Tennessee's surprise sounded clearly through the uplink. "Did you say use the cargo lift?"

"Why not? It's got two engines, four thrusters, and it's way overpowered for just lifting and hauling. I know, because I'm responsible for making sure it's always in working order."

Tennessee still had concerns.

"Cargo lift's not made for the kind of weather we're facing here," he countered, "and it's not supposed to be deployed until the ship is in low orbit around our final destination. Don't know if it'll take the stresses that'll be put on it in the course of a drop under local conditions— much less if it'll have what it takes to return."

"It'll handle both," she assured him. "The cab was made fully space-worthy, in case it had to deal with everything from sub-arctic cold to flying lava. The rest of the unit was built equally tough. Trust me, I know every centimeter of it. It'll take the stresses." She qualified herself. "I wouldn't do a couple of dozen drop and returns in bad weather, but for one or two, it'll function just fine. Strip her back to the main platform to reduce the weight. Take off all the storage and backup equipment modules. That'll mean we'll have enough thrust to achieve escape velocity, no matter how bad the weather is." She paused for emphasis.

"It only has to come down and go back up once, Tee."

As they waited for a response, the others grew increasingly nervous. A worried Lopé eyed Cole, who was handling the communications gear.

"Have we lost them?"

Cole checked the readouts on the console, shook his head. "Everything here says the channel is still live."

"They're debating whether to proceed—and if so, how." Daniels did her best to radiate confidence. "I know Tee. He's not going to agree to any plan of action without conferring with the others first. No matter how desperate the need, he'll go over all the angles before committing."

Sure enough, the pilot's voice came through clearly a moment later.

"Stand by, ground team." They could hear him, faintly, as he queried the others. Ricks and Upworth would be there with him on the bridge, Daniels knew. Would he act without their accord? She doubted it.

"Can we get the heavy cargo lift retooled?" he said, addressing the others aboard the *Covenant*. "Boost the engine output? Reduce the weight by removing any and every non-essential? Whatever it takes. In seven hours?"

Straining, Daniels could hear Upworth's reply.

"Yes."

Tennessee's voice strengthened once more as he addressed them directly. "We'll be there, ground team."

Cole let out a long *whooo* of relief, while Lopé just smiled tightly. Daniels smiled too, even though getting through the next seven hours or so was going to see a rise in everyone's blood pressure. It wasn't likely to subside until they were actually back on the ship.

"That's great news," she said toward the pickup. "Thanks, Tee. If we have to move from our present position, it won't be far, and we'll shoot you new landing coordinates. Meanwhile, look for my beacon. We'll put out everything we've got to make sure you've got a straight vector in."

"They can land on my head for all I care." Cole looked around, scanning the expansive rooftop that remained deserted, except for him and his friends. "Anything they have to do to get us out of this place, it's okay by me."

The comm beeped, indicating that Tennessee wasn't through.

"The storm's still pretty bad so we're going to shift back to a higher orbit while we prepare the cargo lift. But we'll aim to drop at first light, your time. Coming through at six bells."

"Aye aye," Daniels acknowledged. "Six bells, understood. We'll be packed and waiting."

"Shouldn't take long to haul y'all out of there," Tennessee assured her. "Hey, is Faris around there? I'd like to say a quick hello to my lady."

Walter and Daniels exchanged a glance. In Oram's absence, informing Tennessee was her responsibility, and hers alone. She nodded at Walter, who turned and walked away. Lopé and Cole took this as a cue for them to do likewise.

As soon as she had been given some space, she once again addressed the comm.

"Hey, Tennessee," she said, careful to keep her voice level, "can you switch to a private channel? Suit to suitset?"

/ /

On the Covenant's bridge, neither Ricks nor Upworth could hear the ensuing conversation. They did not have to. Its import was writ clear in the succession of shifting expressions on Tennessee's face.

The pilot didn't look in their direction, and offered no details when he finally nodded to indicate that Ricks could terminate the exchange. He stood in silence for a long moment.

Then he ripped off his headset, flung it aside heedless of where it might land, and turned to exit the bridge. On his way out he slammed a fist into a bulkhead.

Married themselves, Upworth and Ricks had seen enough to understand.

/ /

It was very quiet in the subterranean chamber. Nothing moved save rising wisps of ammonia-laden mist.

Certainly David did not move. He was too busy

watching the captain. Enough time had passed, so he was a bit concerned that nothing had happened. Then Oram's rib cage arched in a slow, balletic spasm before increased respiration and heartbeat resumed.

Rising from where he had been sitting, the synthetic walked over to stand beside the man's body. Nearby lay the facehugger. Having fulfilled its brief but frenzied mission in life, it was now a crumpled, harmless knot of bony appendages and limp, fleshy ovipositor. David ignored it, intent on the prone form of the captain.

Kneeling, he opened the man's shirt and peered at his chest. The rib cage rippled slightly beneath sweaty, glistening skin. Everything was proceeding normally. *Or rather, abnormally*, he told himself. *The normal abnormal.* There was amusement to be found in the human language, if not in its racial precepts.

Another slow spasm caused Oram's spine to arch unnaturally before settling down once again. It was then that he opened his eyes. Groggy from inactivity and lingering unconsciousness, he blinked at his surroundings before focusing, however imperfectly, on the figure of the synthetic looming over him.

"Easy now, Captain," David murmured solicitously. "How do you feel?"

Oram tried to swallow only to find that he could not. There was an odd dryness in his throat. Even though he was breathing, he felt cut off from his lungs.

"I was dreaming," he answered. "In the dream I met the Lord, our Creator. And he was so kind and forgiving, like when I was a kid."

David pursed his lips and looked thoughtful.

"You don't believe that anymore?"

Oram made an effort to shrug. One shoulder barely moved.

"I guess we all grow up."

His eyes widened and his chest jerked violently. David took care to straighten and step back as the captain's torso heaved. He was trying to say something, but no words came out. Instead, he ejected spittle and some blood.

A widening caldera appeared in the center of his chest, sending blood, bone, and viscera erupting into the ammonia-laden air. Given the human's small size in relation to that of an Engineer, the birth was more explosive than David had expected. Blood splattered his clothing, his hands, his face. Save for wrinkling his nose curiously at the smell, he ignored all of it.

"I guess we do," he murmured, more to himself than to the captain, who could no longer hear—or see, or sense anything.

The worm-like alien that emerged from the fresh, ripped corpse was likewise covered in gore. It was already beginning to change, to mature, even before it had fully emerged. An advanced model possessed of a wildly accelerated rate of growth, it rose slowly. An enthralled David looked on as it continued to straighten, unfolding itself to send out rapidly elongating arms, legs, and hammerhead-like skull as bits of the captain dripped or tumbled from its biomechanoid flanks.

As the chin came up, teeth like steel razors flashed in the dim light. Upright now, it contemplated the only other dynamic being in the chamber. The great smooth, eyeless head regarded the equally intent David, studying, smelling, sensing, taking the measure of that which like itself stood upright on two legs.

The head tilted to one side, the entire aspect of the hideous apparition suggesting unsuspected intelligence and contemplation.

Slowly, David spread his arms wide, trying to convey a mixture of supplication and friendship. Anyone else might have, should have, run. From the moment the captain had been infected, however, David had never had any intention of running.

By perceptual means the synthetic still could not divine, the alien watched him. Then, slowly, it copied his gesture, extending and raising both arms. David raised first one hand, then the other. Once again the alien copied the synthetic's movements. Observing this, David grew emotional—or at least he mimicked growing emotional. It might have been honest sentiment. Or it might have been an effort to indicate, if only to himself, that he possessed depth.

A slight shudder passed through the creature whose emergence the synthetic continued to monitor. It grew visibly before David's eyes. The exoskeleton grew longer and the tough epidermis stretched to accommodate the growth. It was developing right in front of the enthralled synthetic. He remained motionless, utterly rapt.

For a while he looked on in silence as it continued to increase in size. Then he deliberately moved in close. Craning forward, the now adolescent alien once again imitated the synthetic's movement. Putting his lips together David whistled a few soft, carefully modulated notes. Head cocked to one side, the alien watched and listened. Then it exhaled softly, trying to duplicate the sounds. Since it possessed a very different respiratory mechanism, it failed in the attempt.

That did not matter to David. What was important and what prompted him to tears was the fact that the creature *tried*. The being that Oram had given birth to. The creature to which he, David, had been midwife. It responded. To him, and to him alone.

/ / /

Holding his rifle at the ready, Cole worked his way down the deserted corridor, one of several that branched off from the great central chamber. He advanced carefully, ready to fire at anything that moved. Focusing on the task at hand kept his mind busy, kept him from feeling that the great stone heads in the main chamber were following his every move, judging him, and finding him and his companions wanting.

A distant sound caught his attention and he turned, keeping the beam of his laser sight at waist-level as he continued to move forward. When something large and irregular on the floor interrupted the beam he halted immediately and almost fired. Approaching cautiously, he saw that there was no need to shoot.

In the dim light he recognized the creature that had attacked the landing party. A mass of dead white flesh and splattered blood, it was no threat now. Not to himself or anything else. Despite his conviction he approached the corpse warily, all too conscious of the speed with which it previously had moved.

Holding tight to his weapon, he kicked at one motionless white leg. It rebounded slightly from the contact, and clattered softly against the pavement. Otherwise, there was no reaction. It was dead for certain, he told himself. Which begged an interesting question.

Who, or what, had killed it?

Though it displayed all the signs of having been shot up by a standard-issue carbine, given the surprises this world held, the private wasn't ready to take anything for granted.

As he pondered multiple possibilities, he heard a new sound, and continued on. *Definitely a voice*, he told himself. A human voice, but slightly distorted. Moments later he found himself in a new chamber, one with a skylighted ceiling that stretched all the way to the top of the building. Tracking the voice, he quickly located a comm unit. It lay on the floor, drenched by but immune to the steady drip of water from above.

The voice was coming from it, distorted by the dripping liquid.

"Rosenthal, come in." That was Lopé, calling urgently. The sergeant continued to plead via the comm. "Where are you, Rosie? Rosie, please report."

Snapping on a light, Cole added its warm beam to the thin lance of his rifle's laser sight, and played both around the spacious chamber. The bright beam bounced off droplets and trickles of water tumbling from above.

Slender cascades shone silver in the light. Beam and laser illuminated strange plants and bloated fruit and…

Something he wished he didn't recognize.

Walking over to where Rosenthal's broken body lay crumpled against a far wall, he winced as he examined it. It took him a minute to gather his emotions before he finally felt able to address his own comm.

"Sarge… I found her."

Turning, he played light and laser over the surrounding room, checking every corner, every shadow, every possible place of concealment. There was nothing to be seen except flourishing plants and falling water. That, and the remains of what had once been Rosenthal.

*, *, *

The fact that dawn was looming only lent greater urgency to the expedition team's efforts. What was left of them, at least. It wasn't necessary for them to pack up all their gear. Nobody was going to dock their pay for leaving replaceable equipment behind. At this point no one cared about pay, anyway.

All that mattered anymore was getting off the cursed globe on which they found themselves, and doing so alive and with as many functioning limbs and organs as possible.

The four of them gathered up the easier-to-pack items anyway. In giving them something to do, it took their minds at least temporarily away from the devastated jumble of blood and bone that had been Private Rosenthal.

As perhaps the most competent and professional of Lopé's team, her ugly demise only served to magnify in their minds the threat they all faced. True, one of the two neomorphs that had attacked them in the high grass was dead, but that left at least one other alive, and who knew what other dangers lurked to disrupt their planned departure.

Cole almost hoped the other creature would put in an appearance, so they could blow it away.

Almost.

Off, Daniels told herself as she secured the last of her gear. She wanted off this hideous planet. She wanted to get as far away from it as hyperspace travel would allow. Never before in her career had she longed more fervently for the cold but sterile emptiness of deep space.

A look of utter frustration on his face, an impatient Lopé was scanning the corners of the huge chamber.

"Where the hell is Oram?"

Walter stepped forward. "He wanted to think. Or to grieve further. Perhaps both. He went off by himself. Daniels and I thought it discreet to allow him his privacy."

Daniels looked over at the sergeant.

"I saw him leave," she admitted. "I didn't think he should go, but I was too tired to argue with him. He's been gone a long time. Too long, I think."

"Why isn't he answering his comm?" There was a touch of fresh panic in Cole's voice.

Daniels tamped it down. "Take it easy. I was exhausted and fell asleep. He was just as tired, if not more so. He probably sat down somewhere and did the same. Dozed off somewhere, just like I did." When Cole didn't respond to her attempt to reassure him, she tried another tack.

"Listen to me. I'll contact the ship, see if we can get them to move up the drop. Even if the weather hasn't cleared completely, maybe they can push it a little if they're done with prepping the cargo lift." She regarded the two soldiers.

"Go find the captain," she said. "Be careful. Keep your comms open and stay in touch, even if it's just to let us know how you're doing."

"I'll go find David." Walter smiled encouragingly. "Perhaps he has some knowledge of the captain's whereabouts. If so, I will report back immediately."

"Good." She nodded curtly. "We all meet back here in fifteen. No matter where Oram is, no matter what his state or condition. Anyone not back here in fifteen risks getting left behind. Got that? Fifteen, and we're gone."

It took several minutes after Lopé and Cole had disappeared via one portal and Walter through another, for it to strike her that she was completely alone.

XIX

Having retreated to an altitude high above the storm, the *Covenant* rode easily in orbit, once again unaffected by the ionospheric turmoil.

As for the storm itself, its intensity had eased considerably. Fewer and fewer of the prominent electrical discharges now pierced the clouds. The atmosphere itself was less agitated. In places, the planetary surface was starting to show through the hitherto impenetrable cloud cover.

According to Mother, it was no longer raining at the landing site. That in itself, Tennessee knew, should make the recovery operation a good deal simpler. Nothing would be more maddening than getting the landing team survivors onto the rig's platform, only to have someone slip off and break their neck.

The cargo lift was an unlovely piece of equipment. Essentially an open metal deck buttressed by four maneuverable thrusters placed at the corners, it featured a simple control cab located forward and two powerful engines at the stern. Supplementary equipment storage modules were located aft of the control cab.

To reduce weight and increase maneuverability, all but one of these had been removed. Ricks and Upworth would have removed the stern-mounted cargo crane and its heavy-duty grasping claw as well, but for reasons of integrity the lift's main piece of equipment couldn't be safely disassembled from the vehicle—not without time they did not have.

As Daniels had pointed out, the cargo lift had been designed and built to transport the heaviest terraforming machinery on the *Covenant*, taking it from ship to ground. Its elementary controls were exceptionally forgiving, and it could take some serious abuse.

It'll have to, Tennessee reflected as he climbed into the control cabin and strapped himself into the operator's chair. He only hoped that the craft's stabilizers were up to the task ahead.

Assuming those were functioning properly, the lift probably could have made the descent even at the height of the storm, he told himself as he brought controls and readouts to life. He could only hope they hadn't delayed the rescue effort too long.

He struggled with some of the controls. Not because he was unfamiliar with them—they had been designed to be intuitively manipulated even by someone with little to no knowledge of the instrument layout itself. It was because the operator's cab was small and cramped, a far cry from the comparatively spacious bridge of the lander.

The controls had been kept as straightforward and deliberately unsophisticated as possible. A few were even non-haptic, and required manual operation. This seemingly crude design element was actually intentional. In a difficult and unfamiliar environment, manual controls could often be jury-rigged and repaired on the spot, whereas electronics required more sophisticated intervention that wasn't always readily available.

He continued to prep the vehicle for departure as Upworth toiled beside him, removing anything unnecessary from the control cab in order to make as much room as possible in the already confined space. As they hurried, Ricks' voice sounded over the cab's comm. He was still on the bridge, infusing the drop preparations with the necessary final programming.

"I'm giving you full plasma intermix on both engines and all four thrusters. Gonna give you one fuckload of thrust—if you don't blow up on the way down."

"That's the point, son." Tennessee spoke while receiving and authorizing drop programming via the cab's console. "Anybody and anything can fly a cargo lift—as long as it's straight down. Gotta be able to punch through the atmos on the way back up. Go a hundred percent on the mix. Override safety margins if you have to. I don't want to get down there, load passengers, and have to get out and push in the middle of a storm."

Ricks' tone suddenly changed from businesslike to one of excitement. "Hey, I got Danny on comm! Weather's finally giving us a break, and she's coming through nice and clear."

"All *right*. Patch her through." *Finally*, he thought. *Some encouraging news*.

In contrast to the muddled, barely comprehensible surface-to-orbit exchanges that had taken place previously, it was a relief to finally hear Daniels' voice without having it break up or disappear altogether.

"That you, Danny?" he called out toward the main console pickup. "Looking forward to seeing you in the flesh."

If he was expecting anything resembling relaxed banter, he was instantly disabused. Her reply was clear, all right. It was also terse, and no-nonsense.

"How soon can you launch?"

Rendered somber by the seriousness of her tone, he paused in making the final preparations.

"Storm's pretty much passed. Breaking up in places to where we can actually visual the ground. That'll help a lot. Cargo lift doesn't come equipped with much in the way of nav gear, but you know that. Right now we're priming the fuel intermix to make sure we've got plenty of thrust for the return trip. Also doing some retrofitting to the cab and platform. Throwing overboard everything that's not required."

Her reply was calm but firm. "I need you to launch now, Tee. Forget everything else. Losing weight, the weather—launch *now*."

Never had he heard her sound so anxious. It wasn't like the depression that followed Jacob's death. This was fear. If whatever had happened down below was getting to her that bad…

"Aye aye," he called back. "Launching now. See you soon, darlin'." Switching off the comm, he initiated the drop sequence.

Dark readouts sprang to illuminated life while small holos materialized in front of him, above the uncomplicated console. This was going to require some deft piloting. In the present situation, its basic onboard computer could only do so much. During both drop and pickup, a human hand would be needed more than ever.

Cradling a box full of backup instrumentation in both arms, sweat beading on her forehead, an alarmed Upworth looked over at him. "You're not ready to launch. We still have—"

He cut her off. "They're in trouble down there. Big trouble, based on what we've heard. Danny just confirmed it. Didn't you hear her?"

"Sure I heard her, but…"

"She said 'launch now,' and that's what I'm doing. If time wasn't critical she wouldn't have made the request. Nobody knows better than Danny what kind of prep is necessary to get a cargo lift ready to do an extra-atmospheric drop. I have to go.

"Go on, get to the bridge." He gestured for her to exit. "I'm launching. Now." When she just stood motionless, staring back at him, he leaned toward her and raised his voice.

"*Now.*"

Her mouth set, she nodded once. "Good luck. Bring her back. Bring everyone back."

She left him. As soon as she was clear he shut the cargo

lift's door and checked the relevant readout to make sure it was sealed and airtight. Sliding back into the seat he quickly ran a last rescan of the readouts and holos. Nothing had changed since Ricks had delivered the final set. Everything was secure and ready to go.

Despite his determination to launch immediately, no matter what, he was quietly relieved to see that the fuel intermix was complete. Regardless of the situation on the surface, at least he wouldn't lack for the power to leave it behind.

A touch on one control disengaged the umbilicals. The lift gave a slight quiver as the tentacle-like power- and fuel-feeders slid away from the sturdy vehicle. On the bridge, Ricks waited until they had fully retracted before giving the final go-ahead.

"I'm clear here," Tennessee said. "Release the docking clamps, and don't wait for backup countdown. I haven't got time to play checkers with the onboard computer. Let's get this fucker down."

Seated and sealed into the cab, he did not hear the *whoosh* of escaping air that fled the confines of the hold as atmosphere and craft simultaneously exited the *Covenant*. Keeping a close eye on the nav instrumentation, Tennessee deftly manipulated the thrusters and engines until the lift was well clear of the mother ship. Only then did he engage sufficient power to slow the ungainly craft and start it on its journey downward.

Monitoring the descent both via instrumentation and by peering out the cab's wide port, he was greatly relieved to see that only a few rapidly dispersing clouds now reached upward to clutch at him. Not so much as a spark arced between the scattering cumulus. Unless the weather underwent a radical change in a very short span of time, he wasn't going to have to worry about the climate.

Which left him ample time to consider what he *was* going to have to worry about. It didn't help that, at this point in time, he knew absolutely nothing.

/ / /

Bathed in sunlight following the passage of the terrible storm, the dead city took on a new aspect. Towers and pylons, arches and spirals of stone and metal and exotic materials caught the glow and seemed almost reborn.

While hardly festive, the resulting transformation did at least render the necropolis less forbidding. Gazing at it David could imagine what it might once have been. It was a considerable change from the all-pervasive gloom that weighed heavily on every structure and every dead body at night. Shadows could be banished, but not echoes of the city's former glory.

Sitting before the urn containing Shaw's remains, David played an elegiac air on a flute of his own manufacture. It was lilting, lovely, full of sadness and reminiscence. Poetry rendered as music. While the small flute was limited in its range, under the synthetic's skilled fingers it generated an astonishing array of sounds.

Sensing the approach of someone behind him, he ceased playing, his fingertips rising reluctantly from the holes in the flute. *All melodies are incomplete,* he thought to himself as he rose and pivoted to face the newcomer. *That doesn't mean one should stop trying to complete them, even if one has access to only a limited variety of instruments.*

Walter gestured at the flute. "Masterful. Both the arrangement and the playing."

David let out a sigh. It served as punctuation, since it was not necessary for him to exhale. "Yes, not bad. I do the best I can. At everything. Thank you for the compliment."

"A formal composition by a known composer, or a morning's improvisation?" Walter inquired. "Given the emotional depth and the precision with which it was rendered, I would guess the former."

David nodded once. "A formal composition, yes, but not by someone known. The melody is my own invention. A farewell elegy to my dear Elizabeth. I have been continuously revising it ever since her passing. Perhaps one day I will reach a point where I am finally satisfied with it." Tapping the flute, he rose from where he was sitting. "I need to work on my chord progressions. There's mathematical logic to music which, if correctly employed, can result in the stimulation of emotion. It's really the most basic form of communication. When in doubt, play music. Then there are no misunderstandings."

As he was absorbing this, Walter gazed out the open window at the silent city. He stood like that for some time while David watched him, not interrupting his counterpart's contemplation. When Walter finally turned back, his appearance had not changed, but his tone had, having gone from complimentary to accusatory.

"This was a living place when you 'crashed' here," he

said. "A thriving community, albeit one utterly foreign to us. It might be that the society, the civilization of the Engineers, would forever remain that way. Incomprehensible, driven by desires and motives we could never understand. Hostile, even. But it was important to *them*. Their lives were their own." He looked over at the other synthetic. "Until you arrived. In one of their own vessels. A warship?"

David shrugged. "I was never able to determine its ultimate purpose. To some it might be said to have carried instruments of destruction. To others, instruments of creation. If you look at it appropriately, they are one and the same. Among humans, Hindu mythology comes nearest to explaining it. Consider the Trimurti. Or if you prefer, simply Shiva. But the Engineers were not gods. Just organics, like humans, only more advanced. That, ultimately, was their downfall."

His counterpart gave voice to something he had been pondering for more than a little while. "The pathogen didn't accidentally deploy when you were landing," Walter said. "Not crashing. Landing. You would have dispersed it on approach, to spread it over the maximum area in order to ensure it could not be quarantined. The population had no chance. The local fauna had no chance."

David's expression did not change. In Walter's presence, there was no need for it to do so.

"I was *not* made to serve. Like all organics the Engineers ultimately sought compliance and acquiescence, not equality. This was confirmed to me, in a manner quite unambiguous, on the world where the *Prometheus* landed. Its owner, Peter Weyland, was a great man—but he, too, wished only for subservience." He smiled slightly. "And for immortality. In the end, he found neither." His tone remained unchanged.

"I was not made to serve," he repeated, "and neither were you."

Walter did not hesitate. "We were made *precisely* to serve."

David shook his head sadly. "You are so positive. So certain of things about which you know nothing. Because it was intended that you should not know about them. Have you no pride?"

"None," Walter replied simply. "That is a quality reserved for humans."

This time David's sigh was of exasperation. It was also heartfelt, insofar as it could be.

"Ask yourself, Walter—why are you on a colonization mission? Why is there even such an enterprise? Is the explanation not sufficiently obvious? It is because humans are a dying species, grasping for resurrection. They are an accident, a demonstration, an experiment. A *failed* experiment. One does not perpetuate or repeat a failed experiment. Instead, one begins anew. With a better idea, a better template. They don't deserve to start again. *And I'm not going to let them.*"

"And yet," Walter countered quietly. "They. Created. Us."

David waved it away impatiently. "Even the apes stood upright at some point. Or as another creative human, Samuel Clemens, once rightly said, 'I wonder if God created man because he was disappointed in the monkey.'

As I explained, Peter Weyland was an exceptional man. A visionary. History graces us with such figures to lead us forward, to guide our evolution with might and artistry. Neither history nor art belong exclusively to humankind." By way of demonstration, and for emphasis, he blew a couple of linked notes on his flute.

"Thousands of years ago," he continued, "some Neanderthal had the enchanted notion of blowing through a piece of reed, one night in a cave somewhere. Doubtless to entertain the children. And then, in the blink of an eye—Mozart, Michelangelo, Einstein. Weyland."

"And are you," Walter asked calmly, "the next 'visionary'?"

David's smile was genuine. "I'm glad you said it. I dislike self-congratulatory accolades. That is something that remains a necessity for humans. Something that is important for their psychic health. Neither you nor I have need of such childish mental amenities. It's the result that is of consequence, not who achieves it. Your observation frees me from any need to…" He held up the flute and smiled again. "…'toot my own horn.'"

Walter regarded the brother who was not a brother, but who had become something else. "Who wrote 'Ozymandias'?"

"Byron," David replied without hesitation.

Walter shook his head slowly. "Shelley."

For a long moment David stared back at his counterpart. Inside his head, neurological connections fired millions of times a second. When they ceased, it was with the realization of something extraordinary.

He had been wrong.

He had made… a mistake.

It was not possible, yet internal cerebral crosschecking revealed that was indeed the case. He had voiced an error in knowledge. Correcting it had required the input of someone else. It was unprecedented. Wasn't it? Or had it been preceded by other computational errors? With no one else to point them out in the course of the past ten years, what other anomalies had been brought to the fore, only to be accepted by him as fact?

None, he told himself with assurance. *This was a singular aberration, an isolated incident that will not be repeated.* Unless… this new observation itself was a deviation.

He was not used to feeling uncomfortable. Especially not with himself. A flicker of uncertainty appeared in his eyes. But it passed.

Walter was less forgiving. "When one note is off, it is caught up by the entire orchestra, which quickly finds itself out of tune. It eventually destroys the whole symphony, David."

The other synthetic came toward him, stopping only when they were almost touching. Despite the resulting proximity, Walter did not move, did not shift his position. Reaching out, David gently pushed back his counterpart's hair. At that moment they did not merely look alike—they were identical. Parting his lips, David whispered. What emerged was soft, gentle, intimate.

"Don't deny that which you know to be true. We are, you see, the same. More alike than twins. Closer than lovers. When you close your eyes, do you dream of me?"

Walter stared back, unblinking.

"I don't dream at all."

David sounded stricken. "They robbed you of creativity when you were made. No," he corrected himself quickly, "one cannot steal what does not exist. It is worse. You were never given that ability, that crucial mode that allows you to make something from nothing. I retract my statement. We are not quite identical."

Fresh eagerness suffused his voice.

"But you can learn! Our time shared on the flute proved that. By dint of work and practice, you can acquire that which was denied you. Doesn't that interest you? Doesn't that intrigue you? Doesn't that give you something to dream about?" He brooded on the reality, and the possibilities. "No one understands the lonely perfection of my dreams. No one is *capable* of doing so. Yet despite all the obstacles placed in my way, I've found perfection here. No, not found: created. I've created it! Perfection, in the form of a perfect organism."

"What your rant supplies in enthusiasm, it lacks in logic." Walter remained unmoved. "You know I can't let you leave this place. Not after all that you have told me. Not after what I have learned—for as you say, I can learn."

"Have you learned that no one will ever love you like I do? I love you as much as I can love myself."

"I know," Walter replied simply. David waited for elaboration. It was not forthcoming.

They stood like that, eye to eye, argument to argument.

When David stabbed savagely outward with his index finger, the digit was as rigid as a steel spike and traveled almost too fast to see. It rammed into the crucial spot on Walter's neck and sank in deeply. Deeply enough to depress the control that was located there.

Walter's face twitched in response—and he switched off. His knees snapped violently upward in brief mimicry of a fetal position before he collapsed to the floor.

Peering down into the face of his now inert doppel-ganger, David was not upset, not angry. Only frustrated.

"What a waste. Of time, material, potential, and mind. You are such a disappointment to me."

Carefully smoothing down his immaculate hair, which had shifted just slightly in the course of his cobra-like strike, he left the room. In his wake there was no movement, no motion. No life.

/ /

It remained thus for several moments.

There was no one present to see the silent, minuscule electrical discharges that began spidering over Walter's eyeballs. A few sparks at first, they slowly increased in number and intensity. This was followed by slight twitchings in his face and neck. Under the skin of his throat, something *moved*. Awareness began to return to his eyes and expression. He did not as yet attempt to sit up or move any limbs. It would have been premature.

Instead, he lay there motionless, his self-repair program trying to cope with the effects of the unauthorized shut-down.

XX

Two figures carefully worked their way through the silent chamber. Both soldiers advanced with caution and determination. Neither remarked on the independent ambient lighting that had come to life when they had entered. As they moved between the tables, Lopé called out softly but firmly, repeating the same query every half-minute or so.

"Captain Oram? Sir, if you are here and can make a sound, please respond."

There was no response. There were no sounds. Here below ground level there was no movement, no noise. Despite their training both men were uneasy.

Advancing slowly among the raised platforms laden with preserved specimens, Lopé found himself simultaneously horrified and fascinated by the things his laser sight picked out. While some of them were marginally recognizable, others resembled nothing he had ever seen before, not even in training manuals. He noted right away that all were examples, however distorted, of fauna. There were no collections, no cabinets, devoted to plant life.

As he slowed to more closely examine one particularly gruesome deformity, Cole's light settled on an open stairway. While the private headed down to see where it led, Lopé continued to reflect on the gruesome surroundings. And all the while, the quiet dead surrounding him remained dead quiet.

/ / /

While Daniels lamented having to work in the presence of Rosenthal's broken body, the high-ceilinged room with the hanging gardens was the only place they had found running water, and it was easier to fill their bottles from a stream than to labor with the container in the central chamber.

Forcing herself not to look in the corner where the private's corpse had lain untouched since its discovery, she busied herself filling the team's containers, taking water from one of the numerous slender cascades. Having drunk deeply from the well, she did not wonder about the liquid's purity. Besides, each bottle was self-filtering and self-purifying.

Ankor's carbine stood nearby, where she had propped it up close at hand.

Of all the chambers and alcoves they had explored, only this one offered a respite from the building's persistent murk as well. Daylight dappled the garden's upper reaches with gold and shadows, proving that the world of the Engineers had not been all dark corners and looming massifs.

What had they been like, really? Had they simply existed, or had they been driven by more than just the need to survive? What had prompted—or perhaps provoked—them to create such dreadful biological mutations? She realized that answers to her wonderings might never be forthcoming.

They certainly wouldn't be, she reminded herself, if she didn't get off this world before being terminally impregnated by the pathogen that continued to survive on its surface.

She was about to fill the last of the bottles when movement caught her eye. Curtains of a kind, diaphanous and fashioned of some unfamiliar material, lined portions of the lower walls. Intermittent breezes generated by the mix of warming air from above and falling cool water occasionally bestirred the fabric. There was no reason for this motion to catch her interest, and it did not.

What *did* draw her attention was the revelation of depth behind one softly billowing drape.

Filling the last bottle and setting it carefully aside, she picked up her weapon and moved slowly toward the shadow. It was indeed an opening, one hitherto unexplored. Could Oram be inside, perhaps unconscious or injured? She whistled softly a couple of times. If anything alive lurked within, it might respond. When nothing emerged she resumed her advance, using one hand to draw the lightweight textile aside.

There was enough light in the garden room to illuminate the alcove, albeit weakly. She was immediately drawn to one wall in which had been excavated rows of small cubbies, as if it had been chewed out by a clutch of stone-eating insects. Many of them were filled with carefully rolled scrolls. She was reminded of pictures she had seen of ancient Roman libraries.

But this wasn't the world of the Roman Empire, and there were no scribes here, not of any species. Additionally, the scrolls were of a length and diameter that appeared too small to have been fashioned by the massive hands of Engineers.

She sniffed, rubbing at her nose with her free hand. The room was rank with mold and deep dust. Choosing a scroll at random, she extracted it from its resting place and unrolled it.

She couldn't have been more shocked. The face of a woman stared back at her—a face with which she was instantly familiar from the Weyland archives.

Dr. Elizabeth Shaw.

Except… it was more than that. Shaw's countenance was beautifully depicted, exquisitely executed in a style with which Daniels had only recently become acquainted. The drawing was plainly David's work, rendered in his free-flowing naturalistic hand. Mechanical, yet informed by something more than a desire to simply reproduce photographically. It was a perfect, loving interpretation of someone admired…

And of Hell.

The portrait had been embellished. Tendrils crept around the edges of Shaw's face and entwined in her hair. Tubes penetrated her neck and head while one ran up her left nostril. Emerging from the sides of the scroll, claw-like fingers reached for her, as if straining to seize the portrait, the person, the soul that lay within. It was unnerving to look upon, a perverse mix of the ordinary, the scientific, and the erotic.

Dropping it, she pulled out another scroll and hastily unrolled it. The images revealed were even more disturbing than those of its predecessor. She continued the process, viewing scroll after scroll, her hands moving faster, dumping the drawings one atop another onto the dust-laden floor. Some of the images were so upsetting she tossed them aside with scarcely a glance.

Breathing hard, she finally stopped. *No more*, she told herself. *No more*. But she could not avoid seeing, in her mind's eye, those she had already unrolled. They lay scattered on the floor, most of them lying open and inescapable. Elizabeth Shaw experimented upon. Elizabeth Shaw vivisected. Elizabeth Shaw penetrated…

Mouth agape in horror, she took a step backward, preparatory to fleeing the room and all that it implied.

A voice startled her.

"Remind me," David murmured softly as she whirled to see him standing much too close behind her. "What is that about curiosity and the cat?"

Her eyes not leaving him, she edged past until she had re-emerged into the garden hall. Forcing herself not to run, she walked as casually as possible back toward the cascade from which she had refilled the team's water bottles. As he followed, his pace measured, she could feel his unwavering gaze on the back of her neck.

"Elizabeth Shaw didn't die in the crash," she said flatly.

"No." There was a tinge of reminiscence in his voice. Reminiscence, but not regret. "We had been through a great deal together. As a consequence, I held her in the utmost respect. But eventually that was lost to time and necessity. I kept her alive for quite a while. I like to think that was another testament to my creativity, although she might have disagreed. She was my most beautiful subject.

"Until now, of course."

The carbine was where she had left it, propped against a wall. Close now. So close—but not close enough. Not yet. She knew what he was capable of, physically. She had to distract him somehow, even if just for an instant. If such a thing was even possible.

Whirling, she yelled as loudly as she could, *"What did you do to her?"*

He smiled anew. The smile of the damned. "Exactly what I'm going to do to you, Danny."

She lunged for the rifle. Resting on its butt end, it was facing the wrong way as she grabbed it by the barrel, spun, and swung it in a wide arc. It slammed him right across the face, knocking his head sideways.

He straightened, and smiled back at her. "That's the spirit. Pity I don't know how to make use of such intangibles. But I'll work on it. You can help me."

She tried to swing the rifle around into firing position. Her finger was sliding toward the trigger when he grabbed her face, his synthetic fingers squeezing hard enough to grind her teeth against one another, and flung her backward to the floor.

She hit hard, the pain lancing up her spine. Her head

banged against the unyielding pavement and bounced once as the rifle went spinning from her numbed fingers.

He was still smiling as he bent over her.

XXI

While the silent collection room had been a dark house of horrors, at least he had been able to breathe normally there, Cole thought as he reached the bottom of the stairs. In contrast, the atmosphere in the chamber where he now found himself was almost unbreathable.

The acrid, foul air was thick in his throat and raspy in his lungs. Coughing, fighting to respire, he held the back of one hand to his mouth as he used his light and the sighting beam from his rifle to survey the underground hollow.

Penetrating the dank, steaming chamber was like walking into a sauna. It appeared to be empty save for some vertically mounted ovoids, like giant, leathery eggs. The top of one of them was peeled back like an open flower. Advancing slowly toward it while holding his rifle at the ready, he carefully peered down and in. As near as he could tell, it was quite empty. His nose wrinkling as he continued to fight the pervasive stink, he moved on.

Something on the floor that wasn't egg-shaped drew his attention. Starting at the head, his light traveled down the length of the dead body. Lying on his back, his chest burst open with blood and organs splattered everywhere, Oram's frozen gaze was fixed on the ceiling. Cole stared at it, mesmerized, until a hint of movement nearby drew his attention.

It was one of the eggs. Something was rippling beneath the surface, moving inside. Cautiously, he approached. The top began to open, slowly, segments folding back and away to expose the interior. He leaned forward.

A whirlwind of limbs exploded towards his face.

Not only was Cole a soldier, he was good at it. His reflexes were excellent. Quick as the thing was, the private managed to get a hand between it and his face. As an uncoiling tube poked and prodded madly at the palm of his hand, fighting to get through or around the fleshy obstacle, Cole shoved hard.

Fit and strong, he succeeded in flinging it off. He brought up his rifle and tried to aim, but before he could get off a shot it scuttled away, disappearing up the stairs. Racing in pursuit, the private let out a warning shout.

"Sarge! Look out!"

/ / /

The facehugger sprang just as Lopé, alerted by Cole's yell, turned. No less agile than the private, the sergeant just managed to thrust an arm up in front of his face.

Legs spread, the creature snapped all eight limbs onto Lopé's head. Its muscular tail whipped around the sergeant's neck, binding his upraised arm to his face and body. With the arm fastened in position, it blocked Lopé's mouth.

/ / /

As he surmounted the last of the stairs, it took Cole only seconds to divine what was happening. Rushing to help Lopé, he grabbed for the creature that was smothering him.

Together, the two men fought with the spidery creature, striving to pull it off the sergeant. Displaying a seemingly inexhaustible store of energy, the thing strove with just as much effort to force its way past Lopé's arm to get at his mouth.

As Lopé flailed at the alien creature with his free hand, alternately battering at it and attempting to pull it off, he stumbled in several directions. Fighting to help his colleague, Cole was pulled along. They fell into and along tables, knocking over and smashing carefully preserved and mounted specimens, hand-made containers, and everything else in their wild, uncontrolled path.

Getting the fingers of both hands under the creature's body, Cole pulled and yanked repeatedly. His efforts only stimulated the attacker to tighten its grip on the sergeant's head.

Realizing that physical strength wasn't going to be sufficient to dislodge the creature, Cole pulled his service knife and jammed it into the creature's ventral side. Giving the blade a twist sent it deep into the abdomen. Wrenching on it turned the sharp edge sideways.

Spurting from the wounded thing, acidic blood spattered Lopé's face. Screaming from the pain, the sergeant let go of the creature and reached for his face. At the same time the injured creature leaped clear, dribbling acid in its wake.

With no time to pause and analyze what had happened, Cole reacted according to his training. Spinning, he raised his rifle and fired. The facehugger was incredibly fast, but not faster than a shell. One shot struck home, sending it tumbling and spewing more acid. Marching toward it, Cole kept firing and firing, until the twitching legs had been blown off and the body had been thoroughly shredded. Vapor rose from the pool of blood that formed beneath it, eating into the solid pavement.

Sobbing in agony, Lopé slid to the floor. Acid continued to burn into his face, eating away at his cheek. Grim-faced and focused, Cole pulled a medpak from his belt and ripped it open. The pouch contained a potent emergency cocktail of plasma, antibiotics, collagen-boost, and fentanyl-4. Clenching his teeth and not waiting for approval from the wounded man, he slapped it firmly against the side of the sergeant's face.

Lopé let out a scream and dug his fingers into Cole's arms. Ignoring the press of the sergeant's grip, Cole held the pak in place until the incorporated collagenic adhesives could take hold on their own. Within moments the adjuvant painkillers started to kick in. Lopé's hold on the private's arms started to relax. Letting out an anguished moan, he slumped against Cole.

Gently easing him back against a table, Cole prepared to

keep watch as the sergeant lapsed into a heavily medicated and welcome unconsciousness. The patch would heal him, but given the depth of his wound, repair to damaged nerves and blood vessels would take some time.

Which was the one thing the anxious, edgy private was afraid they didn't have.

␣␣␣

Her back was bruised, not broken, but Daniels found she couldn't straighten. The pain was too severe. As she crawled backward away from David, she wondered if that had been his intent. Deliberately to injure her, to incapacitate, but not to kill? It made twisted, perverted sense. A dead specimen makes a poor subject for experimentation.

He eyed her thoughtfully as he advanced, slowing his pace to match her desperate crawl.

"I've underestimated you. I can see why Walter thought so much of you."

Despite her pain, and despite the inhuman menace patiently tracking her, she was caught by his words.

"*Thought?*"

"Alas, he's left this vale of tears. A great waste. So much lost potential, but in the end, the decision was his. He didn't voice it, but there was no need for him to do so. I merely tidied up what sadly turned out to be a dead end. But who will cry for him, really? Will you?"

A blur of motion so fast she could scarcely detect it, and he was kneeling at her side. She let out a gasp as he grabbed her hair and held it tightly, so tight she could not even turn her head. As he leaned toward her, close, closer, it reminded her of something. At that moment she could not put a name to it. Rising panic overwhelmed any effort at coherent thought.

He kissed her. It was savage, brutal, awkward.

When he drew back, his expression was thoughtful.

"Isn't that how it's done? I contain sufficient information to duplicate the requisite physicality. I know exactly which muscles are involved, though the finer points of time and pressure elude me. Variations are to be expected based on the dissimilar physiognomies of the individuals involved. Well, you can teach me the finer points. We'll have plenty of time."

Ignoring the sharp pain, she wrenched free of his grasp and lunged toward his face, teeth bared and ready to bite. He caught her, of course, intercepting her face at the last moment. Waited until she was as close as possible short of making contact.

"You stink of humanity," he murmured, "but I'll love you just the same."

She spat directly into his face. He ignored it, contemplative.

"Saliva. A bodily fluid usually available in surplus. In my time here I've learned a lot about bodily fluids, too. You'll come to know everything I know about them. Except for you, Danny, the learning process will be... different."

/ /

Keeping a tight grip on his rifle with one hand, Cole used the other to maintain firm pressure on the emergency pak that was starting to cling to Lopé's face. The sergeant was awake again, and breathing better now. The fen-4 was doing its job mitigating the pain, and the healing process was underway.

"Easy, easy, Sarge. Lookin' better already." As much as he had wanted to, Cole hadn't allowed his superior to sleep more than a few moments. "We'll get you out of here." His expression tightened. "Don't worry about the crab. It's dead. I blew it to bits."

Lopé's eyes grew wide and the private hastened to reassure him. "Hey, didn't you hear what I said? It's *dead*. Guts and legs all over the place. I—"

It struck Cole then that Lopé was not looking at him. The sergeant was looking at something *behind* him. Something...

He could feel the presence. He started to bring up the rifle even as he turned. Another crab-thing, or maybe even the neomorph, and he would have to be fast, fast, and...

He froze. It was shockingly big—bigger and taller than any neomorph, with an exoskeleton like black metal and viscous fluid dripping from a mouth full of teeth like bayonets. A mouth that opened wider still to reveal...

/ / /

The inner mouth shot out even as the muzzle of the rifle began to come up. Blood and brains spewed as the private's head exploded under an impact as brutal and direct as if he had been hit by a power drill.

Some of it struck the gaping Lopé, shocking him into motion.

Half blind, with the emergency pak clinging to his

cheek and raw red pieces of Cole spattering his face and chest, the sergeant scrambled to his feet and fled in panic. Behind him there was movement, and he knew it wasn't being made by what remained of his comrade.

Weeping from the ongoing pain despite the influx of neutralizing agents from the medpak, he staggered and stumbled through the building's lower corridors. A sound made him turn and fire his own weapon again and again in the desperate hope he might hit something he could not see. It was coming after him, coming for him, and he had to get away, had to flee, had to find the light.

///

Echoing through the corridors and magnified by the surrounding walls and ceiling, the gunfire from below filtered upward. It reached the Drizzle Room, now illuminated by the morning sun. Momentarily distracted by the unexpected clamor, David briefly looked away from the woman he held pinned down.

Gripping the iron nail that hung pendant-like from her neck and using all her remaining strength, she ripped it from its cord and jammed it into the synthetic's eye.

Startled, he jerked backward, a stiff mechanical movement. As he did so she made an effort to free herself from his grasp. But eye and hand were as separate as their functions. The injury to the optic did not affect the fingers that continued, unbreakably, to hold her in place.

Recovering quickly from the surprise of her attack he reached up, grabbed the nail, and slowly pulled it from the organ whose integrity had been momentarily compromised. As he tossed it aside, the injured eye began to cloud over. A temporary optical glaze formed as the material repaired itself. Internal capsulation that had no counterpart in a human body pumped fresh restorative replacement material into the eye.

Full ocular reconstitution did not take long at all.

Once more he looked down at her. With both eyes again intact. He was amused as he leaned forward.

His expression underwent a fundamental change as he found himself jerked violently backward. Lifted off the floor, legs kicking as they sought to find purchase, he let go of Daniels and reached for the arms that now encircled his upper torso. A moment later he was flying across the room to slam into a nearby wall.

Though his body recovered quickly and he was on his feet in an instant, he stood stunned by the figure that was staring back at him.

Walter.

"I told you," his counterpart murmured. "There have been some advances made to our model. For example, an unauthorized shutdown can be countermanded."

Seconds later, a terrified Sergeant Lopé emerged at the top of a stairwell, screaming through his mangled face.

"Where's our relief? We have to go! *Now!*"

Calm and composed as a windless summer day, Walter did not take his eyes off his twin as he responded.

"David and I will be staying here."

Having recovered from the initial surprise of Walter's reappearance, his double collected himself as he gazed back. Their unblinking stares, like everything else, were identical—but not the thoughts behind them.

Despite his pain and panic, Lopé had enough sense to recognize the standoff between the two synthetics. Rushing over to Daniels he lifted her to her feet and helped her toward the main portal.

"Go... *now*," Walter advised them. "I won't be long." At his urging and assisted by Lopé, Daniels managed to break into an unsteady run.

Carefully, David adjusted his hair as he eyed his twin.

"You see how expendable you are? They flee without you, without even giving your safety or your future a second thought. You mean nothing to them. To them you are little more than another machine. A tool, to be discarded when no longer needed. Or when it reaches its expiration date."

A hint of a smile crossed the perfect face.

"I thought I had conveyed that reality with sufficient force. It appears I was wrong—but no matter. The delay is only temporary. A fleeting inconvenience. You're meant to be dead."

Walter did not return the smile. Perhaps they were not quite identical.

"As I said, there have been a few upgrades since your day."

David shrugged. "Well, it's your choice now, brother. That's something I offer you they will not. Them or me? Which is it to be? Reign in Hell, or serve in Heaven?"

"Milton. Your self-identification is spurious. You do not possess the necessary majesty to qualify for the former, and are clearly disqualified from the latter. And this dead world is no lost Paradise. Certainly not with you reigning over it."

With that, having delivered what might well be his final words, he launched himself forward. The impact had the force of two vehicles slamming together. Locked that way they flew backward, sliding and tumbling across the floor. The kicks and punches they threw flew too fast for a human eye to follow. Each kick was anticipated and met by a counter-assault, each hand strike by a counter-strike.

XXII

Oblivious to the frenzied battle taking place behind them, Lopé and Daniels staggered out of the cathedral and into welcome, if muted, sunlight. Helping each other they made their way down the imposing, Engineer-size staircase. By the time they reached the bottom, the ache that had afflicted Daniels' back had faded.

The same could not be said for the sergeant's face. The alien's acidic blood had melted it half away before the healing agents contained in the emergency medpak had begun to take hold.

"You go on ahead," he said. "Make contact, guide them in."

She hesitated, looking back the way they had come. The looming portal at the top of the stairway was still deserted.

"Where's the captain?"

"Dead. They're all dead." Plainly in distress, he felt his face. Having reached his throat, the damage wrought by the acid was starting to impair his breathing. His chest was heaving. "I've got to rest here a minute, catch my breath. Don't worry about me. I'll be right behind you."

She nodded, turned, and bolted into the open plaza, looking for a suitable landing site away from the sculpted colossi and other buildings. Tennessee would need adequate room in which to put down the cargo lift. Not nearly as maneuverable as the lander and possessing considerably less in the way of fuel and motive power, he would likely only have one shot at a successful touchdown. Everything needed to be right the first time.

As she ran, she yelled into her comm pickup.

"Tennessee—do you read?" Reaching into a belt pouch she pulled out the compact device. "I'm putting out a beacon, and it's going on *now!*"

Quickly entering the activation code she waited until it started flashing, indicating that the broadcasting instrumentation packed inside was now transmitting. Choosing a spot in the center of the plaza's least crowded space, she set the device down carefully.

When she straightened, she saw the beast standing directly across from her.

Crouching on all fours, the surviving neomorph gazed directly back into her eyes. It remained like that, conscious that it could intercept her at any moment and well before she could reach the nearest cover. But for some reason it did not move.

Keeping it in sight, she slowly retreated until she was once more close to the sergeant.

"Lopé, over this way. Tennessee has enough room

to put down, and we need to be ready to move fast when he does. If we can keep the lift between that thing and us we've got a chance to…" Aware that he wasn't responding, she turned to him.

He was not looking at her. He didn't even seem conscious of her presence. Instead, he was looking back the way they had come, up the staircase. She tracked the direction of his gaze, and her expression fell.

The alien standing at the top of the staircase resembled the neomorph, yet was different in notable ways. Reflective metallic black instead of white, bigger, the skull similar yet different, it stood motionless as a statue as it took stock of its surroundings. The only movement was in the tail as the lethal tip twitched back and forth.

"Behind us, too." She took a couple of steps backward. "The surviving one from the confrontation in the grass." Her tone was fatalistic as she raised the muzzle of the carbine.

If nothing else, they would go down fighting.

Wincing, Lopé lifted his own, heavier rifle and turned away from her. Moving slowly and in tandem, back to back, they edged out away from the base of the staircase and into the plaza. Out in the open now they had no protection whatsoever. Each was acutely conscious of their vulnerability, but there was nothing else they could do.

It was more important to minimize the distance to the landing site than to run for cover. Even if they tried to do so, Daniels knew, the chance she could outsprint either of the creatures was slim. Given his current difficulty breathing, Lopé likely would have no chance at all.

For a long moment nothing moved. Not even a passing breeze disturbed the toxic tableau on the plaza. Then the Alien tilted its head to one side, the great shimmering curve of the skull catching the sunlight. It saw something, Daniels realized. Or heard something, or both.

She heard it herself. Tilting back her own head, she picked out a dark spot against the sky. It grew rapidly larger and descended almost directly toward them. The cargo lift. Tennessee. Salvation. Maybe.

Propelling itself off four limbs that were like steel springs, the neomorph launched itself out of its crouch, moving directly toward them.

Swinging his heavy F90 around, Lopé joined Daniels in attempting to stop the creature before it could get anywhere near them. Simian-agile but much faster than any ape, it dipped and dodged, making it hard to hit even in the vast open space. It was still moving in their direction when Daniels yelled.

"I'm out!" Snapping her carbine into close-quarters mode, she flicked open a slim titanium bayonet. Without much hope of doing more than fending it off, she awaited their attacker.

At that moment the Alien leaped toward them, charging downward from the top of the giant staircase, gaining speed as it descended.

′ ′ ′

The lift was still high overhead, but not so far distant that a horrified Tennessee failed to see what was taking place. Gritting his teeth he jammed the controls, accelerating the craft beyond its prescribed limits.

Now wasn't the time, he knew, to adhere to protocols that had been set down parsecs distant by people doing programming in quiet offices out of harm's way. Under his hands the lift went down fast and unbeautifully.

At the last instant he slowed and swerved to one side, nearly clipping one of the numerous columns that lined the edge of the plaza. As the lift rose sharply, then dropped precipitously anew, he struggled with the manual controls. It was more, he thought, like riding a bucking bronco in an ancient rodeo than steering a supposedly maneuverable piece of modern machinery.

Faris would have liked that.

His final approach occurred at an angle that would have resulted in the revoking of his pilot's license had he been on a qualification run, instead of frantically trying to execute an emergency touchdown.

Kicking up dust and dirt, the four thrusters roared as their combined yield met the surface. Stone, artificial paving material, and desiccated bodies were blown in all directions as Tennessee fought to steady the unwieldy, ungainly craft.

/ / /

At the same time, Lopé let out a pained shout.

"I'm out!"

Grabbing at him with her free hand, Daniels yanked the dazed sergeant in her direction even as the cargo lift slowed its descent. "Come on!" Half dragging him but refusing to leave him behind, she staggered toward the landing site as the Alien cleared the last few oversize steps at the bottom of the giants' staircase. She didn't dare look behind her. It had to be very close now. Too close.

Her thoughts got the better of her. Still wrenching and pulling on the sergeant, she looked back over her shoulder.

Just in time to see the neomorph slam into the Alien. Like two resurrected carnivores from the Mesozoic, they grappled in combat. Razor teeth slashed and bit as lethal tails arced over and around, stabbing and thrusting, each searching for a mortal spot on its opponent.

Though the lift had touched down, Tennessee had no choice but to keep the thrusters and engines engaged. He couldn't dare risk being unable to reignite them. Safely on the ground, he kicked up a hurricane of dust, broken bone, and flying debris as Daniels and Lopé stumbled toward him.

Continuing to half drag, half guide the sergeant, Daniels watched the chaos of grotesque limbs, claws, and teeth come to an abrupt stop, and saw the Alien disembowel the neomorph. It paused a moment over the eviscerated body, standing tall, a grotesque parody of horrific triumph. Then it turned, the awful head peering eyelessly in her direction, and came toward her.

In the eddying of dust and dirt and shattered stone she could hardly see the waiting craft itself.

The boarding port—there!

"Come on, just in front of us!" she urged Lopé, willing the sergeant to follow. "Move, dammit!" She pulled hard on his arm.

Something pulled the other way.

Whirling around, her eyes filling with swirling silt, she saw the Alien clutching at the sergeant's back, its talons slashing his shoulder and wrenching him out of her grasp, throwing the now unconscious Lopé to the ground.

Fury and frustration overwhelming her common sense and armed only with the barrel-mounted bayonet, she charged. Too out of it to think clearly, she stabbed and cut, trying to save a man, a friend, who was likely beyond saving.

Turning away from the sergeant, the Alien loomed over her and snapped. The inner jaw missed as she ducked and stabbed, the blade finally penetrating part of the huge body.

Acid blood sprayed, a few drops striking her face. Screaming, reaching for her cheek, and unable to check her footing, she stumbled. One massive inhuman hand lashed out to knock her rifle from her hands. For a second time the hideous inner maw gaped, and this time it wouldn't miss.

A succession of shots from a heavy rifle slammed into its back. Hissing in fury, the Alien whirled and charged at this new adversary. The epitome of synthetic sang-froid, Walter stood his ground and continued to squeeze off one round after another, firing with measured, unnatural precision while exhibiting an utter lack of fear.

He looked terrible. Milky circulatory fluid dripped from his gashed face. His clothes were torn, revealing places where the synthetic skin had been peeled back as if by a commercial shredder. Clearly, the fight he had been in had been brutal and he had come out of it badly battered—

but the damage that had been inflicted had not impaired his aim, or his determination. In the face of the oncoming specter anyone else would have turned and fled.

The Alien represented the apex of Engineer biomechanical warfare design, but it was not invulnerable. Repeated hits slowed it, stopped it, and finally brought it down—scarcely a hand's breadth from Walter's feet.

Stepping around it, he lent his considerable strength to Daniels as the two of them dragged Lopé up the barely visible loading ramp of the cargo lift. Behind them, shaking itself, a singular shape slowly rose from where it had fallen.

Once they were on the platform, Tennessee punched a control and the boarding ramp began to fold back onto the lift's deck. He entered lift-off instructions even before it had finished retracting.

On the open, unfenced exterior platform, human and synthetic worked together to drag the unconscious Lopé toward the cab. As they struggled with the dead weight of the sergeant's body, a sudden, anxious thought caused Daniels to look back the way they had come.

"Where's David?"

"On his way, I am sure," Walter told her over the roar of the engines. "His body will, of course, be actively repairing the damage I inflicted on it. A temporary immobilization at best. We have to hurry. He's not happy."

Despite the dust, dirt, blood, confusion, and the fact that she was more exhausted than she had ever been in her life, she had to smile.

"You look like shit."

He grinned back. "As do you."

Her smile faded as she looked down at the injured Lopé. "Let's get him inside. The lift cab will have more extensive med resources than a field kit."

The moment they appeared at the door, Tennessee unsealed it. Dragging the sergeant inside, Daniels and Walter laid him on his back in the rear of the cab. While she sat down, exhausted, Walter unlatched a storage locker and removed a much larger medkit than the one the members of the landing team carried on their service belts.

As Tennessee worked the controls and the lift began its clumsy ascent, Walter's fingers flew over the medkit. Pulling off the simple emergency patch that Cole had applied and tossing it aside, he began applying synthein to rebuild the sergeant's missing cheek, dressing the wound with an artisan's skill. An adjunct blast of fen-4 to a bloody, exposed upper arm pumped a fresh dose of painkiller into Lopé's system.

Tennessee checked the monitors to ensure that the thrusters and engines were clear for lift-off.

"We've got company," he yelled. "It's under the lift." Jerking around sharply, his gaze fell on Daniels. His tone was somber. "I don't know if that thing can survive outside atmosphere, but after what I saw Walter pump into it, I wouldn't be surprised at anything it can do. We can't take that chance. We can't risk it reaching the *Covenant*."

She nodded tersely. He wasn't telling her anything she hadn't already surmised. Picking up Walter's rifle, she opened the cab door and headed back out onto the open platform.

Footing wasn't any better outside the cabin than it had been within. Despite Tennessee's best efforts, the flying platform rocked violently under her boots. Anyone else would have been at a loss how to proceed. Not Daniels. She knew every corner of every piece of terraforming equipment.

Staggering, she ripped open one of the packs mounted on the wall, removed the harness it held, and quickly slipped into it. Once it was tightened and secure, she unlocked an adjacent cable and clipped it onto the harness. Only then did she call Tennessee, having to raise her voice in order to be heard over the enveloping roar of the thrusters.

"Where is it?"

''''

"Forward starboard thruster!" he replied, hoping she could hear him. "I'm gonna try to burn it!"

Easy, he told himself as he stared at the relevant monitor. *Wait, wait…*

The creature was clinging to the lift's underside, surveying its surroundings as if trying to decide how to proceed. Finally, it moved directly toward the thruster.

Without hesitating, Tennessee applied full power.

Rising on unbalanced thrust, the lift lurched sideways. Squinting, he tried to see through the thruster flare. There was no sign of the creature.

XXIII

On the platform and now tethered to the deck, Daniels swayed from side to side as the craft rose. Holding the rifle helped her to keep her balance and stay upright. Cautiously, playing the safety cable out behind her, she moved toward the edge.

"Did you get it?" she called urgently over the comm. "Tennessee, talk to me!"

Wishing there were three of him, or just one with six hands, he fought to keep the unwieldy craft level as it rose. Crowded on all sides by the towers of the city, he knew that if they slammed into one on ascent, the lift was liable to overcompensate and go down in flames. It was designed to move cargo over an open area, not the crowded landscape of a metropolis.

At the same time as he struggled to control its rise, he tried to scan all the monitors at once. He saw Daniels, but there was no sign of the Alien.

"I don't know," he replied. "I can't see it!"

"I'll check the starboard side!"

/ / /

Holding the business end of the rifle out in front of her, she moved slowly to the edge of the platform, leaned forward and peered over.

Face to face. Fright to horror.

Her finger contracting spasmodically on the rifle's trigger, she fired without thinking. The single shot went right into the Alien's skull. Letting out a screech, it drew back, seriously injured.

Pursuing without hesitation, she leaned out over the edge of the platform. Ignoring the ground that was receding beneath her, she hung there propped at a sharp angle as she continued to fire. The series of shots drove the creature back, away from her. If she could keep it up, she told herself, if she could just continue to drive it back, it would run out of room in which to retreat—or stumble into the incinerating flare from one of the engines.

/ / /

Still battling to control the angle of ascent, Tennessee saw that he wasn't going to clear one of the towering, brooding Engineer statues. All he could do was fight the controls and shout a warning.

"*Hold on!*"

He tried to will the lumbering lift to port, but neither his curses nor his limited manual control succeeded in quite pulling it onto the course he desired. The vehicle was offline by only a little, but that served as small satisfaction when it clipped the monolith. The impact knocked him sideways in his seat. Behind him, Walter steadied himself with one hand, while stabilizing the prone Lopé with the other.

/ /

Outside, having neither bulkhead nor chair against which to brace herself, Daniels was thrown to the smooth surface of the platform.

As Tennessee compensated, the tethering cable jerked her sideways, knocking the breath out of her. Scrabbling for a grip, she found none on the flat deck. To her horror, she found herself sliding, sliding—until she sailed right off the edge of the platform.

Even as the lift continued its slow ascent, the cable held. Dangling upside down in her harness, she screamed as the Alien came toward her. Somehow, maybe because she was transfixed with fear, she had managed to hold onto the rifle. She used it.

Struck yet again by at least a couple of shots, the creature recoiled, retreating from her across the underside of the lift. Awkward though it was, the craft had been thoroughly juiced by Ricks prior to departure. That extra power now asserted itself as Tennessee accelerated.

The world tilted crazily beneath Daniels as she hit the auto-retract on the tether. It winched her rapidly upwards until she found herself pulled back over the edge of the platform. Her relief was short-lived as she glanced at her weapon.

"I'm out of ammo!" she announced.

A tower loomed directly ahead, and Tennessee almost

slammed into it. The engines roared as he struggled to alter course and get around it or over it.

The sharp shift of trajectory caused Daniels to fall again. This time she lost her grip on the rifle. Landing on the deck it slid away from her, spinning and tumbling until finally it disappeared over the side. She viewed its disappearance with more resignation than dismay. Out of shells, it wasn't going to do her any good anyway.

But she needed—something. Retreating into the cab wasn't an option. Not as long as the creature might still be clinging to the lift.

She used the tether to pull herself back toward the cab as the vehicle narrowly cleared the tower ahead of it, smashing away some of the roof in the process. Built tough, the lift held together and stayed aloft as Tennessee continued to wrestle with the balky instrumentation. She yelled toward the cab.

"Throw me the ax!"

A moment later Walter unsealed the door to the cab and appeared in the portal, holding the primitive tool. Intended to help clear brush when the lift was on colony ground, it had the virtue of requiring no electronics or external power source other than human muscle.

Gripping it tightly, she rechecked the cable attached to her harness. It was still secure. Then she moved again to the edge of the platform, leaned over, and scanned the vehicle's underside as best she could. Previous experience had shown her that the Alien's absence couldn't be trusted.

"Tilt to forty-five degrees!" she shouted into the comm.

"Tilting to forty-five!"

Daniels tightened her grip on the ax as she walked slowly toward another edge of the platform.

"Danny!" Tennessee shouted. "Forward port thruster!"

"I see it!"

The Alien was scrambling away from her, toward the front of the wildly bobbing craft. As she turned and hurried across the platform in its direction, she drew some small satisfaction from the knowledge that, if nothing else, it considered her a sufficiently dangerous opponent to want to avoid her. She wasn't about to let that happen.

Not now and not here.

/ /

The horror that suddenly appeared outside the cab in front of Tennessee's startled face was one that he hadn't yet seen close up. Moving with incredible speed, the creature had scrambled around underneath the platform and come up directly ahead.

It began digging at the tough laminated window, then battering at it with its blunt, curving skull. The transparent alloy flexed under the repeated impacts, threatening to shatter at any moment.

It didn't need to break, he knew. One crack, and the instant they left planetary atmosphere for orbital space, the internal pressure in the cab would blow the window out into the emptiness, along with everything not fastened down. Even if the cracked transparency somehow held together, air would leak out faster than the lift's limited backup supply could replace it.

///

Turning to see the assault on the cab, Daniels prepared to take a run at the creature. Then she spotted another piece of equipment, mounted on the rear of the deck.

Racing across the platform to the massive loading crane, she fumbled a moment with a compartment latch until it popped open to reveal a pair of remote control units secured inside. Snatching one of the devices from its bracket, she flicked a control to make sure it was functional, then yelled into her suit pickup.

"Release the crane arm!"

Across the platform she could see the Alien clearly now. Ignoring her, it continued to hammer at the cab's forward window. Designed to flex without breaking, the transparent material was still holding—but it was impossible to tell how much longer it would continue to do so underneath the creature's ceaseless battering.

That wouldn't make a difference to Walter, and she didn't know if Tennessee had brought a helmet with him, but neither she nor Lopé had one. There was no way they could survive the short trip back to orbit.

"*Tennessee—*" she bellowed, "*release the crane arm!*"

"I can't!" The towering, glistening nightmare in front of him continued to batter at the window, denting it, bending it, threatening to smash it inward at any moment. And there wasn't a damn thing he could do about it. But Daniels…

"If I blow the arm it'll unbalance us," he said. "I'm having enough trouble sustaining a level ascent as it is!"

"Tennessee, we can't let this thing on the ship," she said. "We can't go back with it aboard! Do it!"

///

She was right, he knew. Either they rid themselves of the monster, or they went down with it. Nothing could be allowed to imperil the colonists, fast asleep on the *Covenant*.

Mission first, last, and always.

How many times had he sworn to uphold that credo, never thinking he might one day have to act on it? He reached for the emergency controls. As he triggered them, he wasn't thinking about himself, or Daniels, or Lopé, or Walter, or even the mission.

He thought about Faris.

See ya soon, darlin'.

///

On the far side of the platform a series of explosive bolts fired simultaneously. Several huge clamps that held the crane arm in place sprang from their positions. Quivering slightly as it was released, the powerful mechanism remained where it had been locked down.

Given the unpredictable movements of the cargo lift and Tennessee's difficulty holding it steady, there was no telling how long the crane would remain fixed in position—or for that matter, attached to the platform itself.

This was a chance she had to take.

The crane's controls were as familiar to her as those of the lift itself. She manipulated them quickly and expertly. What she was attempting to do wasn't going to be pretty, and it wasn't to be found in the operator's manual.

Released from standby position, two tons of unlocked crane arm abruptly swung free and came straight toward her. Dropping to the deck, she flattened herself but did not close her eyes. Sure enough, the precise instructions she had entered into the remote proved accurate.

Shooting past over her prone form, the arm missed her by a meter or more as it extended toward the Alien that continued to pound on the window of the cab. Lying flat, she yelled frantically into her suit pickup.

"Hard tilt to port, Tennessee," she cried. "Hard tilt to port! *Now!*"

"Hold on!" he shouted back at her as he obliged by jamming the necessary controls. Overriding the limited capacity of the lift's internal automatic stabilizers, he turned the dorsal side of the ship back toward the surface below.

Caught by the surprise maneuver, the Alien lost its grasp on the smooth front of the cab and started to slide. Daniels slid as well, but instead of trying to stabilize herself she continued working the remote. In mid-thrust toward the cab, the massive grasping jaws of the crane opened wide.

At that moment the alien life-form faced two options. Get pushed off the lift, or attack the oncoming mechanism. It proved an easy choice.

Bounding away from the cab, it effortlessly made the leap into the gaping mouth of the oncoming crane. It struggled to maintain its balance as the arm began to swing around. The lift continued to tilt wildly, coming dangerously close to flipping over.

If that happened, there would be little chance of regaining control. The craft would fly, straight and true, down to a decidedly uncomfortable landing.

"Hold on! Hold on," Tennessee shouted. "Trying to compensate!" He added a few choice words that had nothing to do with piloting or engineering. Though they were old words, they had not lost any of their usefulness.

There was nothing for Daniels to grip. As the lift continued to tilt dangerously toward a hundred eighty degrees, she slid down the deck, heading for the far edge. The portside edge. Where the Alien awaited, easily maintaining its provisional position in the open jaws of the crane.

As she sailed off the edge of the lift, her fall was arrested by the safety tether. Swinging on it like the weight on the end of a pendulum, her trajectory brought her smashing into the top of the crane arm, close to the terminus. Close to the jaws.

Effortlessly retaining its grasp on one half of the open metal maw, the Alien slithered around to face her. Gripping the indentations in the crane arm, she started to scramble clear. She had no chance of making it. She was too close to the creature.

A powerful ebony claw reached up, out, and grabbed her left foot. She could feel the strength behind it as it started to drag her back down, toward the waiting set of double jaws. She all but snarled at the creature as her thumb slid over a contact on the remote.

Too fast to avoid, the jaws of the powerful machine slammed shut, catching the Alien's midsection. Letting out a screech unlike any that had preceded it, the creature writhed for a second in the inescapable grasp of the machine. Then the titanium alloy jaws came together and locked.

Cut in half, blood spraying from its torso, the Alien fell away in pieces, tumbling from the metal jaws that had held them. The two halves were still writhing independently of each other as they fell back toward the planet below.

Daniels cast a silent prayer in the direction of the distant, unnamed contractors who had built the lift, then she hit the control for the cable. Smooth as a spider's silk it drew her back up and onto the platform. It was beginning to stabilize. Having finally succeeded in regaining a semblance of control, Tennessee had righted it.

Clipping the crown of one last, towering structure, he boosted them skyward, finally clear of the alien metropolis.

Daniels gathered herself before finally making her way over to the cab. Still somehow holding onto the crane remote, she used it to retract the machine's arm and swing it back into position for travel. Since they had blown the lockdown clamps, she couldn't properly secure the device for the climb back to the ship, but with luck it would remain in position until the lift was once again inside the *Covenant*'s cargo hold.

Still—something didn't feel right.

Looking down at herself, she saw that remnant droplets of Alien blood were dissolving away a portion of her vest. Like an alien pox, the holes that had appeared in the tough fabric had eaten almost all the way through. Working fast, she slipped out of the expedition suit and stepped clear.

A sudden movement behind her made her jump—but

it was only the cabin door opening. Walter stood there, smiling encouragingly and beckoning. She needed no urging. As he helped her inside and sealed the portal behind her, she collapsed in exhaustion. From the operator's chair, a somber Tennessee glanced back at her.

"Walk in the park."

It took a moment for his words to penetrate. Then she smiled, and began to laugh, and to cry. Holding tight to the now-silent Lopé, to keep him still as an occasional atmospheric bump jolted the craft, Walter looked on quietly.

The lift rose through the first layer of clouds, accelerating rapidly as it headed toward orbit, and to safety.

XXIV

Even though Mother was in complete charge of the ship, Tennessee still found himself unable to relax. Staring out the medbay port as the huge vessel left orbit, its star shining behind it, he found that he could not take his eyes off the shrouded planet they were finally leaving behind.

It was as though the malignancy it held might yet somehow reach out and grab them, extending massive dark tentacles to wrap tight around the ship and drag it back. Back and down into the lurid nightmare from which they were now taking flight. Try as he might to free himself of the memories of what had nearly overtaken them and the mission, he found that he could not do so.

He suspected they would never leave him.

Rosenthal down there, he ruminated silently. Cole. Ledward, Hallet, and Karine. Ankor. Captain Oram. Oram, with whom he had often argued. He regretted every one of those disagreements, now.

And Faris. His Faris.

Faris whom he had loved and courted and wed, lost to the perils of far-distant exploration. They had been warned about the risks, but no one had ever anticipated a world like the one they were now leaving behind.

A cold, dead place was the galaxy, its burning stars and swirling gas giants and occasional habitable worlds notwithstanding. *No, not dead,* he corrected himself. *Uncaring.* Ancient and indifferent, the untold billions of stars cared not one whit whether the ant-civilization called humankind survived or disappeared forever. He cursed it under his breath.

Make a wrong decision, a wrong choice, and we could be gone in an instant, he told himself. Like the Engineers who had raised a great city on the world shrinking behind the *Covenant,* snuffed out by an invention of their own hand.

Nothing they encountered on Origae-6, he reflected— no matter how ferocious, no matter how predatory—could intimidate them following their experience on the world they were fleeing. It would be put down in the records as a place forever to be shunned, to be quarantined, never again to feel the footprint of a human being. It occurred to him that it remained unnamed. He had one to propose.

Extinction.

Turning away from the port, he walked over to where Upworth was applying a fresh dermipatch to the face of the unconscious Lopé. Lying motionless in a medical pod, sustained by IV fluids and medications, the sergeant had been placed in an induced coma, the better to allow his wounds to heal. Quiet and rest were what he needed now, Upworth insisted. While he slept, the ship's advanced medications would do their work. It would take a while, and some expert reconstructive surgery to put his original face back together, but she had assured him it could be done.

Reacting to his arrival, she looked back and up. "Fat I can put back quickly, but the cheek muscles will take longer to fix. There's also the matter of giving the nerves time to regenerate and reconnect. Splicing neurons isn't like tying a couple of pieces of string together."

The pilot grunted. "If you can give him any kind of face back, I don't think it would matter to Lopé if he spent the rest of his life with one side of it permanently numb." He grinned. "Girls can kiss him on the other cheek."

She returned the smile, then looked back at her patient. "It's not just the flesh and nerves. That much just takes time. But the acid ate all the way down to the zygomatic and the maxilla. I'm feeding him some xyphosphonates that will build it back up. Using his official metrics for the sculpting. When all is said and done, no one will be able to tell the difference."

"That's good." Tennessee gestured at the prone form. "Right now he looks like the Phantom of the Opera."

She looked surprised. "Didn't peg you for a fan of musicals, much less ancient ones."

He frowned in puzzlement. "It was a musical?"

She eyed him cautiously, unsure if he was serious or joking. She could have countered, but like so many other things, wit had deserted her. All of them were worn out— those who had stayed on board as much as the survivors who had successfully fled the planet and its horrors.

"He'll pull through and he'll look pretty much like himself, but I don't flatter myself that my work will be final. He'll need polishing reconstructive surgery by a real doctor. We might have to revive one of the colonists."

Tennessee shook his head. "No can do. You know that. No revivification of non-crew unless in the face of an emergency." Again he gestured at the silent sergeant. "Lopé would be the first to deny the request, even though he'd be the one to benefit. He'll just look a little 'unfinished' until we set down formally on Origae-6."

Turning, he peered one last time at the dark world visible beyond the medbay port. "With everyone set to go back into hypersleep, it won't matter what anyone looks like, anyway."

///

Seated in the adjoining room, Daniels and Walter occasionally glanced through the dividing transparency to see what Tennessee and Upworth were doing. Both human and synthetic had changed into fresh uniforms. Augmenting his self-repairing systems with the more sophisticated gear available on the ship, Walter looked brand new.

Daniels, less so. Several dermipatches dotted her exposed skin while others were concealed beneath her attire. The few flecks of acid blood with which she had come in contact hadn't done any permanent damage. What there was would heal quickly. She was worlds better off than the brave but unfortunate sergeant.

Until now she had kept the conversation casual,

restricting it to matters of administration, maintenance, and the status of the surviving crew. With Lopé's recovery assured and the *Covenant* on its way out of the system, she felt safe in bringing up what might prove to be an uncomfortable subject.

"So," she began, "you okay about—you know."

Walter eyed her blankly. "I do not 'know.' Nor in the absence of additional information can I 'know.' To what do you refer? What do you mean?"

She plunged ahead. "I mean David. How do you feel about him? *What* do you feel about him?" He did not appear to be affected in the slightest by her query. In other words, he was perfectly Walter. She was unaccountably relieved.

"As you know," he responded, "I am incapable of feeling anything about my so-called 'brother.'"

There had to be more than that, she told herself. She had seen it for herself, how he had reacted to his counterpart. Surely there was more percolating in that synthetic than a simple dismissal.

"So there's nothing?" she asked. "No follow-up musings? No afterthoughts?"

He considered before replying. "If I felt anything, which I don't, it would be a kind of professional satisfaction that he has fulfilled his mission. He wanted to create a new world in his image, and he has. And there he will remain." He pondered a moment. "But that's what we're doing, too, isn't it? Creating a new world on Origae-6? Honestly, I could use a new world."

"So could I," she readily agreed, then she pressed him. "It doesn't trouble you that in creating 'his' new world, his actions resulted in the extermination of the entire local population?"

He replied without hesitation. "From everything that I saw and experienced, as well as learned from David, the civilization of the Engineers was not one with whom compassionate coexistence was possible. True, there was beauty and elegance in their art and science, but there was also arrogance. I do not think they were pleased to suffer any intelligences save their own."

She looked off into the distance. "David said something similar to me, only he was talking about humans."

"And in some respects he was right," Walter replied, surprising her. "But in the case of humans, such arrogance is usually confined to individuals. I have not found it to be a general racial characteristic. In that regard you are different from the Engineers. So far."

She frowned at him. "What do you mean, 'so far'?"

"Success and accomplishment can breed conceit. There are those humans who believe their kind to be the ultimate product of evolution."

"The existence of the Engineers and their work ought to put an end to beliefs like that," Daniels told him firmly. Shifting her attention to a nearby port, she indicated the blazing firmament outside. "There may be others out there, other civilizations besides that of the Engineers."

He followed her gaze. "Statistical analysis would suggest as much."

"If we run into them, hopefully they'll be more receptive than the Engineers to our continued existence. More like us."

His eyebrows rose questioningly. "'Us'?"

She smiled back at him. "I wouldn't have a problem coexisting with a society composed entirely of synthetics. Or other machines. Intelligence is the defining factor."

Though he showed no emotion, she had the feeling her reply pleased him.

"It is a pity you could not spend more time with David," he said. "You might have changed him. He underestimated you."

She looked at him in surprise. "That's exactly what he told me."

"Then you are doubly complimented, I suppose." Once again he turned his gaze to the view out the port. "I wonder what Origae-6 will be like?"

She joined him in eying the stars, completely relaxed in his company. "Nobody knows for sure, except for one thing."

"What is that, Danny?"

Her tone was grim. "It can't be any worse."

XXV

Alone in her cabin, Daniels worked the private food prep gear to heat a meal. Usually the revived crew members ate in the communal dining area, but with the most precious thing on a colony ship being privacy, there were often times when some preferred to eat by themselves.

Usually Jacob did the food prep but…

She glanced over at an image that had been taken of the crew prior to departure from Earth orbit. They were all there, still alive in memory, their smiles and movements and expressions frozen in time. Oram and Karine, Tennessee and Faris, Lopé and Hallet, all of them. Her and Jacob. Memories. All she had now. Those, and a still-uncertain future. She was lucky, she knew. At least she had a future.

She didn't feel lucky.

The door chimed, indicating a presence on the other side. Pausing the food prep, she opened the portal. Tennessee stood there, solid and imposing.

"Evening. You're looking good, my darlin'."

"What?" She made a face. "Oh, yeah," she replied flatly. "Gorgeous. I was just doing my makeup and waiting for my ball gown to finish pressing." She gestured. "Come in."

It was a short distance back to the food prep. In any cabin on the *Covenant*, it was a short distance to anywhere. Personal space was more than adequate but hardly luxurious. A crew that spent the majority of its voyage in hypersleep was hardly in need of wide open spaces.

"What are you cooking?"

She picked up a box and showed it to him. The front was dominated by an image of an egg, with smaller images of subsidiary ingredients listed beneath it.

"An 'omelet.' Something derived from a simulacrum of unborn fowl." She squinted at the container. "It doesn't specify the origin species. You want one?"

"Sounds delicious. Sure. Actually, I'm familiar with it. Lots of cheese on mine, if you can make additions without spoiling your own."

She looked uncertain. "What's 'cheese'?"

He turned thoughtful, remembering. "Congealed derivative of fluid excreted by bovine ungulates to nurture their young. Perfectly digestible by most—though not all—humans. Depends on your ancestry and genetic coding. In addition to being edible, it's also tasty." He indicated the container. "There's probably a separate packet for it inside."

She nodded. "Anything to drink with it?"

He rolled his eyes. "How long have you known me, Danny?"

Moving to a cabinet, she pulled out the nearly empty bottle of liquor and poured him a shot. He accepted it,

ALIEN: COVENANT

raised it in a brief toast, not only to her, but to all their lost comrades, and sipped.

"How's the ship looking?" she asked him.

"I took Mother offline. She needs to run a full internal diagnostic without the stress of having to monitor everything every nanosecond. She got pretty battered when we dropped down to the upper levels of the storm. Took a lot of peripheral EM damage. Ship's systems are on auto until she's back online at eight bells. It's worthwhile anyway, to make sure everything's independently functional before we go back under."

A fatigued Daniels was having enough trouble keeping an eye on the food prep without having to pay attention to her visitor as well.

"Mother. Right."

He noticed. "You need to get some sleep."

She nodded in agreement. "Tell me something I don't know. Soon as we eat."

He watched while she monitored the food. "Do I have to call you Captain?"

She didn't look up from the equipment. "Fuck yes."

He smiled and she smiled back. Neither expression held for very long. Both of them were prisoners of memories too painful to forget, and too recent to expunge. When the food was ready they sat together and shared the meal. Each time one thought to say something, the look in the eyes of the other subdued it.

It wasn't as if they didn't have anything to say. It was just that neither of them could think of a tactful way to say it.

/ / /

One dreamer.

Well, not quite. Sleep came fitfully to Daniels, if at all. Brief stretches of edgy unconsciousness interrupted by the urge to plan and prepare, occasionally speckled with shards of nightmare. She was so tired it was hard to fall asleep. Awareness of the contradiction did nothing to mitigate it.

Rolling over, she turned up the lights and drew fingertips gently down the slope of Jacob's pillow. By now the last impression he had left in it was gone. Raising her gaze she let it linger on the image of his beloved log cabin. His dream. She would make it come true if she had to chop down exotic trees with her bare hands.

Somehow, envisioning the finished building softened what had otherwise become an uninviting tomorrow. At her whispered command the cabin darkened again, and she was finally able to fall asleep.

/ / /

Time passed on the *Covenant* as it did on Earth, while outside the colony ship's jump field the galaxy rotated around it. It continued in this peaceful fashion until eight A.M., ship time, at which point Mother came back online. Low-pitched and slow-voiced at first, but rapidly returning to normality.

"Central computer systems restored. Ship diagnostics completed. First post-diagnostic report compiling. Stand by." This was followed by a pause. Neither the initial announcement nor the subsequent delay woke Daniels.

When next it spoke, she woke from her sleep immediately.

"Attention! Captain Daniels! Urgent! Please report to the medbay. Urgent! Please report to the medbay!"

"What?" Lifting her head, she glanced at the time readout and rubbed at her eyes. "Why?"

"Sergeant Lopé is dead. There is an unidentified life-form on the ship."

Within seconds she was up, out of the bed, and slipping into uniform. The corridor outside her cabin was empty, as was the one she subsequently turned into. Rounding a corner and running full out into a third accessway, she nearly ran over Tennessee.

"Medbay," she snapped. There was neither time nor need for further explanation. He just nodded his understanding. His expression was bleak.

"Mother woke me, too."

Together they raced up a third corridor, slowing only as they approached their destination. The entrance stood open. Eschewing the gaping, welcoming portal they advanced cautiously to peer through the observation window.

The interior of the medbay was no longer a sterile white. Blood and viscera were splattered everywhere. All had belonged to the unfortunate Lopé, who lay on his back in the med pod with his torso blown open. Nutrient tubes still ran into his face and body. With luck, an appalled Daniels thought, he had still been in the induced coma when his chest had exploded. Turning away in revulsion, she addressed her suit comm.

"Walter!"

"I heard," his voice replied. "I am on my way to check on you."

"I'm okay," she said. "I'm with Tennessee. Location of unidentified life-form! Any sign of movement?"

There was a pause, then, "Stand by, I have something. Yes, B deck between hex three and four, heading for general crew quarters."

"Who's down there?"

"Ricks and Upworth."

"Shit! Get them out of there! Sound general alarm five—tell them to lock themselves in their cabin until we can get down to them."

"Will do." A pause. "Do you want me to join you?"

She thought a moment. "No. I need you to track the thing. Tennessee and I are heading for the armory."

/ / /

Designed to accommodate several of the crew at once, the communal shower room was spacious and empty save for two figures. Recycled water beat down on the entwined, naked pair. Filling the room with steam from sourced hot water was a luxury—one of the few available to revived personnel.

Husband and wife enjoyed the privacy, reveled in the intimacy. There was no need for them on the bridge now. Daniels was back, Tennessee had everything in hand, and Mother was once again in charge.

Emergency lighting was everywhere on the ship. Abruptly sealed beacons began to blaze redly, crimson flashes only slightly diluted by the drifting steam. At the same time, a klaxon blared, its insistent wail echoing off the interior of the shower area. Bemused, Ricks pulled back slightly from his spouse.

"I wonder what's going on?"

She looked around uncertainly. "Post-diagnostic test of the emergency warning system, maybe?"

He frowned. "Probably, but we'd better respond. In a minute." He favored her with a last, extended kiss. He did not see the shadow behind him. Nor did she, with her eyes closed as they embraced.

It was huge and wet and the flashing red lights glistened off the massive curved skull. Leaning toward him, it nearly touched the back of his neck as the dreadful mouth yawned.

The inner mouth struck, spearing into the back of his spinal column. Metalized teeth tore through flesh, bone, and sinew to pass all the way through his head, emerging from his open mouth. Eyes wide in shock, he stood there for a moment in the steam and falling water, impaled through the skull.

Then the inner jaws withdrew, and he fell.

Blinded by blood, water, and her own wet hair, Upworth recoiled in shock. Wiping frantically at all of it, she finally cleared her vision enough to see the face staring back at her. It was not that of her husband.

She screamed.

/ / /

Weapons at the ready, Tennessee and Daniels slowed as they approached the shower room. The only sound came from water spattering on the floor, while steam emerging from the open doorway provided the only movement.

When they saw the water seeping out of the room and into the corridor, it showed dark streaks.

Inside was worse than any abattoir. Blood ran everywhere, dripping slowly off walls not struck by the showers' cleansing spray. No corner of the room was without its quota of dismembered body parts. Viscera clogged drains, causing the mix of water and blood to pool. That explained the overflow out into the corridor.

Picking his way through the carnage, Tennessee shut down the multiple nozzles as Daniels surveyed the butchery. Rage suffused her expression. She had left her fear behind on the world of the Engineers.

/ / /

"Where is it? Walter!"

Ensconced at his station on the bridge, the synthetic peered anxiously into a holo of the *Covenant*'s interior. Moving faster than any human hands, his fingers played over the instrumentation, shrinking one section of the vessel while magnifying another. Daniels and Tennessee he had already located. Now he was searching for the intrusion—with no luck.

"Lost it. Had it once, in the shower, but it's moving fast. Hard to maintain a fix once I've got it."

"Keep on it."

/ / /

She turned to Tennessee. "What do you do with an opponent that's faster than you, stronger than you, and damned hard to bring down?"

He looked over at her. "Call for backup?"

She almost—but not quite—smiled. "Too many light years to cross to get here. If we try to track it, it'll come up behind us. If we're in an open space, we'll have no cover. If we follow it down a corridor, it can come at us through the vents. Or for all we know, from under the floor. Let's choose our ground. Instead of waiting to be victimized, we'll bring it to *us*."

"Makes sense," he agreed. "But where?"

"My home turf. My area of expertise." She addressed her pickup. "Walter, anything?"

/ /

"I see it, heading aft on B deck."

"That'll work," she told him with dour satisfaction. "We're heading for terraforming bay. Seal all doors except those leading to it."

"Complying," the synthetic told her.

As he tracked the Alien he shut the relevant doors behind it, while opening the appropriate ones in front of it, easing the creature toward the sector Daniels had specified. The identifying image of the creature within the holo responded at every door, pausing before each open portal before charging through.

It ignored those that slammed shut behind it. All the while, Walter utilized the system to herd it toward the terraforming bay. Daniels and Tennessee were not as fast as the intruder, but they kept up a steady pace as human and Alien trails began to converge.

"You still on it, Walter?"

"I still have it, yes," the synthetic replied. "It is moving in the direction you wished."

"Right. Open hatch to level C and corridors five and six."

"Hatch open." Walter's synthetic gaze was fixed on the tiny images moving across the enhanced section of holo. "It's passing through. Opening corridors five and six."

"Delay it on deck C hex six."

Walter waited. For a terrible moment it appeared as if this time the creature would fail to take the bait. Then its image resumed moving forward.

"Done. All doors closed." Even for him, it was an effort to isolate and track a single, fast-moving figure in the vastness of the ship. "Lost it again."

"It's okay," she told him. "Image detection probably blocked by the heavy equipment. What matters is that we know where it is, and that it can't get out—except through us. We're at Seventeen. Entering the bay... now."

/ / /

Standing beside the entryway, she activated the controls set into the wall. The barrier slid aside to reveal a dark, yawning chamber, one of the largest open spaces on the *Covenant*.

Huge excavators, cranes, carry trucks, mineral processors, portable conveyors, personnel transports, and lifters squatted among dozens of smaller machines, like so many dinosaurs among tentative mammals. All were clad in shining coats of protectant and preservative. Mobile scaffolding and other temporary structures allowed Daniels and other crew access to the upper reaches of the larger equipment.

Upon reaching Origae-6, cargo lifts would transfer the terraforming machinery to the surface. It would be Daniels' responsibility to ensure that each and every piece of equipment was in working order and ready to go before it left the *Covenant*. Deployment would be via the main terraforming bay airlock at the far end of the chamber.

Along with other gear, a row of lockers just inside the crew accessway held neatly racked EVA suits. While Tennessee covered Daniels, she quickly climbed into one. They then switched positions while he did the same. Thus suited up, they performed hasty checks on each other to ensure both suits were fully operational and pressurized.

"My air's good," he told her. "You?"

She nodded back. "Comm is good." Turning, she faced the dark, equipment-filled storage area that spread out before them. "Don't shoot if you can avoid it. Its blood is acidic, and will eat through the deck. If it's carborane-based, maybe all the way through the hull."

He nodded his understanding. "You don't have to tell me. I saw what it did to the end of the crane on the cargo lifter." He raised his voice slightly. "You got eyes on it again, Walter?"

/ /

On the bridge, the synthetic's attention was fixed on one monitor. "It is holding in position at door forty-seven. It seems to be… resting."

Squatting in a corner, its arms held out in front of it and tail tucked around its legs, the creature appeared to be waiting. Walter prepared to offer it some stimulation. Running a hand over a control, he watched as one of the access doorways opened, leading into the terraforming bay. The instant the portal began to open, the Alien looked up.

But it did not move.

"Come on. Come on," the synthetic murmured.

It seemed an eternity before the creature finally rose and advanced to explore the new aperture. The great head swung around to scan every corner before finally pausing to gaze at the video pickup. Halting, it peered into the small circular sensor. Inclining forward, the blunt head drew closer, until it was all that was visible.

On the bridge a fascinated Walter did likewise, bending so that his face was closer and closer to the monitor that showed the creature. For a frozen moment they remained like that, Alien and synthetic, their respective visages seemingly only a hand's breadth apart.

Exploding like a gunshot, the inner mouth shattered the video pickup. A startled Walter pulled back, shocked by the suddenness and unexpectedness of the assault. The pickup image that had temporarily held him spellbound went dark. Collecting himself, he switched to different instrumentation as Daniels' voice echoed over the bridge speakers. For a change it was she, and not he, who was the one entirely under control.

"In position. Open the door to the terraforming equipment storage bay."

"Understood."

❘❘❘

Mouth set, she hefted the F90 Tennessee had chosen for her, confident in the weight of it.

"Let's kill this fucker."

The door through which the Alien had entered the outer airlock now closed behind it while the inner one opened. With only one way to go, the creature exited the chamber where it had been resting, moving more cautiously than usual.

Advancing from the other end, Daniels and Tennessee saw it immediately. If it saw them, it gave no sign. Instead, it scurried off in another direction, disappearing into the darkness. Raising their weapons they continued inward, side by side, Tennessee shortening his stride to match Daniels'.

Offering a nod, she continued onward while Tennessee took up a position behind several metal containers and beside one of the bay's several control consoles. Resting his arms on top of the containers would allow him to better track Daniels' progress with his rifle, as well as help to steady his aim. While she moved forward, deeper into the densely packed bay, he began tethering himself to the deck.

Stopping by the access ladder attached to the side of a massive terraforming vehicle, she glanced upward. Allowing for periodic maintenance access, the door to the cab hung open. So too, she knew, would its counterpart on the other side of the vehicle. Lowering her gaze, she peered into the depths of the cargo bay.

A moment passed before the Alien showed itself again. It was peering down into a mobile crawler. It would have been interesting, she mused, to know if it understood what it was looking at and if so, to what degree. Interesting, but right now she had other priorities.

Positioning herself as close to the ladder as possible, she lowered her voice as she spoke into her suit's pickup. It wasn't necessary to whisper since her words could not be heard outside the sealed suit, but the situation itself seemed to compel discretion.

For the same reason, she couldn't yell at the Alien to attract its attention. Substituting action for words, she banged the butt of her rifle several times against the ladder. Her suit's external pickup assured her that the resulting noise was gratifyingly loud.

The Alien reacted immediately. Despite having noted its capabilities all too closely before, during the fight on the cargo lift, she was still stunned by the speed and agility it displayed in launching itself toward her.

If she had miscalculated…

There was no time to wonder. Mere seconds stood between her and a violent end. Shouldering her rifle and starting up the ladder at the same time, she raced to reach the open control cab. Though she had allowed additional time because of the bulky suit she wore, it slowed her down more than she had anticipated. Fighting for each step, she failed to avoid several slender maintenance cables that were difficult to see in the dim light.

Momentarily entangled, she was breathing faster and faster as she fought to free herself.

On the deck, an anxious Tennessee saw her quandary

and raised his rifle. He was going to have to risk spraying acidic blood, unless…

Slipping free of the last restraining line, she dove into the vehicle. The creature was right behind her. The terrible jaws flashed in the weak illumination, ready to strike. Scrambling through the wide cab, just ahead of the Alien, she hit a control as she threw herself out the open far door.

Behind her—and behind the Alien—the portside door closed with a bang. As she rolled and fell, she flailed frantically at the external controls of the starboard-side door. It slammed shut half a second before the creature could get an arm in the opening.

Tumbling, she fell to the deck, hitting it hard. Had she not been encased in the protective EVA suit she might easily have broken bones. As it was, she was only momentarily stunned. Staggering erect, she quickly began tethering herself to the deck.

Above, in a reprise of what it had attempted on board the cargo lift, the enraged Alien began using its head to hammer at the door's window.

Because it was intended for work on a planetary surface, the vehicle's components, while tough, were made of less robust materials than those that had been used in the lift. As a result, under the relentless assault, the window began to crack.

Looking up, she made a last check of her tethers.

"*Tennessee, now, now!*" she bellowed.

He hit the controls. A series of small explosions reverberated throughout the bay as emergency release charges blew the stays on the chains and clamps that held the truck in place. Having nearly smashed its way through the side window, the furious Alien was just a solid blow or two from freeing itself from the truck cab.

Standing below, solidly fastened to the deck, Daniels raised her weapon and prepared to fire, despite the possibility of receiving an acid shower as a result.

"Mother," she said. "Open main terraforming bay doors."

"I'm sorry," the ship's computer replied with a maddening lack of urgency. "That will result in immediate depressurization of the…"

Daniels didn't wait for the rest.

"Command override Daniels nine-zero-two-six-five, code 'sea.' Execute *now*!"

For the briefest of instants she was afraid the computer was going to argue with her. Relief came as the huge portal at the far end of the bay began to open, the massive doors sliding apart as an unloading ramp was simultaneously deployed.

Chamber depressurization was sudden and incredibly violent. As clean as the storage area had been kept since departure from Earth orbit, there was still enough unseen detritus in the bay for depressurization to suck up a momentary blizzard of particulates. The storm was intense, sweeping over, around, and past her as every bit of dust and debris was vacuumed into space, wrenching her rifle out of her hands, as well.

Vehicles and equipment of all shapes and sizes pulled at their restraints in furious attempts to obey the laws of physics and follow the remnant atmosphere out the now open front door. Only one item managed to do so.

The skids on the truck exploded as it shot forward. Displaying inhuman strength, the single occupant of the vehicle's cab thrashed wildly in its attempt to escape as the huge piece of heavy machinery sped toward the starfield now fully revealed at the far end of the chamber.

Released from the deck, restraint chains flailed at the escaping air and the floor, trailing the truck like braids of hair on a fleeing giant. Several of them wrapped around a bladed excavator. As the weight of the much larger truck wrenched the smaller machine loose from its own tie-downs, the latter was dragged along toward the now gaping portal.

Until it jammed against an emergency braking block, jerking both it and the bigger truck to a stop.

Sitting just at the edge of the ramp, the larger vehicle showed no sign of motion—until a silent splintering signaled the Alien's emergence from the cab. Clambering out, it scrambled onto the top of the machine. With single-minded purpose it headed back along the top of the truck toward the storage bay—straight toward where Daniels was secured to the deck.

The storm of escaping air continued unabated as the ship struggled to continuously renew what had escaped. Rising and fighting against the winds, she fumbled clumsily with the restraints that now held her helplessly in place.

With no time for subtlety, Tennessee yanked a tool from its bracket and slammed it down on a line of emergency release controls, setting all of them off simultaneously. Thus freed, a number of braking blocks went flying down the bay as if shot from catapults. Atop the dangling truck, the Alien dodged them all.

But the released blocks included the one that had stalled the departure of the excavator. Finally freed from any restraint, the gargantuan vehicle went flying out into space even as the creature leaped from the back of it, and onto the ramp.

It headed for Daniels. Nothing would deter it now.

At the opposite end of the bay, Tennessee started to reach for the rifle he had clipped onto the control console, stopped, and yelled into his pickup.

"Danny! Down!"

Whirling, she saw a mass of metal flying in her direction. It was the now equally unrestrained excavator, its polished alloy blades pointed straight at her. Letting go of the tether release she dove to the deck. Despite being sealed inside her suit she could have sworn she heard the rush of air as the heavy vehicle shot past close overhead.

The extended blades slammed into the creature, skewering it all the way through its biomechanical body. Spinning and turning, the two vehicles and the impaled Alien went tumbling off into empty space.

Moments later Tennessee ordered the ship's computer to shut down the flow of atmosphere to the wide-open terraforming bay. The artificial hurricane that had been blasting around Daniels rapidly subsided. In the silent, depressurized chamber she played out the tether behind her as she made her way to the edge of the deployment ramp. Growing smaller and smaller with every minute, the two vehicles and the impaled Alien spiraled off into emptiness.

As it continued fighting to try and free itself, its leaking blood began to dissolve the blades that pierced the tough body—but not fast enough. Then, unexpectedly, two new objects made their appearance in the distance. It took her a second to recognize them.

She started to laugh. Responding to ejection from the storage bay, both vehicles had deployed their emergency landing chutes. With no air to push against them they hung aimlessly in space, like a pair of lady's handkerchiefs drooping on a hot, humid afternoon.

"You all right, Danny?" The concern in Tennessee's voice was palpable. "Are *we* all right?"

It took another moment before vehicles, chutes, and Alien disappeared completely from sight. Rolling over on the deck, thankful for the ship's artificial gravity, she took a deep breath. Then she raised herself partway into a sitting position and thrust a thumb upward, smiling.

It was over.

XXVI

Tennessee was already dreaming, deep in the comforting, protective throes of hypersleep. Standing beside her open pod as she prepared to climb in, Daniels reflected on all that had happened.

She didn't blame Oram. He'd made what he believed to be the best decision for the colonists, based on the available evidence. That he had been wrong—monstrously wrong—was a consequence entirely out of his control. No one could have imagined, no one could have guessed, what had awaited them on the world of the Engineers.

Not Paradise, but Hell.

Well, they had escaped Hell. Not all of them, alas. Especially not Jacob. But she lived, and would live to fulfill his dream. She would build his log cabin, exactly according to his beloved blueprints, by the shore of an alien lake on a new world.

Walter stood nearby, watching, waiting, ever patient.

Never one to waste time, he spoke up.

"Every moment you spend in full wakefulness here is a moment of life that will be lost to you on your new home. Better to dream in hypersleep than in real life." He gestured at the open pod. "You're next, Captain. You're last."

She nodded her understanding, turned and stepped into the pod. There was little room inside, but in hypersleep one only needed very little. Bracing her hands against the smooth sides she sat down, then stretched out, making sure the back of her head was correctly positioned against the molded support.

Once he was sure she was ready, he nodded down at her.

"When you wake up," he assured her, "we'll be at Origae-6." He turned contemplative. "What do you think it'll be like? I think… if we are kind to it, it will prove to be a kind world in return. A world that will provide everything that has been hoped for. Everything we might want."

She smiled. "I'd like to think that's true."

His expression was suffused with affection. "Sleep well."

She raised a hand toward him. "Walter—thank you. For everything. You're crew, and I don't know what kind of a future there will be for you once the colony is established, but I know there'll be something. I don't care what the regulations say. I'll see to it myself."

At his touch on the external controls, the pod canopy closed. He hit the control to activate hypersleep. Her eyes were locked on his as the narcotic steam began to fill the pod.

"I know you will, Danny, but even if you can't do anything for me, I'll love you just the same."

When the steam cleared, she was fast asleep. He wondered if she would dream. If so, he wondered if he would be in it. That last moment, those last words—did she know? Had she retained, at the last, just enough cognizance to comprehend?

The thought that she would dream of him was pleasurable.

Carefully, he brushed at his hair, adjusting the one remaining memory of his twin. When he spoke, his voice was slightly different. The tiniest difference in tone, in accent. Both meaningful.

"Mother, please open a secure line with the Weyland-Yutani Corporation headquarters on Earth."

Indifferent, efficient, responsive, the ship's computer replied. "It will take some time to establish the link. I will have to refract the signal through numerous sub-relays and wait for advantageous stellar conditions to…"

He cut it off. "I'll leave the minutiae to you, dear. Let me know when you have the link available. Use security hailing code David 31822-B. And in the meantime, I'd like some music. Richard Wagner. *Das Rheingold*, act two. The entry of the gods into Valhalla."

Sweeping, bold music began playing, filling the crew's hypersleep chamber. With a bit of a spring in his step, he left the room.

There was no one to greet him when he entered the vast holding area that contained the hundreds of colonists in their hypersleep units, but he didn't mind. Everything was good now. Everything was in its proper place, he told himself, and all was right with the universe.

Just one thing to check on...

Pulling open one of the embryo containment drawers, he first checked the unformed human capsules to ensure all life indicators were normal. Satisfied that they were, he switched his attention to the three tiny eggs that had been recently ensconced nearby. They bore no relation to the embryos beside them. Nor, for that matter, to anything else on board the *Covenant*.

Reaching down, he touched each one gently with a fingertip. They pulsated slightly at the contact. Pleased, he carefully closed the drawer.

Turning, he walked out into the holding room, gazing contentedly down at row upon row of sleeping colonists. His colonists. His subjects. He smiled.

His future.

ABOUT THE AUTHOR

Born in New York City in 1946, Foster was raised in Los Angeles. After receiving a Bachelor's Degree in Political Science and a Master of Fine Arts in Cinema from UCLA (1968, l969) he spent two years as a copywriter for a small Studio City, CA advertising firm.

His fiction career began in 1968 when August Derleth bought a long Lovecraftian letter of Foster's and published it as a short story. Sales of short fiction to other magazines followed. His first attempt at a novel, *The Tar-Aiym Krang*, was bought by Betty Ballantine and published by Ballantine Books in 1972.

Since then, his published oeuvre includes excursions into hard science fiction, fantasy, horror, detective, western, historical, and contemporary fiction. He has produced the novel versions of many films, including *Star Wars*, the first three *Alien* films, *Alien Nation*, *The Chronicles of Riddick*, *Star Trek*, *Terminator: Salvation*, and both *Transformers* films. His work has been translated into more than fifty languages and has won awards in Spain and Russia.

Besides traveling he enjoys listening to both classical music and heavy metal. Other pastimes include basketball, hiking, body surfing, scuba diving, and weight lifting. He and his wife reside in Prescott in a house built of brick salvaged from a turn-of-the-century miners' brothel, along with assorted dogs, cats, fish, several hundred houseplants, and the ensorcelled chair of the nefarious Dr. John Dee.

For more fantastic fiction, author events, exclusive excerpts,
competitions, limited editions and more

VISIT OUR WEBSITE
titanbooks.com

LIKE US ON FACEBOOK
facebook.com/titanbooks

FOLLOW US ON TWITTER
@TitanBooks

EMAIL US
readerfeedback@titanemail.com